WHAT THE END WILL BE

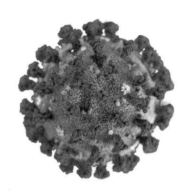

WHAT THE END WILL BE

"I WILL GO, I SHALL GO
I'LL SEE WHAT THE END WILL BE."

By

Dennis de Freitas

ISBN-9798554948213

Printed in the United States of America.

Published by
Calzypher Publishing
calzpher@gmail.com

DEDICATION

This story was inspired by the writings of
Thome Luiz de Freitas, (1873 -1951).

Thank you, Connie Jean for your sharp mind and eye.

TABLE OF CONTENTS

THE KILLERS

They come at us with an intent to kill. They don't charge at us with a frontal assault swinging a sword. And they won't step out of a dark alley toting a gun. It won't be that obvious. They'll do it with little infestations of bacteria or viruses. We've tried to stop them for centuries but nobody has yet figured out their origin. These little killers seem to be stalking humans as if we're their prey. We may eventually knock them down, but they always seem to come right back again.

Many have speculated why they perform this dastardly deed and why they can't be tamed like any other animal. Perhaps it's because these things grow and change, like soldiers wearing bushes of camouflage in a tropical jungle. You know they're out there somewhere, but you can't see them or feel them, until they attack. These things continually evade our understanding.

Pandemics aren't a new thing. Since the beginning of mankind, there have been silent killers spreading over the world. The first know pandemic was in about 165. The Antonine Plague killed about 5 million people when the world's population was about 200 million. In today's numbers, that is the equivalent of 156 million deaths, 78 times more than deaths from Covid-19 as of October, 2020 at 1.1 million.

Other historic plagues like the Black Death (Bubonic Plague) killed an estimated 200 million of the world's 475 million people. In the 17th century, there was a series of "Great Plagues" that routinely ravaged cities across Europe. More recently there was Cholera, the Third Plague, Yellow Fever, the Russian, Spanish, Asian, and the Hong Kong flu. Not to mention MERS, SARS, HIV, Ebola, and Swine Flu.

Now the world has COVID-19. Where did it come from? Rumors suggested China made it, but that is just a theory. Nobody really understands where these novel bugs originate and why they try to kill us. In 2008 Ed Rybicki, a virologist at the University of Cape Town in South Africa, wrote in "Scientific American" the following:

" At the end of the day, however, despite all of their common features and unique abilities to copy and spread their genomes, the origins of most viruses may remain forever obscure."

The mystery has evaded science generation after generation. Maybe, just maybe, there is an answer that nobody has considered. That answer might be within our grasp.

THE HOMELESS

He came to them as they slept,
No disrespect, no emotions yet.
No glory no wallow would he bask,
Just finish it as he was asked.

For the past decade, Wallace Granger aimlessly roamed the streets of San Francisco. He had few friends, little money, and no real place to go. Yet he was content because unlike other cities, San Franciscans seemed to welcome people like him. They were kind-hearted and didn't mind him carrying a sign saying, "Vietnam vet, please help," even though it was a lie. He assumed that's because it wasn't locals mostly who walked along Powel Street; it was tourists. San Francisco had a love-hate relationship with people from out of town. Particularly those from cultures that didn't tip. Locals felt terrible for the restaurant and bar workers so they chipped in with larger than normal tips. Locals also were generous with him, giving him a little money, used clothing, and occasionally their perfectly good discarded shoes, like the almost new Nikes he now wore. One of the friendly residents threw them to his feet as they drove by in their shiny new 1975 Lincoln Mark V up Powell Street, probably headed for the Union Square parking lot with good access to the high-end shops in San Francisco.

He liked his Johnston & Murphys, even if the laces were missing, had holes in the soles, and the tongue hung out like an overheated dog. These Nikes were almost new. The laces were even clean. Though they were casual and didn't present the sophisticated image he preferred, they fit, and that was good enough.

Another thing that bothered him was that nagging voice. Others on the streets had theirs too, and mostly they all just lived with it. Complaining did no good, even though they tried to persuade it to keep quiet. Some of them came to San Francisco to rid themselves of it, but they all knew that no matter where they lived it would follow and be with them. Like the others, a voice pestered and demanded he do things. Things he had no interest in. Someone told him even the President of the United States had one and maybe it bothered him too.

Wallace didn't remember any family other than those he met on the streets. And neither did he remember where he was born or even if he had any relatives. No mother or father or uncles or aunts or cousins or siblings. He just knew he was here and came to San Francisco from somewhere up north in Oregon... Portland he thought, but even how he got to Oregon was a blank. Life before his life on the streets was an empty chapter in his life. As far as he could tell, he was born in his tattered clothes and worn-out shoes on a cold, wet night in Portland.

Those winters in Portland made him seek another location where the streets were a little more hospitable and the climate a little warmer, not to mention a lot drier. Because of San Francisco's reputation of being friendly to street people, he hitchhiked south, seeking the warmth he thought was there. It wasn't. In fact, during the average July the temperature in San Francisco was 67 degrees to Portland's average of 80, but it at least was drier.

Here he wasn't harassed by the police forcing him to either get treated for his addictions or get a job or do some other despicable thing. Yes, there were shelters he could go to, but they didn't allow drugs or alcohol, so he preferred one of the hundreds of doorways along the streets of "The City," as the locals called San Francisco.

On those cold foggy summer mornings, he sometimes wandered up Powel Street to the Grace Cathedral, an Episcopalian Church on Nob Hill. They offered a free meal program that fed the poor and homeless. Rummaging around in his plastic bag, he found his cleaner clothes and decided to take the hike. From experience, he knew a polite escort out would be in the offing if he was too disrespectful.

He didn't like the term "poor" or "homeless." He was neither poor nor was he homeless. He had a home and plenty of money. His home just didn't have a roof, kitchen, bedrooms, or a bunch of other useless space. His home was a terrific deal. There are no property taxes on discarded refrigerator boxes, and they don't have upkeep expenses and/or house payments. It didn't need painting, and the water heater never broke, nor did the dishwasher. The dishwasher was in the kitchen of the places with free meals. They paid the repair bills and painted the rooms, and he didn't. And he preferred the treasure hunt of digging through trash cans to mowing, fertilizing, and edging a useless lawn just to make it greener than the neighbors. He wasn't homeless; his home was just different.

As he walked along, he hardly noticed the soft rumble beneath Powel Street. The cause was the cables under the roadway coming from the powerhouse at Washington and Mason Street, there to pull the cable cars through the city. He knew cable cars had no motors. Instead, a 'gripman' yanked back on a lever that caused a mechanical grip, much like pliers, to grab the cable which then pulled the car causing it to glide motorless along the street. Once the car gripped the cable, it freed gripman to merrily ring the bell to warn everyone another load of tourists was coming up the hill. Locals seldom used crowded cable cars, preferring trollies and the new BART trains instead.

The rumble and bell ringing on the picturesque cable cars didn't mask the melody of the forty-four-bell carillon of Grace Cathedral. Those bells seemed to be beckoning him forward. By the time he reached the top of

Powel Street, he was out of breath. He stopped and looked up California Street eyeing one more steep block he would need to trek to reach the fabled Nob Hill, so named, someone once told him, from the Hindu word "Nabob," that meant a very wealthy person. And that was true because the area overlooked San Francisco below and was where the famous railroad and mining barons built their mansions.

After that last steep block running past the ritzy Claremont Hotel, he stopped in front of the exclusive Pacific-Union Club, a historic brownstone home built by silver mine mogul James C. Flood in 1886. From there, he gazed up at the Cathedral's twin bell towers out of breath but satisfied that he was close to a nice meal.

Crossing Taylor Street, he continued halfway up the block along California Street and walked in a side door to the Cathedral. Once in, he thought he heard the singing of a choir. Curious, he followed the sound toward the chapel listening intently to the enchanting words of the music. Still, just as he rounded the corner, the music stopped. He scanned the area and except for a few people praying, the chapel was empty. Walking toward the middle of the chapel, he studied the area but still saw no choir, yet the sounds and words of the song continued to play in his mind.

I open my mouth to the Lord, and I won't turn back.
I open my mouth to the Lord, and I won't turn back.
I open my mouth to the Lord, and I won't turn back.
I will go; I shall go to see what the end will be.

Wallace shook his head as he walked. "What the heck is that? Did the voice hire a choir to sing to me?" he wondered.

As he approached the lunchroom, a smartly dressed black man greeted him.

"Welcome to Grace. Help yourself to something to eat," the man said.

"That's kind of you. Thank you," Wallace replied.

Stepping to the back of the food line, he took one of the military surplus metal trays and began working his way along the line. Wallace slid past the lady serving Brussels sprouts but stopped at the hamburger patties with mashed potatoes and gravy. He was ready to bring his refrigerator box home and park right there. Instead, he slid to the dessert, taking a little extra of something that looked like an apple turnover. When his tray was full, he looked out over the group and spotted a place to sit. Making his way to the picnic-like table, he threw his leg over and sat down to eat.

Across from him, another man was slowly savoring the almost delicious meal. His eyes came up to meet Wallace's when he said, "We're lucky this is here, aren't we?"

"You're right my friend. This is much better than the dumpsters off Market Street," Wallace said.

"Yeah. If they had Olympic medals for dumpster diving, someone from San Francisco would surely win gold," the man said.

Wallace couldn't help laughing.

"Did you hear a choir singing when you came in?" Wallace asked the man.

"No. I didn't hear nothin', maybe because I haven't had a good meal in a week and all I could think about was food," the man said.

Wallace too was hungry, but he couldn't shake the sounds of the choir. He changed subjects and asked, "Know any other good places to get a meal?"

"Yeah, a couple," the stranger said but offered nothing. People on the street tended to keep valuable information to themselves.

Wallace sat silently eating waiting for the man to say something, but nothing came. He decided not to press the issue and watched as the man gobbled down his food. After cleaning up his tray, the stranger stood and bid Wallace goodbye.

"See you around," the man said and walked away.

Wallace, scraping some of the gravy from the tray with his metal spoon, then stood, stepped out, and made his way over to the scullery where he dropped off his tray. Hoping to find a place to sit and something to read, he headed to the meeting hall.

As he walked by the man that greeted him, he asked, "Did you enjoy your meal?"

"Yes, I did. Thank you," Wallace replied

"Just to let you know today's meal was brought to you by Beebe Memorial Cathedral in Oakland," he declared proudly.

"Well, thank you for the meal. Are you the pastor there?"

"No, I'm just one of the church volunteers. We have a great community over in Oakland," he said

"Is the choir from your church?" Wallace asked.

The man looked at him puzzled.

"What choir?" he questioned.

"I swore I heard a choir singing when I first came in," Wallace said.

"Where did you hear it?"

"In the chapel," answered Wallace.

"No choir that would be singing in the chapel at this time of day. If one was planned, it would have been ours, and ours isn't here. What were they singing?" the man wondered

"I don't know the name, but I remember the tune and the words," Wallace told him.

"Can you sing me a few bars?" the greeter asked.

Singing a little off-key, Wallace repeated the song he thought a choir was singing.

"Oh, I know that one. It's called 'Open my mouth to the Lord.' It's from an old 'negro' spiritual that slaves and ex-slaves sang," he explained.

The man described that it and others like it were called "sorrow songs." He said the last few words change slightly in other versions to "...see what the end's gonna' be," or "...what the end is going to be." Those slight variations were most likely due to the song being passed down by singing, rather than a music score, from generation to generation.

As they stood talking, a few others came over who he assumed were from Beebe Memorial too. The greeter spoke to them, saying, "This fine gentleman was talking about one of the songs you have our choir sing, Jonathan."

"Jonathan is our music director," he said, looking at Wallace.

"He was commenting about that song, 'Open your mouth to the Lord,'" the greeter said.

"Yes, it's a very old song that came from several Bible passages that discussed going to heaven to meet the Lord. It seems the song was referring to the fight for equality in more modern times," he explained.

"Is that where that last line, 'Seeing what the end is going to be,' comes from?" Wallace asked.

"Generally, it means coming to end of life, yes. But it could also mean the end of some quest or fight, not necessarily something in the Bible, more like coming to the end of a road, something like that. Nobody knows. Personally, because it's speaking to the Lord, it has a reference to what happens when we die and even why and how we exist," he said.

"You mean it could be about why we come to this life and how we leave it?" Wallace asked.

"Yes. I believe it's about our total existence," he said.

"I too wonder what the end will be," Wallace said as he headed for the hall.

With no chairs left in the hall, Wallace decided to leave. The walk back downhill was as tiring as the one coming up, but he navigated his way down to Market Street with a full stomach. He made his way to his shopping cart hideout and began pushing it along Market searching trash for discarded cans. Later, he went to the theater district with the used Styrofoam cup that he had scratched into the soft foam, "Please help" on the top line and under it, "God bless."

After the theaters let out and his cup was partially full, he scraped the coins and bills out and stuffed them in his pocket. It looked like he had enough for breakfast in the morning so headed back to his doorway for a good night's sleep. As he dozed off, something came to him.

"Get up little man. I have her pinpointed. We'll catch her asleep and you will be able to complete your job."

"What? Who?" Wallace thought.

As if the voice could hear his thoughts, it came back to him, saying, *"The one you missed when I sent you to the desert a few years ago is now here. Now leave and walk up that long diagonal street that goes from the water up over the hill. I will guide you."*

Wallace knew the voice meant Market Street, but he also was aware the voice didn't know the name of anything. It merely described things, just like it described Tucson as the desert, but guided him there perfectly.

He hesitated but was not yet ready to defy the voice because it helped him get the heroin he needed and he required its guidance for his supply. Once he was off the stuff, something he was considering, he would ignore it. But for now, he would obey.

He slid from beneath his blankets, pulled on his new Nikes, grabbed his cap, and stood up sleepily... still in a semi-state of dream. He didn't understand why it was important he go now, but there was no sense in even thinking about it. The voice didn't answer questions; it just promoted and coaxed him. When he ignored its commands, it would say simply, *"Do you need a fix?"* and he would do whatever it asked.

"She's asleep now and won't be trouble. Deleting her will help us win. That Whip Titanium guy has way too many points and is gaining on us."

"Who? What's that about?" Wallace wondered out loud.

"Begin the walk to the location, and I will guide you. We must get our work done before the others."

"What others?" Wallace thought. He had no idea what the voice was talking about.

Since it was past the time when other street people were out, he felt relaxed leaving his sleeping place and his cart behind. He covered the cart with a black plastic can liner and rolled it into the doorway where he slept. Hopefully, he would be back before someone tried the door.

Through the drizzle, head down, escaping from the fog, he began trudging up Market Street. He pulled his coat up around his neck, fastened to the top button, hoping to repel the chill. He walked briskly westward away from the city up toward Twin Peaks and the Sutro Tower. He wasn't sure how far or how long he would walk. After about forty-five minutes, the voice said, *"Go down this street."*

With no street to the right, he looked left and could see directly down Guerrero toward the Mission District. Crossing Market, he walked along

Guerrero, wondering how far the voice would have him walk this time. Hopefully, he wasn't on his way to Daly City.

"See that subway-looking station? When we are finished, we'll hide there. Keep walking."

The voice didn't know the name of the BART station, again demonstrating it couldn't even read, but was still commanding him. "How dumb am I?" he wondered.

In another four blocks, the voice came to him telling him to cross a particular street then the next corner where he was to turn again.

"Stop here."

He stopped and waited for further instructions.

"There is a small opening under those trees to your right. Go through there, climb the fence into the back yard immediately behind this house with the green steps."

Wallace looked around and saw the house with the green steps, the tree, and the narrow opening between the green-step house and its neighbor.

"Yes. That one."

Wallace was sure the voice had cameras connected to the back of his eyes since it seemed to know what he was looking at most of the time.

"When you climb the fence, you will be in the back yard of the house behind this one. That's the house we want. The first floor is a garage... do not go in the garage. It leads nowhere. Climb the back-porch steps and open the door that connects you to the laundry room. There you will find a bucket that contains several aluminum softball bats. Pull one of them out slowly and quietly, then go to the bedroom at the end of a long hallway. That is where you'll find the rising star of Congress, Sara Worthington. We must delete her."

There was a long pause as Wallace looked around the area. Then the voice came back saying, *"I must be AFIB while you work, but I will return in just a little while."*

AFIB? What did that mean? Wallace knew from his use of public library computers what AFK meant from the AOL chat rooms. It meant the person you were chatting with wouldn't respond because they went to the bathroom or the refrigerator for a beer, and they were Away From the Keyboard. But he had never heard of AFIB. Away from...what? Idiot Boneheads, he wondered?

Complying with the voice's commands, Wallace quietly made his way through the narrow opening next to the house with the green steps. He climbed the fence and walked across a small back yard to the steps leading up to a laundry room. Quietly, he made his way up the steps, testing each one for an inevitable squeak, until he got to the top. Twisting the knob, he found the door wasn't locked so he opened it slowly and made his way inside.

There he found himself in an almost-dark laundry room that seemed to be added to the house after it was built. In this section of San Francisco, the homes were built around 1920 and only 1% had indoor plumbing. He wondered where they had put the bathroom.

Looking around the room, he spotted the bucket with the aluminum bats that seemed almost luminous in the diffused light. In the stillness of the house, he reached down to pull out a bat from the galvanized trashcan that was jammed full. Trying not to make noise, he pulled up on it but couldn't quite get it loose. Reaching for the handles, he moved them around as quietly as possible until he found one that seemed extractable. As he pulled, there was a soft scratching of aluminum against the tin sides of a bucket that seemed to be working as a trashcan amplifier.

"Got it," he thought to himself, wondering if the scraping noise had awoken anyone in the house.

THE DELETE

Stay quiet now with catlike steps,
The targets here; no pesky pets.
Do the job; get out fast,
Let's make it back where we can rest.

Wallace stopped and listened to see if the noise had caused a stir. If someone opened the door to come and investigate the sound, he was close enough to the back door to escape without being recognized. After a few minutes of hearing nothing, Wallace made his way into the kitchen, where he spotted an opening to the hall. Stepping into it, he could see it was the typical layout of the traditional "railroad" house in San Francisco. Because of the limited acreage in The City, homes were built narrow to maximize limited space. The hallway ran almost the length of the house with rooms off the hall, one behind the other, as the passage ran from front to back.

As instructed, Wallace walked to the end of the hall where he found a room with the door slightly open. He nudged it a little further open and saw a bed and someone seemingly asleep. Cautiously, he slid in. Light from the street glowed of the yellowish window shade revealing a shape in the bed. He hesitated but remembered the words of the voice repeating his commands. *"Delete her."* He raised the bat over his head and brought it down just as the woman in the bed rolled over.

"Puff," came the sound as the bat smacked the pillow.

The girl began rolling over to the opposite side of the bed attempting to escape her attacker. Before she could utter a word, Wallace quickly raised the bat again, this time finding his target. The simultaneous smack and splash of slushiness made him wince.

"What have I done?" he thought to himself.

Instantly a feeling of sickness raced through his body, and before he could stop its surge up his throat, he bent over and violated the homes new carpet.

He moved over to the bed and, through the dim light, looked at the beautiful face that stared back at him. Her forehead resembled a wad of clay thrown with force on the table, but her beautiful face was smooth, soft, and untouched.

Quickly, he jerked his eyes away, wondering how he could have taken this life, but understood that he had only performed his duty like a soldier at war. Then he had second thoughts. Did the Third Reich soldiers working at Auschwitz also believe they were without guilt because they were only doing their duty?

He thought that to be true, but he knew the history of WWII and the terrible atrocities committed simply because someone felt it was their duty. He had done his duty, and it was a ghastly one, yet he had no time to think about remorse. Now he had to get out of there.

Though he was sad, sick, and ready to cry for the life he had taken, he quickly turned, stepped out of the room, and moved into the hall. Just as he began working his way back down the hall, he was called to a sudden stop.

"Wait! Not her. This isn't the one. You're in the wrong room. I said in the bedroom at the end of the hall. This is the front of the hall."

Wallace stopped. He thought about that for a moment. It had been years since he had even been in a house, but he knew when you walked in, you kept walking to get to the end, just as he had done. Then it dawned on him that he had entered from the back and had walked toward the front. He had it reversed.

"Shit," he thought to himself.

He was still confused since this was the only closed -- even though just partly closed -- door off the hallway. The kitchen where he entered didn't have a door and as he entered the passage and worked his way along, there was another opening to his right, but it didn't have a door. The door he entered was the only one at the far end of the hall.

The half-moon window of the front door cast a faint shadow down the long foyer. Did he see another door at that end? He couldn't be sure, so he decided to investigate a little further.

Using his bat on the wall like a blind man's white cane, he slowly moved along half feeling his way along the semi-darkened area. Before reaching the end, he felt one of the openings he passed. Was this the "back" bedroom?

Cautiously he moved into the open area that was faintly lit by a dirty window on the far wall. There was no yard, no flowers, no view, only the neighbor's flaking, painted wall. He shifted his gaze to the right and saw a passageway to the kitchen. Then he looked back in the room to see if there was anything he missed. There was a chair, a couch, and a lamp, but no bed. Feeling around, he found a piece of cloth lying across the chair, so he picked it up and wiped the bat's business end. Without a bed, this obviously wasn't the correct room either.

Clumsily, he bumped into a floor lamp, quickly grabbing it before it fell. To the right of the lamp, he made his way through the small passageway that led past a sink. He stopped, turned on the water, washed his hands, and splashed some on his face, then stepped into the kitchen. He saw the door where he came in and moved toward it.

"You haven't finished your job."

Irritated, but still obedient, he again stepped into the passageway. He turned and looked in the direction he'd gone and could see down the long narrow corridor and the front door with half-moon window at the top.

"That's the front, this has to be the end of the hall the voice is referring to," he thought to himself.

Recognizing his mistake, he turned to his left, where the hall ended, and saw another door. He cocked his head, listening for sounds. Pressing his ear against the door, he heard a slight rustling and some soft footsteps behind the door. Faintly, he could hear whispering as if someone was softly talking, saying a series of numbers.

"Was it this address," he wondered. Carefully, he placed his hand on the round doorknob and twisted, hoping for a silent release. There was resistance. Not the kind one would feel if there was a metallic block like a lock. It was a soft resistance causing the knob to feel as if it was being held from the other side. He stopped and thought. If it is a girl, he should be able to overpower her easily, but she seemed to have the strength of two women or a powerful man. He laid his bat against the wall and grabbed the doorknob with two hands. With all his strength, he twisted it and felt it grudgingly move. As it did, he pressed against the door, but still couldn't get it open. He knew she must be placing her foot or some other object at the bottom, holding it closed from the other side. With his shoulder he pressed far enough to slip his foot between the door and the jamb.

He had it partially open slid his foot in the door opening. He reached for his bat that was now out of reach just as a sharp pain accompanied by a loud thunk caused him to quickly withdraw his foot.

Falling to the floor, he again reached for the bat that had fallen on the floor a few feet away. Retrieving it, he laid it against the wall and got back up. This time when he forced the door open, he would wedge the bat in the door, not his hurting foot. He again twisted the knob, pressed the door slightly ajar, grabbed his bat, and forced it into the opening. Using it, he pried the door open a little further.

As he was about to enter, he heard sirens in the distance. Was he imaging it, or were they getting closer? He wasn't sure. He knew he would have to complete his task quickly and get out.

Forcefully he worked his body into the partially opened door. There was the soft resistance of someone holding it, but it wasn't something he couldn't overcome.

"Watch it!"

11

Wallace caught the hint of movement and heard something slicing through the air. Instinctively, he jumped back, pulling the door with him. There was a crash of something substantial against the doorframe sending splinters flying and forcing the door back against his body. Turning quickly, he swung his bat toward the direction he thought the other person might be. He felt a soft thud and a muffled cry of surprise as a body fell to the floor.

The sirens in the distance were now just outside, and heavy footsteps were climbing the stairs, followed by a crash as the front door flew open. He turned and ran through the kitchen for the rear door. He couldn't be sure if he hit his target or just a clump of clothing hanging over the door but knew he couldn't wait around to find out.

As he ran, he wondered what would happen if he had failed to delete her.

THE TARGET

They'll come for you as you sleep,
Don't give your life, don't take that leap.
They'll appear to you in your dream,
Hold it back, you cannot scream.
The lessons learned not long ago,
May guard you from his murderous blow.

In her dream, Aunt Rachel was cooking up her famous stew, stirring it in mother's large metal pot as she hummed some unknown melody beneath her breath. When she was through, Rachel rapped on the side of the pan with her spoon, letting the family know she was finishing the meal.

Then the dream jumped going to when Sara was small and Rachel and she would sit and color the day away. Like a broken record, the dream jumped again and Sara, through sign language, asked Rachel to tell a story. Though Rachel was not blessed with the gift of speech or hearing, she made her way through the world with an unrelenting love. Rachel went through a story using sign language and facial gestures, telling her a fairy tale that Sara heard before but loved.

Even without a voice, her love sparkled through her actions and her smile. It wasn't just coloring, Sara also remembered Rachel playing games with her like hide-and-seek or jump rope or even a little stickball. Sara was somehow magically lifted from her bed and moved toward the kitchen of their apartment with anxious anticipation. She felt the eagerness of seeing Rachel wanting to throw her arms around her and give her cheeks a zillion kisses. She longed for those great Rachel hugs, warm smile; delicate touch; soft caresses; and those sweet "butterfly" kisses she gave with her eyelashes on Sara's cheeks.

Floating slowly toward the sounds, Sara felt herself drifting effortlessly above the bedroom floor. In her dream, there was no familiar shuffling of slippers over the smooth bedroom carpet; no footsteps pattering their way along the hallway; no doors opening or closing. In the half-sleep, she drifted toward the sound as if on a magic carpet riding a moonbeam toward a deep, heartfelt love. In the kitchen, Rachel's back was turned facing the empty kitchen wall left of the stove. She carried no pot and no spoon. Instead, she stood motionless, almost department store mannequin-like.

Sara's loving feelings began to change. Once Head and Shoulders clean, Rachel's black hair now seemed oily, dirty, and unkempt. Her typically fresh and stylish dress looked dirty, wrinkled, and torn. Sweat streaks lined her filthy legs down to her feet. Strangely, her feet were adorned in an old pair of grimy softball cleats Sara recognized as hers from years ago on Arizona's women's softball team. Rachael's head turned, tipped, and looked down toward the floor as if gazing at something. Sara's eyes darted down to where Rachael was looking, and there, in a sprawled heap, was a lifeless Christiana, Sara's roommate. Christiana's glassy eyes were staring blankly at nothing. Her golden hair pointed in a thousand directions incrusted with splattered dark dried blood that seemed to have escaped from the depression in her skull. Her broken arms with palms facing skyward seemed to be fending off an invisible force.

Most gruesome was Christiana's one leg that was bent at the knee, forcing her shoeless foot to point toward her blood-stained hair. Beneath her, and bright as a polished San Francisco hook and ladder, trickled a syrupy liquid substance she knew was blood. Sara gasped, but couldn't scream. With all her strength, she tried to call out but couldn't muster a sound, so she decided to turn and run, but her legs wouldn't move, and she could only float petrified in fear. Rachel now had the pot and spoon and kept stirring unaffected by Christiana's poker-chip-eyed corpse gawking skyward. Again, Sara tried to scream, but her voice only mimicked Rachel's. Finally, for some odd reason, Rachael laid the pot aside and holding her arms out toward Rachel she signed, 'Scream!'"

Rachel then looked down at Christiana as she emotionlessly went back to stirring and creating that metallic sound. Then something strange happened. Without moving her legs, she slowly rotated as if she were a turning store window display. When she completed the rotation, Sara could see that the stirring sound wasn't from a spoon or even a kitchen utensil. Instead, Rachel was clutching the large metal bat trashcan. She was slowly stirring it with a blue and silver aluminum softball bat. Her eyes shot from the bat up to Rachel's face that no longer revealed the sweet loving Rachel she had known as a child. The soft lips that once seemed to form a perpetual smile and the dark eyes that always had a twinkle were missing. That face was drawn and cold, white and lifeless. Rather than love and kindness, it showed anger, hate, and resentment. As Rachel released the bat and the metal kettle, the two seemed to hang in the air, and Rachel signed something quickly back to Sara that jolted her awake. Her fingers slowly wrote out, "He is here to kill you." Rachel's shrill scream jolted Sara out of her dream.

*****

As she came out of the dream, wet with sweat, Sara's heart was pounding in her chest, but her senses were heightened. On edge, she listened carefully to the dark house. She heard a slight scrap of something against the wall in the hall. She turned her head and listened again, intently. She heard a muffled thump that reminded her of a neighborhood kid hitting a watermelon with his bat. She abruptly sat up, trying to comprehend what she'd just heard and the visions she saw without realizing it was a dream. Even in confusion between consciousness and sleep, she knew that Rachel couldn't be there in the kitchen. After all, Rachel had been brutally beaten, robbed, raped, and murdered in the safety of her home one dark, moonless night when Sara was just ten.

Hearing the sound, Sara sat partially upright, resting back on her elbows. She could hear the sound of an occasional car driving down Dolores Street and the soft scream of a siren off in the distance. Her sense of sound now so acute she could hear the leaking faucet in the shared bathroom and the ticking of the clock on her bed stand.

Then there was something else. She heard a shuffling of feet. Slowly she slid out of bed and quietly glided over to the bedroom door where she stood listening and heard it again along with a distinct squeak in the hardwood floor. Her biggest fears were right; someone was there.

She wondered if it was her roommate Christiana. Perhaps she had gone to the bathroom and was just heading back to bed. But the shuffling wasn't her familiar barefooted footsteps. It was more the sound of something standing or slowly trundling along the hallway. She wondered if maybe Christiana brought home a friend who was spending the night. But she didn't think so. If she had a friend staying over, she would have told her. And even if Christiana were going out, she would have left a note. Christiana wasn't the type to pick up some guy in a bar and bring him home. Sara knew it had to be something or someone else.

It was then that she realized the sound she was hearing wasn't Christiana or a friend. It wasn't a mouse, or a rat, or someone's dog or cat; it was an intruder. Someone had come into their flat, probably through the rear door that leads from the kitchen into the house. That door had a broken lock, but flats in that section of the city sat directly adjacent to each other with no side yard space to the street. The only access to the back was through the garage under the flat, and it was locked by way of an electric garage door opener. She thought the only way was for the intruder to jump the neighbor's fence behind them. That house had a side yard.

They'd discussed guns in the house but dismissed it since most gun deaths were attributed to people who lived in the house, not intruders.

15

Besides, she hated guns ever since the time she'd been shot and her Congressman was killed down in Guyana's forests. Her actions that day helped in her being elected to take his place in Congress.

She kept her favorite aluminum softball bat in her bedroom. She'd hit a game-winning home run in the bottom of the ninth to beat rival Arizona State, so this one was special to her. She didn't keep it with those on the back porch. That's when a lightbulb went off. The sounds she heard in the dream with Rachel stirring something metallic could be related to what she understood now. She'd distinctly listened to the sound of a bat hitting a watermelon so concluded that the dream and the melon sound interrelated, and someone was in her hallway. Sara became concerned. There was a danger in the house to her and to Christiana.

Sara considered her options. Her staff purchased one of the new brick-sized cell phones and demanded she carry it with her at all times. Cell phones were a new technology in San Francisco, and they wanted to reach her when a critical situation came up. This certainly was one of them. But if she used it, whoever was there might hear her, might have a gun, and then she wouldn't have a chance.

She considered that if they just wanted their television or stereo system, they'd just let them take their stuff and leave. She'd recalled a public service announcement that preached confronting an intruder was dangerous and could result in the homeowner being hurt. Still, she had to be prepared to do something.

The floor squeaks seemed to quiet down and she assumed the intruder had turned off the hallway into the living room looking for something to take, so she decided to take the chance of making a call.

Stepping away from her bedroom door, she moved quickly to her bed stand and searched around in the darkness for the bulky cell phone. She fumbled, knocked the small clock radio off, but luckily caught it before it hit the wood floor. She found the lamp's base to orient her hand, then moved slightly forward, found the phone, and pressed 911.

She heard the sounds of ringing. Once, twice, three times, then an answer.

"911. What is your emergency?" the calm voice said.

Whispering, she said, 'There's an intruder in my house.'"

"What is your location?"

"1743 Delores. Please hurry."

"Ma'am, not your address. What city are you calling from?"

"City? I'm in San Francisco. Where are you?"

"This is the regional 911 center. I'll transfer you, and they will help you."

San Francisco had not yet implemented PSAP, the Public Safety Answering Point, that would automatically locate and transfer cell phone calls to the appropriate agency. Though the FCC was in the process of requiring all cell phones to include accurate GPS information, the system was not in place for her call.

Waiting felt like she was in the BART tube with the train speeding down on her. By the faint sound of the old home's creaking wooden floors, Sara sensed the intruder was moving toward her. She suppressed an urge to throw the phone on the floor and run for the back door. Sara realized that it could be a fatal mistake. Besides, if there was an intruder, she couldn't leave Christiana alone to deal with it.

There was silence on the line as the call was transferred from the Regional operator to San Francisco emergency. After a few moments, an operator came on the line saying, "San Jose emergency."

Sara wanted to scream.

"San Jose? I'm in San Francisco, you idiot. Get them my address 1743 Dolores," she whispered forcefully."

"I'll transfer you," was all the operator said.

"I can't stay on the line and I need help…NOW!"

In frustration, she threw her cellphone toward her bed, hoping it would land softly. Next, she grabbed her bat and firmly placed her bare foot against the bottom of the door. She held the doorknob securely, hoping to prevent someone from twisting it. It wasn't long until she felt someone from the other side begin to turn it.

With her foot and weight against the door and her hand on the knob, she continued resisting. He was stronger and got the door partly open. Sara saw a foot slip between the door and the jam so she took the slugger up and drove it down hard enough on his foot to let the intruder know it wasn't going to be easy. She heard the guy let out a scream and his foot quickly retracted, allowing her to close the door and grab the knob again, this time more firmly.

With the next attempt, he again overpowered her ability to keep the doorknob from twisting. When he got the door open a crack, he stuck in an aluminum bat, using it to pry the door open further. As he was about to enter, Sara heard sirens in the distance. He seemed to stop and listen himself then went back to trying to force his way in. He worked his body into the partially opened door.

Sara could see the outline of a guy in the dimness. He stopped his movement and waited, listening. She took the opportunity to take a swing at the intruder's head, but he ducked. The door was now free to swing open, and the shadowy figure swung his bat that caught Sara on the shoulder. Many balls had hit her in her softball life in college, so it shocked more than hurt her, but still, it sent her stumbling and falling to the floor.

The sirens she heard in the distance were now just outside and heavy footsteps were climbing the stairs followed by a crash as the front door flew open. The stranger turned and ran through the kitchen for the rear entrance to the back yard and escape.

THE SOLDIER

There is that place,
Where souls do dwell.
For some it is heaven,
For others it's hell.

Mark Gorman survived his teen years, but not without consequences. Like his friends, he was competitive, energetic, fearless, and like so many who didn't survive those years, reckless. Combining those four factors can make a strong and healthy adult life, or they can place a young man in dangerous situations. It was the latter that committed him to the maximum time of service to the government.

The government assessed all young people for aptitude and personal strengths. For example, unlike those reckless boys, others were introverted, lethargic, cautious, and careful. For the cautious, careful, studious type, it might be higher education and jobs as accountants, scientists, or research. Or if their grades aren't high enough, government service could mean working in parks as a groundskeeper or delivering mail.

There was one more option for those in the competitive/energetic classification: the military. The country had been at war as long as an eighteen-year-old could remember. As Mark Gorman reached that critical age, his destiny was determined by those last two government measurement factors: fearlessness and recklessness.

It happened one night when he was out with friends. He and his buddy Pete took their dates to a local bar for one of the girls' eighteenth birthday. They were having a good time shooting pool, playing the jukebox, telling jokes, dancing, and laughing. The evening's tone changed when a pair of rugged-looking guys a little older than they were entered the bar. They wore identical dirty blue overalls with a circle logo with the letters S and D in the middle. The logo stood for Sewer Department that had recently been renamed from Sanitation Department when the new practical-oriented Mayor determined there was nothing sanitary about sewers. Under the logo, the government went to the extra expense of embroidering their name in an attempt to make everyone friendlier. Dick, the larger of the two, seemed to be the leader. He walked with purpose toward the bar and pressed his way between a pair sitting there and ordered two beers with a snarl and two-fingered signal. When they arrived, he took one over to his companion, a smaller but still stout and muscular man standing by the jukebox.

"Here you go, Harry. This is your brand isn't it?" Dick said.

"It'll do," Harry shouted over the song playing from the jukebox.

The two sipped and drank, plunked more coins into the jukebox, and took turns going up to the bar for beer. Not far from where they were standing, the four eighteen- and nineteen-year-olds were still playing pool. The girls were watching when one of them noted the name tags on their overalls and whispered something to her friend. She looked over at the sewermen watching them and began giggling.

The two sewer workers saw the girls poking fun at their expense. The bigger one, Dick, walked over to the pool table and approached Mark.

"What so funny?" Dick roared.

Mark looked at him, somewhat surprised but said nothing.

"I'm talking to you, punk," the sewerman working snarled

Mark, lined up to sink the nine ball in the side pocket, slowly pulled the cue stick back and stroked the cue ball into the nine and watched it slowly roll into the pocket. Without turning, he began walking around the table to line up the eight ball.

Harry slid over to stand beside Dick more as a backup than wanting to interfere with his fun.

Out of the corner of his mouth, Dick said, "Your girlfriend likes me better. I think she was laughing at that pussy little face of yours."

He elbowed his buddy Harry, and the two took a sip of beer and began laughing.

Still getting no reaction from Mark, Dick finally said firmly, "Get your ass away from that table, punk."

Mark continued eyeing the table lining up his important eight-ball shot.

"Did you hear what I said?" the man yelled. The bar went silent, and patrons turned their attention to the group as the man grabbed Mark by the shoulder, spinning him around.

Again, one of the other girls cupped her hand, whispered something to her friend, and the two began laughing uncontrollably.

"Damn it, what's so funny?" Dick yelled across the table.

"You two," Mark's date giggled.

"Funny how?

"You mean funny like a clown? Funny because we tell funny jokes?" Harry piped in.

"No," she said, laughing again.

"What's so fucking funny?" Dick yelled.

"You two are Harry and Dick. Get it? Harry dick," she finally said as the beers they had helped the humor spillover.

"Fuck you, bitch. I'm coming over there after I make your boyfriend my bitch," Dick said.

"With lightning reflexes, reminiscent of the doctor's red rubber mallet against a knee, Mark fired a straight right fist into the man's nose, sending him flying backward. With blood trickling out of his nose, the man came charging back at Mark. Mark stepped aside just as Dick went for a tackle, causing the man to hit the pool table, planting his face on the granite-backed green felt surface.

Harry slid back and grabbed a cue stick from the rack as Dick picked up one propped against the table's side. Dick spun off the table and took a swing at Mark. Seeing it coming, Mark quickly ducked, causing Dick to spin around like a home run hitter striking out. Pete spotted Harry pull the cue stick from the rack so he stood in front of him, keeping him away from the fight.

After the miss, Dick pulled the stick back again and took another swing at Mark, who grabbed it in midair. Mark yanked the stick and pulled Dick toward him and, at the same time, threw a right hand directly into Dick's nose. Blood gushed out and Dick staggering backward and fell, hitting his head on the pool table railing with a sickening thud. Dick slumped and fell to the floor, stone-cold dead.

The bartender called the police and Mark was taken into custody. Though he hadn't started the fight, the judge learned he'd been in other fights. Most were in sanctioned boxing and wrestling matches with a few outside of school.

"Your love of fighting and your temper has gotten you into trouble before, Mr. Gorman. Those were minor; this one is serious. I think you are a threat to the public safety until you learn control. I'm going to give you a choice of prison for thirty years or the military for the rest of your life or until they believe you'd be safe in public. They can use fighters like you in the war, so make your choice."

He was held in custody until the Army came by and took in him in shackles to their stockade. After a few days, he went through a battery of aptitude tests. He scored the highest in puzzle solving and computations. When he was called in to meet with Major Johnson, the head of recruiting and placement, he was told he would be off to tech school to learn about the Army's technology if he would agree to something else.

"What else do you want me to do?" Mark asked.

"We have an annual competition in mixed martial arts between the other branches of service and the General wants the Army to win this time. We've had our ass kicked in the first round by even the fucking Navy. I want to send you for some training and we'll see if you can compete with our current team. If you can, you'll be part of that team in addition to tech school. If that's not agreeable, we have lots of openings in the infantry."

It didn't take long for Mark to make his decision.

"I sure wouldn't want to let the General down, sir. Where do I sign?"

At first, Mark was just a regular "grunt" doing as he was told, training and fighting just as he'd always fought, but this time with more learned skills. He attended the tech school in the evenings and trained for fighting during the day.

The military worked off the rough edges of his amateur boxing and wrestling moves and his street fighting techniques and trained him to become an even better fighter. He'd be there for the rest of his life, so why not become even more proficient at something he was already good at. He understood that the 'rest of his life' could be as near as the next battle.

THE BATTLE

Soldiers fight and solders swear,
The enemy charges;
From who knows where?
For youth it's glory;
The challenges there.
For the soldier it's misery,
That's filled with terror.

Tossing and turning, trying to break out of the dream, Mark grabbed the spare pillow to defend himself. The tormented sleep ripped away any sense of clean sheets and soft pillows. It seemed his team had walked and run miles attempting to break out of the surrounding enemy. They were out of ammunition and left to defend themselves with their bare hands. Mark had one weapon left: a pillow. And it was now the only weapon he had to fight off the tattoo-faced enemy. He had no gun, no knife and no grenades. All he had to face the ruthless enemy was his spare pillow. He saw the snarl on their faces and the redness of their eyes as they closed in from all sides. As they broke through, his violent swings didn't faze them. And as the feathers flew, a bayonet sparkled in the sunlight headed straight toward his eye. The flash brought him suddenly awake, as it did every morning at daybreak.

To Mark, the pillow was a symbol of guilt. Guilt because it felt so luxurious compared to where he'd been. There is nothing comforting in war. One of the first things he obtained after buying a queen-sized bed was that extra pillow. Having just one was a luxury compared to the rucksack he used as a pillow in the field. In that makeshift pillow, he carried first aid kits, spare batteries, his metal mess kit, binoculars, an extra radio, and several other things, none of them soft. In the field, he sometimes used it because it was softer than his steel helmet, but he might as well have used a rock as a pillow. Softness was something a soldier rarely experienced, so having just one pillow was a treat; the other pure luxury.

Rolling over to the side of his bed, Mark tried to force himself awake. Sitting up and laying his feet on the floor, he let his head drop down into his palms. His mind shifted to other thoughts, but none seemed to stick. Unwillingly, he kept going back to the dream. Finally, he let himself go and slowly succumbed to the need for sleep. He laid back down on his pillow and drifted off to the darkness of terror.

Their bunker had a four-inch tube extending up through the meter-thick concrete roof. The air tube included iron bars crisscrossing the inside to prevent the enemy from dropping a grenade down it, but in the dream, that shaft was a Santa Claus-sized chimney.

When the attack started, Butch was firing through the slit in their bunker. Mark struggled to get to his side, but he couldn't make himself move through the sticky tar on the concrete floor. He could hear the enemy beating drums and blowing bugles as they progressed closer. An enemy soldier dropped down the chimney and opened fire on the two of them. His kind had an orange skin that turned a burnt umber during battle. It was easy to distinguish the enemy no matter what uniform they wore. In his world, orangeries were hated and killing them was necessary or they would dominate and use his kind like cattle.

Bullets began ricocheting off the walls of the bunker, one grazing his leg. In the dream, the sting was vivid, and his body recoiled in pain, causing him to kick off the blankets of his bed.

When the fighters in the dream came closer, an explosive dropped through that air intake and exploded, knocking both the enemy soldier along with he and Butch to the concrete floor, numbing his senses. As they lay there, the enemy casually walked over to the door of the bunker as if nothing had happened and opened it. Mark frantically reached around for his weapon sliding his hands along the dirty floor. Finding nothing, he reached over to the bedside table knocking off his reading lamp. Finally, after rising to his knees, he crawled to the foot of the bed, frantically searching. Still nothing. Where was it?

Sweat rolled down his face as he rolled back up to his pillow, wrapped his arms around it, reached down, pulled up the blankets, and climbed under. He laid his head back down, groggily wondering if he was in that recurring dream or was this real. No matter, he had to fight. The enemy was at the open door carrying long swords with blades reflecting shimmers of light. Then there was that roar of the sword's handle with its built-in lasers firing and reverberating off the walls. He knew he must defend himself or die, but how without his weapon?

On the next search, he found the other pillow he'd somehow knocked to the floor. Grabbing it, he brought it to his shoulder, pointing it in the direction of the intruders. Frantically he reached for the trigger, but it wasn't there. No trigger, no return fire to the enemy, no bang of his laser, no kickback of a powerful gun. Finally, he threw the pillow in the direction of the imaginary invader and the resounding crash as his trophy fell off the chest of drawers startling, but not waking him from the nightmare.

Eyes squinted, as if that would help him see through the darkness, he saw something. In the dimness, the image of Harry "Butch" Thompson slowly drifted further and further away.

"Wait! Don't go. We have a better chance in here than out there. We can do it together," he shouted.

Mark attempted to leave his perch and run over to grab Butch, but he couldn't move. He fought hard, but the harder he tried, the more his legs seemed to be cemented in place. He'd kill them all with his bare hands and Butch would be back to help him. But then he realized Butch would be of no assistance missing that large portion of his head.

Just as a snarling, facial-tattooed, steel-helmeted enemy soldier came at him, raising the laser sword over his head, Mark woke up wet and almost out of breath.

****

Following the instructions of the military psychologist, he began taking slow, relaxed breaths until he could feel his heart rate begin to stabilize. The attack was so firmly etched in Mark Gorman's brain, it was like an internal brand: never going away and never fading. It lingered there ready to pounce at the slightest provocation.

They'd been under attack for several days but firmly held their position. Their objective was to hold that position to the last man. The high ground was the holy ground. From there they could see the enemy approaching from every angle. Even though they were in a superior defensive position, the cost in human life was extremely high. More than seventeen soldiers were killed in the last attack. But as soon as they were lost, they'd be replaced, making them no more than chess pieces on a grimy battlefield chessboard.

He'd seen so many of his men killed, including his most productive Squad Leader, Corporal Butch Thompson. Butch was hit by a shot to the head almost decapitating him just as Mark was about to pat him on the shoulder for doing a great job defending the platoon's flank. Mark didn't know he'd been hit until the fight was over. There was an open gash in his head and blood was flowing like someone emptying a polluted canteen. Mark reached up, felt the wetness and shook it off, telling his troops it was just a scratch. It was worse than a scratch. After the Navy destroyed the attackers with their attack bombers, the fighting stopped. In the lull, the medivac helicopter came in to pick up the wounded. Before they got to Mark, things went black. The next thing he recalled was being in a hospital somewhere behind the lines.

Mark served gallantly as a platoon leader and was awarded the rank of Captain in the hospital. After the surgery to repair the gaping wound, he was offered the opportunity to move into a new section of the military that required more training in computations for their modern BAAD or Battlefield Advanced Analysis Division. He was sent to attend a civilian college where he excelled and was an instructor assistant after becoming one of their outstanding students. Being away from the war was a welcome respite and, though he would miss his fellow fighters, he enjoyed this new assignment.

THE TEACHER

Don't just stand there.
Wishing you could be there.
Do it now so you can go there.
Instead of to that ghastly war there.

Spilling over with aromas of a thousand faraway places, the bustling college town café stirred with a din of excitement stemming from the recent win of the football team over the school's hated rival, the Red Scorpions. In the background, the music of the anthem softly played unheard by the students assembled in huddles gabbing about the victory the night before.

Mark Gorman was a regular at the café after he was appointed a teaching assistant to the head professor of the computations department. He got the position not so much because he needed the money to supplement his military pay, but because the professor was impressed with Mark's test results, his participation in class, and his maturity... a maturity resulting from his age and military experience.

He grabbed a cup of "Today's Special," not even knowing what it was, then leaning forward with his backpack he nodded a friendly hello to some of the students he recognized and headed toward the back of the café. Balancing his drink and trying not to spill the slew of papers under his arm, he searched for a table. Finding a dime-sized café table, he slid out a metal chair then conspicuously laid out his belongings spread over the entire surface to dissuade disturbance from any table-seeking students.

Mark appeared as fit as any of the school's jocks with his solid, lean, muscular build more that of a wide receiver than a linebacker. His dark hair hadn't been surrendered to clippers since the Army gave him this opportunity. Not cutting it was partly a demonstration of his new freedom, partly an expression of his individualism, but more it helped prevent answering questions about the scars that stood out when his hair was short. One of the professors suggested he pull it back into a ponytail to make him look lawyeresque, but he had no desire to look like anything or anyone. He just wanted to get through this with a plan to find the golden ring and free himself from the requirement to return to the ages-long war.

The Army sent him to school to recover and learn more about computations. He fully expected to return to the war when he finished. But he got lucky. That first year, Congress passed legislation called the "Creative Reimbursement Accelerated-Discharge Program," something the enlisted people called C.R.A.P. The design of the program was to help the stretched and shrinking national budget by reducing expenses and raising revenue. To do this, the soldier needed a substantial cash sum and provide the government with proof his future tax revenues would exceed his value as a soldier. The buyout program was his objective now if he could just figure out how to get some quick money and a secure job. He hoped the nightmares would stop if his subconscious mind knew he wasn't going back into battle. But he had a job to do first. He'd have to work on this pile of student grades, but though he tried hard, his thoughts always went back to making it big financially in the shortest time possible. He had just one more school term to accomplish it, and time was running out.

The longish hair couldn't hide all his scars. One, on the side of his yesterday-shaven face, wasn't grotesquely disfiguring, but it did signal a rugged past that was typical of soldiers who often appeared they'd been in a knife fight in a telephone booth. If he caught someone's eye moving to that side of his face, he wondered if they were thinking, "Should I ask him?" If they did ask, he simply said it was a car accident then changed the subject.

While that cheek scar stood out like a beacon, others resided deeper inside, appearing only to those who could use their energy to see his nightmarish dreams. He'd suffered through the pain, but the psychological scars hid in the corners of his brain, jumping out whenever they chose. Thankfully, unlike so many of his friends, he'd survived. But survival came with a price, something he'd have to work his way through for the rest of his life.

THE STUDENTS

Fast, fast, fast, and faster.
Find the thing that you can master.
Do it quickly, big and bold.
Save your life
Get that gold.

Mark reached into his camouflage backpack to pull out some neatly typed papers along with some handwritten ones. For posting the scores, he also opened his iBoard. First, he'd work on grading the papers and he'd review his notes and some programming ideas he had.

The background of chitter-chatter and the soothing background music of the anthem helped him focus on the task. The elevator music anthem played softly in all school buildings. Psychological studies demonstrated that music softened and mellowed, hence it was never played in any military installation. There the music was loud, intense, and boisterous, creating the feeling of aggression. In this community, the music was intended to prevent civil uprisings by making citizens think about what their end would be.

His notes contained programming concepts from one of the classes, along with some of his ideas for implementation. He would hack into some grid sites to document and demonstrate his prowess of cracking code, then sell himself as a security consultant. He'd focus on major financial firms considering he might be able to obtain an upfront consulting fee. If his idea had the potential of saving an institution million, his consulting fee could be tremendous. As he sat there staring off into space, he hardly noticed a shadowy figure approach his table.

"This seat taken?" a tall, almost skinny young guy with longish, unwashed black hair asked.

Disrupted from his chain of thought, Mark looked up, "Oh... no, go ahead," he said, haltingly pointing at the empty chair. He slid his papers and notes off the table and stuffed them into his backpack.

"Guess I was hogging over the whole table," he added somewhat dejectedly wondering if the guy even noticed he had work laid out on the table.

"No problem. I'm not disturbing you, am I? I could stand over there by the window," the stranger said.

Mark looked around the room and noticed the crowds and occupied tables. But people come and go in the place. He wished the guy would stand by the window and wait for another place to open up, but his mother had always taught him good manners, so he lied, "No. Not at all. You can sit down," Mark said, trying not to show his disappointment.

"You studying for a test or something?" the kid asked.

"Not really. I'm just thinking about a few things," Mark said.

The kid wore a grayish-white, short-sleeved, stained dress shirt missing the third button from the top.

His skin was baby pale, smooth, and soft, and if it weren't for his lanky size and the slight fuzzy hint of a mustache, he might be mistaken for a ten-year-old. His black Sta-Prest pants had some stay left but no press. The whitish, faded line running down the front and back hinted of a long-gone permanent pleat. Rather than shoes, he wore black flip-flops that were too short to prevent his prominent, longish second toe, with its dirty toenail, from protruding over the end.

"You must be a new computational science student, right?" Mark asked, eyeing the "Zax Technical Solutions" pocket protector stuffed with pens of various colors any art student would envy. Mark wondered if he had that pocket protector because it gave the impression that the wearer had some affiliation with the company.

"Yeah, it's my first semester," the kid said. "My name's Duncan, Duncan Moore," he said, sticking his right hand across the table and balancing his cup of hot something in the other.

"I'm Mark. Nice to meet you. Do you work for Zax?" Mark asked.

Blushing, Duncan reached up to the pens, "On, no. I found it in the trash in one of the classrooms," he said.

Mark had a lot on his mind but would have to delay his in-depth thinking for a while. The kid seemed polite and perhaps he'd just sit and read something after their introductory pleasantries. Besides, the manager might make Mark leave if he hogged over a table for himself.

"You majoring in computational science too?" Duncan asked.

"Yes," Mark replied.

Looking past Duncan, he noticed someone else looking for a seat. She was strikingly beautiful, more mature than the typical school-age girl, scanning the room holding books and a drink looking for a place to sit.

He saw the expression on her face change from searching to flight as she seemed to recognize someone to her left.

She shot her head quickly to the right and immediately detoured away. Head lowered, acting as if she wanted some camouflage, she made her way toward his table, hauling an iBoard backpack. Spotting the spare chair at Mark's table, she walked over and tapped Duncan on the shoulder.

"Hi, Duncan. Mind if I sit here?" she asked.

Duncan quickly jerked around.

"Oh, …hi. No. Sit down, Sue," Duncan offered.

Like the typical nerdy, space cadet, computation geek, Duncan hadn't even considered Mark was also sitting at the table. It was initially Mark's table, but that didn't seem to matter to Duncan, who seemed dumbstruck by the attractive female.

After shuffling some chairs and moving some things on the table, Duncan said, "Mark, this is a girl I met in a couple of my classes. I should have asked you if she could sit with us. I'm sorry. Can she?"

"Sure. Sit down, Sue. Nice to meet you," Mark said.

Now he looked more closely at the slender, well-groomed woman the kid called a girl. She sure wasn't a girl; she was every bit a woman. His instinct was to drop his jaw, but he had to shake himself back to his senses mentally. He now knew he'd have no chance for study or review, but what was happening now seemed much more interesting than his original intentions anyway.

Mark wondered who this attractive girl was and why she was taking the same classes as Duncan since few females were interested in computations and why the startled or fearful gesture she made when seeing someone she recognized in the Café. But this new addition to the table made the disruption much more pleasant than just talking to another student.

Sue stuck out her hand, grasped his and, with a firm shake, introduced herself, "Susan Harvey. Nice to meet you, Mark."

Her self-confidence impressed Mark. She carried herself with a fearless posture sending out a signal of pride, but not boastfulness. She was tallish with dark hair and blue-green eyes that complimented her perfect facial features.

Mark wanted to ask why such a beautiful woman would be attending a computation and programming college but held back for now. She didn't seem to fit the stereotypical model of a programmer. She was soft-spoken with a throaty voice that belonged more to a rock star than an iBoard geek. When she smiled, her perfect white teeth seemed to cast light throughout the room.

Her attire was the antithesis of most geekdom majors. She wore a clean, white blouse neatly tucked into a dark, plaid skirt that reached just above her knees. Her long, well-defined, shapely, olive-tone legs didn't require stockings and her stylish, but not outlandish, two-inch heels were a perfect color match to her skirt.

"Duncan and I met in a first term math class and found out we have several other classes together. We discovered we're both iBoard geeks so we hit it off right away. Are you one of the teachers?" Sue asked.

Duncan swung his head toward Mark, looking at him puzzled.

Mark recognized she'd picked up on the apparent age difference between him and Duncan.

"No, no. I'm in my last term of school. I got a late start, so I guess I'm a little older than most students, and though I'm not an instructor, I am an assistant to a professor," he said.

"You must be pretty smart in computations," Sue said.

"Well, I have more experience than you two, so I hope I know a little more. You sure aren't dressed like the other iBoard students I've seen around campus," Mark said.

"Oh…" Sue blushed. "I have to go to work this afternoon. You should see me when it's only a school day," she laughed.

"Work? You work and go to school? That's very ambitious," Mark said.

"I'm an intern at a tech company. I got that position through an uncle who encouraged me to stop wasting my time and go off to school. He knew eventually I'd settle down and start seriously studying programming, so the job kinda fits with school."

"Where are you working?" Mark asked.

"A place called Forrest Labs. I've been there for a couple of years, mostly helping the real programmers with their projects. The lab gives me little pieces of things to do, so that keeps me kind of busy. I also help the security department with projects like looking into the system for potential crackers. Duncan was interested in that one," she said, elbowing Duncan and laughing.

"She works at one of the biggest artificial intelligence companies in the world," Duncan offered.

"Yes, that's their main business, but they are also getting into some grid games as a kind of offshoot and a place to experiment," Sue said.

Mark wasn't too impressed with grid games, but he'd heard of Forrest Labs who'd done some contracting with the military. The company was well known for its developments in artificial intelligence programs and new computational hardware that allowed systems to run more through organic rather than composites.

"I know about Forrest Labs. They produce a lot for the military. It sounds like a great place to work," Mark said.

"Yes. I'm learning a lot."

"I've never worked in the private sector except for a few odd jobs before being taken into the military. I always wondered what it would be like to work in an office with people who weren't trying to kill each other," Mark said with a smile.

"You were in the military?" She asked.

"Actually, I still am. I'm here on assignment," Mark said.

"So this Forrest Labs place. You like it?" Mark asked.

"Very much. I'm a late bloomer going to school and feel like an old lady with all these younger kids," Sue laughed.

"Where's your computing interest, Mark?" Sue asked.

Again, this young lady impressed him. Not only was she beautiful and obviously smart, but she also had a manner of tact that spoke of confidence and maturity. It was most likely because she was about twenty or twenty-one, a couple of years older than the typical freshman. She didn't just hang back waiting for someone to fill her with platitudes, she took the initiative and had a natural curiosity.

"I'm interested in financial grid sites mostly," Mark told her.

"Why there?" Sue asked.

In his experience, not all programmers thought about the whys of programming. They were more interested in the ways. They'd delve into programs to resolve problems or develop a function; they weren't interested in why a company or institution would want the program. Games, grids, systems, telephones, one area would do just as well as another.

"I just figured that if you want to make money as a programmer, go where the money is. Not to steal it, but to protect it from crackers," he explained.

Duncan then turned and spoke something to Sue that Mark didn't catch or even care to catch.

Those two chatted back and forth about things that had transpired in their classes, which included homework assignments, lecture notes, and things to do in lab. Mark feigned interest while trying again to refocus on his notes. As he glanced up, he caught Sue half-listening to Duncan, continually glance over her shoulder toward the other side of the room she'd avoided.

Mark got the impression from their discussions that they still had a lot to learn about school, grades, computations, and life in general. Duncan talked to the young woman like some kid in grade school. His voice inflections were shriller and louder than concerned and soothing. Mark liked his enthusiasm, but still, he seemed a little naïve. She laughed at something Duncan said then turned toward Mark.

"Do you work outside of school?" Sue asked.

"As I said because I'm only on a temporary assignment here from the military, the only outside work I do is as an instructor's assistant. I spend a few hours a week doing that. You know, grading papers and assignments, writing and scoring tests, helping people understand lectures or reading materials, that kind of stuff. Then I teach one of the labs," Mark explained.

"Then you must know this computation stuff pretty well, huh?" Duncan asked.

"Yeah, I guess you could say that. As I said, you'll get there too after a few years of school where you'll have been exposed to almost everything."

Most of the things he'd done in the Army in computations were classified, and what he learned there gave him a head start at school. Still, he couldn't discuss them, so delving into the subject would just make it uncomfortable. Instead, he fired back some questions to Duncan, hoping to divert the interest to the two of them.

"Why did you decide to pursue a career in this?" Mark asked.

"I didn't even want to come to school, but my parents made me after I got caught," Duncan said.

"Caught?" Mark thought.

"Caught him at what?" Now his interest was really piqued and he couldn't hold back.

"Caught you doing what?" Mark finally asked.

"Hackin' into some stuff," Duncan said.

Was the kid hitting financial sites or intentionally harming national security? He was hiding something.

"Hacking. Okay. You a hacker or a cracker?" Mark asked.

To him, the real hacker doesn't exploit technology to harm individuals, governments, websites, or companies. Mark was a hacker too and didn't like people who cracked systems, generating the potential of creating chaos for everyone. He didn't consider hackers as a group of people who used their knowledge of tech to wreck or crash grids. They didn't deploy malicious programs or otherwise hack their way into things for theft or vandalism. Those tech delinquents the real hackers termed as security crackers. To them, they were criminals whose intent is to steal, destroy, or vandalize others' property.

"Crackers break; hackers make," Mark said.

"I don't think you could call me a cracker. I didn't steal anything or screw with someone's identity or anything like that. Primarily, I was just trying to do game cheats. You know, crack the codes of grid games and find cheats to help win. Anyway, I don't do it anymore. After I got caught, the authorities scared me, so I only use my iBoard for programming practice, word processing, taking notes, and playing those no-brain-needed games. I significantly reduced my access to the grid," Duncan told him.

"Probably a good thing. If you were good at it, you wouldn't have been caught," Mark laughed.

"I was good at some things; I just wasn't good at covering my tracks. So, the combination of hacking or I guess cracking into things along with experimenting with equipment from my dad's lab got me into trouble," Duncan said.

"If I'd known you before, I would have convinced you to stop that hackin' around," Sue said.

"I told you I was interested in grid games," Duncan reminded her.

"Yes. Interested is different than breaking in," Sue reminded him.

"It's not too bad a thing if he wasn't stealing or creating havoc with someone's iBoard, Sue," Mark said.

Then turning to Duncan, he asked, "What were you getting into and with what experimental equipment from your dad's lab?"

Mark didn't expect an answer, but he had heard many stories of students cracking into things. All of them were interesting, and some of their techniques were unique and inventive. Information in the programmer world was power and he always sought more information. The students he'd talked to who cracked weren't doing things Mark considered interesting, but if what they did was successful and could be adapted, there might be something he could use with financial institutions or other non-kid grid areas.

Duncan ignored the question about experimental equipment. Shannon Labs, a firm that developed experimental weapons for the military, made things that were top secret. What he took from his father's company must have been very high tech. If anyone found out he had one of their devices, it could mean big trouble for him and his father. To Duncan, it seemed okay because it was only a prototype and not yet in production.

"Did what you borrowed ever get adopted in the military?" Mark asked. He didn't want this kid with something that could harm national security.

"Not the military, no. They were making something for where Sue works," Duncan said.

"Forrest Labs?" Mark asked for clarification.

"Yeah, for them. This thing wasn't accepted, so dad's company was throwing it away. They had plenty of the little things sitting around in a drawer called 'rejects' so one wouldn't be missed." Duncan said.

Duncan knew he wouldn't share with Mark or Sue what he used it for or the tests he'd done with it. It wouldn't be wise to divulge this slipup with casual friends or new acquaintances.

"There are hundreds of grid games out there and just as many hackers trying to find cheats to break them, but as soon as they're discovered, the producers issue fixes to plug the holes. Figuring that all out was more fun than playing the game," Duncan explained.

Sue raised her cup, "Exactly!"

"I have firsthand experience at helping plug a couple of those holes at Forrest Labs even though breaking into their system to solve the game is almost impossible. People are coming up with new attempted schemes all the time. Heck, even if they were to get in, they would never figure out how to crack the essence of the system, the transmission functions," Sue said.

Mark began thinking he needed to be more like a teacher or counselor than a soldier. He'd been through that stage. Now he needed to help kids start thinking about their future, so he moved the conversation to making a living in the real world.

"What about you, Sue? Was it games that got you interested in computing?" Mark asked.

"Not really. I was always pretty good at math and puzzles, and I like building things, so my dad got me an iBoard when I was young and a book on programming. Dad's brother was an engineer and executive at Forrest Labs and the two of them helped me learn. I've been doing it ever since.

I've even taken a stab at cracking codes in some of those grid games, but I'm not a gamer," she told him.

Sue went back to discussing assignments with Duncan while Mark picked up his iBoard and logged into the school's system. He pulled up Sue's class records and saw she was receiving straight A's. One of the instructors Mark knew well had written a footnote indicating that she was the brightest student he'd had in "a long, long time."

Next, he checked out Duncan.

His grades were also very high, but the comment section didn't reflect the same strong endorsements as Sue received.

His best was from the same instructor who wrote he had "excellent potential, but needs to mature."

Mark remembered Duncan had access to some top secret information he'd gotten from his father's lab. He'd like to discover what it was and if it would be of any use in his quest for a big financial take. Setting his iBoard down, he picked up on where the two were in their conversation.

Obviously, they were very talented computators who would blossom with experience. The thought occurred to him that with their minds and his expertise, they might be tools he could use to achieve his goal. These two could be a tremendous help in developing a program that solved a grave and expensive problem.

"Let me ask you to think about something. Can you build a career or business looking for cheats in games?" he asked.

Duncan scratched his scraggly beard and rolled his eyes upward like he did when he knew his parents were right but didn't want to admit it.

"I don't know. I guess you're right; there's not any money in hacking into games," Duncan said.

Then, looking at Sue, then back at Mark, something in games sparked a thought.

"Wait a minute. There is one way you could make massive money at if they get it going," Duncan said.

"Get it going?" Mark asked.

"It's there, but there's no action going on, so there haven't been many payouts," Duncan said.

"That's true," Sue piped in.

Mark wanted to get the talk away from games even if some of them paid out what Duncan thought could be big money. He'd need more than what any game could produce.

"Yeah, okay. I'm sure some games pay big, but what about careers? Games can hinder your career growth. Wouldn't you prefer to get your degree from here faster and enter the job market more quickly? Mark asked.

"Sure," the two said in unison.

Mark explained the problem he saw in trust departments in banks. One of his friends who was just getting into law saying, "There are thousands of class action lawsuits every year that require firms to pay shareholders. The biggest ones are institutions like banks and insurance companies. Because those firms are trading stocks all the time, they don't know if they are eligible for the payouts on these litigations. I want to develop a program that would track their buying and selling of stocks and match it to class action suits. Make sense?"

The two students nodded their heads. Duncan had a look on his face that maybe, just maybe, a light bulb in his mind might come on. He appeared to be getting it.

"I've estimated they're leaving billions on the table by not having the know-how to program their systems to capture the information. Shares of companies are in and out of their systems daily. They know that, they just don't know how to match it to the publicly available class action awards," Mark told them.

Mark decided to float a suggestion and see if the two would respond.

"I checked your records and you're both at the top of the class in computations. I've got an idea that could be worth a lot of money, but I don't have the time to write all the code. Would you two be interested in working on the project?" Mark asked.

"Ah, I kinda do stuff after school right now," Duncan said.

"Games?" Mark asked.

"Well, yeah. I guess so. I love games," Duncan replied

"What about you, Sue? You interested?"

"I'm pretty busy over at Forrest labs... was it Mr. Gorman?" she asked.

"Yes, Mark Gorman. But please, call me Mark."

He went on, "What if there was a way I could help both of you graduate faster with your certification and degree?

"What do you mean?" Sue asked.

"We have an advanced program here at the school. You can accelerate your time here if you meet certain conditions and can test at certain levels. I can help you do that," Mark said.

"Now that I would be interested in," Sue said.

"What about you, Duncan? Does it interest you?" Mark asked.

"Yeah, I guess. If Sue is interested, so am I."

"Why would you want to do that, Mark?" Sue asked.

"Why? It's simple. I want to get out of the military, and I need a big chunk of money and a career that keeps me paying taxes," Mark told them.

"I know you don't want to talk about games, but did you ever consider the new game sponsored by Forrest Labs?" Duncan asked.

"No. Why would I be interested in a game after what I've been telling you about this unfulfilled need in the financial community?"

"Because you said you need a big sum right away, wasn't that right?" Sue asked.

"Well, yes."

"Mark, what Duncan is saying is Forest Labs will pay billions if anyone can beat their game," Sue said.

"Billions?" Mark said.

"That's what they're projecting, but so far, there's not much happening with that game," she said.

"What do you mean?"

"People have gone into the game, but nobody seems to have the key to dominating," Sue said.

"What do you mean, 'dominate'?"

"The game is based on a virtual world similar to our world. The game's objective will be to dominate that world by scoring more points than anyone else in the game. But, you don't have to stop, and the big prize isn't the only way you get paid. The player gains points by deleting the other players' avatars and bots. The one with the most points after the game's preset time period will win a prize. But to win the whole game and the big prize, you dominate the whole world by having the most key followers. Those followers help you delete avatars and bots until the only ones left follow you. That's the general idea," Sue explained.

"That pays the billions you're talking about?"

"Yes."

"Well, maybe I might just rethink that one, but for now, I'd like to get started on the business end, and we can keep discussing that game. How's that sound?" Mark said.

"That might make sense. How about you, Duncan?"

Duncan hesitantly nodded an almost agreement.

"If you two want that accelerated program, I do a little tutoring here at school. I'd trade my time for some help in coding this idea of mine, and my help would get you out of here quicker," Mark said.

Sue sat there, looking a little more committed. The same was true of Duncan.

"You'll also get a share of the proceeds from the program we develop," Mark added.

"And you can accelerate the time to graduation?" Sue asked.

"Yes, I've done that with a couple of others already," Mark said pushing back his chair.

Sue considered this for a while. She looked at Duncan as a safe, unassuming guy, not one of those jock types, like her ex-boyfriend, who seemed to only think about her body. Mr. Gorman -- Mark -- seemed okay and was influential in the school. She didn't see any problem since there were no strings attached and they'd just be writing code together.

"Okay. Sure. But I still have a couple of questions. I mean, how do I pick up the subjects faster by working with you versus simply going to class and reading the textbooks? Would you transmit your knowledge to us using telepathy when we take tests?" she asked.

"That would be cheating, wouldn't it?" Mark said with a grin. "We could just meet once a week and go over your class notes and questions. You're both in the same classes, so that will be simple and maybe our combined knowledge can help all of us. How's that sound?" Mark asked.

Before either answered, he began collecting his things and stood.

"Let's do this. Think about it and I'll give it some more thought myself, and we'll meet again in the school cafeteria after your last class tomorrow, say around 16:00? Will that work for you?"

After affirming the time and place to meet, they finished their drinks, stood and shook hands.

"Nice to meet both of you. I look forward to more discussions," Mark said.

"Nice to meet you too. Duncan and I will look forward to our discussions, won't we, Duncan?" Sue said.

Duncan picked up his things while nodding his head, and the two headed toward the door.

As they made their way toward the front of the café, Mark sensed something was wrong. Sue seemed to be shielding herself behind Duncan as they walked to the door. She was holding her head close to his shoulder, hiding her face from the opposite side of the room.

As the door glided closed, Mark's eyes drifted around the room toward the danger he'd sensed. He spotted a muscular college-age jock holding his iBoard just below eye level, watching the two make their way across the street.

Mark had a feeling that eventually he'd have to deal with this guy.

THE BIRTH

Birth, the splendor mothers wish for,
Children arriving to love and care for,
Filling the love they so have longed for.

True for some who wanted someone
Lost's the child who will have no one.

One Saturday morning a blond-haired man in Dublin, California was enjoying his Saturday morning coffee reading the "Sporting Green," the green papered sports page of the San Francisco Chronicle. For this story dear reader, all you need to know about that man is his name was Bill. He used it to make picks for tomorrow's NFL games. Using the information on the sports page, and the omens he had, he was pretty successful being one of the top pickers of football games at work. Those little hints, almost like a whispering voice, helped him most of his life. The voice was never loud like some of the mumbling homeless people he'd seen on the streets of Oakland or the criminals who claimed, "the voice told me to do it." All his life, the inkling had been very subtle, but this was different.

This one was calling him as if it knew him personally. It was there, determined and clear, demanding, and wanting to be recognized. It almost shouted to him with an ugly piercing stab.

"IS ANYONE THERE?" Came the call.

He flinched, instinctively lifting his hands to his ears.

"Is anyone there?" it asked again.

This time it came through a little quieter as if it was pleading on the verge of giving up hope.

Something like this had never happened before. He'd hear of people hearing voices when something tragic happened. It made him wonder if this was some family member in trouble, but the voice wasn't calling his name or telling him to do something. It was distinctly asking a question: "Do you guys hear me? Is this thing working?" like it was a sinking ship frantically transmitting an SOS.

His mind ran through who he might question about something as strange as this. He didn't want to go to one of his male friends who'd think he was nuts, but his girlfriend was bright, intelligent, and educated. She'd understand, but congress was in session, so she was back in DC and may not be available.

He met Sara about nine months ago on a cruise prescribed by his physician to relieve some stress. As it turned out, Sara was on that cruise for the very same reason. During that trip, he had one of his premonitions, the very thing that had bothered him before. It told him he needed to go out on the deck and toward the rear of the ship. So he set down his drink, forced the heavy door open, and stepped out into the stiff breeze. The ship was cruising along at 20 knots so walking with the wind to his back, he headed toward the rear. He couldn't believe what he was seeing. Someone was fighting with Sara. Her screams, partially masked by the wind, sent a chill down his spine as he began sprinting toward her, but they were still shrill and frightening. She was over the railing hanging on as a figure in black tried to force her fingers loose. First prying then kicking at them. Bill began yelling, causing the dark figure to dart around the corner out of sight.

"Hold on. I'm coming," Bill yelled.

"Hurry please! I'm losing my grip," Sara cried.

Sara's fingers were bleeding and her hold slipping when Bill reached over the railing and grabbed a handful of her light jacket. With all his strength he struggled to get her up to a point where he could pull her with both hands. When she was far enough, she threw her arm over the railing and helped Bill pull her over the top. Crying, she hugged him tight and thanked him for saving her life.

"I thought I was dead. I've never been afraid of a fight, but he attacked me from behind and got me over the rail," Sara explained. "Thank God you came along."

They'd become close before, but that incident made those shallow feelings of fondness intense. After the cruise, they remained the closest of friends and passionately in love.

Bill dialed her number and waited for the third ring when Sara answered:

"Hello, Bill. When are you coming back here to visit?" she asked.

"I'll be there in ten minutes," he teased. "Actually, I'm pretty busy at work right now so it will be a few weeks."

"I understand, but hurry will you? I miss you," Sara implored.

After some fond 'miss you' discussions, Bill got to the point.

"Do you have a minute? I've got something I wanted to discuss," Bill asked.

"Sure. What's going on?" Sara asked.

"Something happened just a few minutes ago that was strange," he said.

"What? Tell me," Sara said, sounding concerned.

"Well, remember I told you of the premonition when you were attacked?

"Yes, I remember we discussed it, but you didn't report it to the cruise company, and I understand why," Sara said.

"I don't want to be considered looney, Sara," Bill said.

"I know. I understand. You're sure not looney to me. Did it happen again?" Sara asked.

"It did. But, this time, it was more than a premonition. It was a voice," Bill told her.

"Go on," Sara said, listening carefully.

"I thought it was on the TV but I did some checking and I don't think it was coming from there. Sara, I think it was an inner-voice, kinda like what that speaker talked about. He called it auditory hallucinations, right?"

"Yes. We went into it over coffee one day," she said.

"He was very informative and told us that hearing things isn't that uncommon."

"True."

"Well, I heard a voice say something to me."

"What did it say?" she asked.

"It said, 'Is anyone there?'"

"That's all?"

"Not exactly. It also said something strange," Bill said.

"What was it?"

"It said, 'Do you guys hear me? Is this thing working?'"

"That is very strange," Sara agreed.

"It was as clear as the two of us speaking right now. It was there, but nobody was there if that makes sense. It shocked the hell out of me and I'm not sure what to do."

Sara too had heard voices and noises, something they shared in common.

One night on the ship, they both heard something strange that nobody else heard." Since we both heard that sloshing, I was wondering if you heard this voice I just heard?" Bill asked.

"No, not this time. You said it said, 'Is anyone there;' right? Did you answer it?" she asked.

"No. I was afraid even to admit hearing it."

"I'll tell you again. You are perfectly normal, better than most men I know, so let's move on this thing. If it happens again, maybe you ought to reply to it. Answer the question it's asking and see what happens after that and let me know," Sara said.

Her reassurance of his seemingly normal behavior gave Bill some hope. Bill decided he'd better just respond to the voice if it came back to him again and get more information.

"If I hear it again, I'll answer it," he said.

"You're not crazy, Bill. Just go with it and come to DC and tell me all about it," she said with the tone of a smile.

He thanked Sara for listening to him and went on to ask her about things that were happening in her life and when they could next meet. She was busy throughout the congressional session and wouldn't be back until the Christmas break. They made plans for him to go back to DC.

"It doesn't seem like it's been nine months since that cruise, Bill. We need to get together soon," Sara said.

"I need to get back to one of our plant locations in Maryland and will do it after the upcoming board meeting. We can have dinner at that crab place," he said.

"I look forward to it, Bill. Let me know what happens with this voice thing, okay?"

"If anything happens, I will. See you soon," Bill said, then hung up the phone.

As he hung up, he took a sip of coffee and made his way to the bathroom for a shower. Reaching in and turning on the water, he waited for the hot to kick in, adjusted it, then stepped in. Pouring some shampoo onto his palm, he ran his fingers through his scalp and soaked up the clean warmth.

As he relaxed, it happened:

"IS ANYONE THERE?" the voice shouted.

Though he'd thought through how he should handle it, he still stood silently with Head & Shoulders running into his eyes. Finally, grasping his chance at courage, he thought with all his mind's forcefulness, "Yes. I hear you."

Immediately came a relieved, "Thank goodness I finally got through!"

Bill almost jumped through the glass shower door. After regaining some semblance of composure, he rinsed the soap from his eyes, hesitantly and somewhat weakly thought, "Yes."

"Who is it?" the voice said calmly and matter-of-factly.

"Bill Delgado," Bill thought back, wondering what the heck was going on.

He glanced around his bathroom even though he knew nobody could hide in there with him.

"Who are you? Are you in my apartment? Are they there?" it said.

"Huh? Is who here?" Bill said.

"The ones I'm working with on this. Ah… Can't come up with the names right now. Never mind. They must have left. I thought we couldn't communicate from here. Now we know we can, so this should make things easier. We just have to get this situation fixed so I can get to work," the voice, whoever it was, said.

"At last, there is somebody who might be able to do something! I've been trying to reach someone for what seems like forever. I think I finally figured it out: telepathy. It's working," the voice said.

"Can you hang on a second?" Bill thought as if he were talking with someone on the telephone. He wanted to say, 'Can I put you on hold?' but thought better of it. He just needed some time to gather his thoughts.

"Sure,' the Voice said. "But I need to get my message to you before it's too late," it said.

Bill couldn't believe what he'd just heard, as clear as an empty stadium's public address system. How could someone, or more appropriately something, be contacting him through what he thought was his relatively sound cerebrum?

Rinsing off and turning off the shower, he grabbed his robe without drying, then dripped his way downstairs to grab a cup of coffee and see where this puzzle might take him. Making coffee in his one-cup pot, he grabbed a notepad, poured himself a cup of Colombian Supreme, and sat down in his easy chair and transmitted.

"Okay. Go ahead. I hear you just fine."

"Good. This could be complicated, so I'll try to be as clear and brief as possible, but please take some notes so you can refer back to them if I forget something. I'm having some memory issues."

"Okay. I've got something to write with. What kind of memory issues?"

"I'll get to that in a moment," it signaled.

"My iBoard and earbuds are in the biggest building in a huge city closest to where the sun rises. It has a name, but we don't know it. Anyway, I need to get to it just as soon as I figure out where I am and what's going on. I need to remember that, so please make a note about the iBoard so I can see it later. That's very important," the voice told him.

"iBoard? Where are you?" Bill asked in his mind.

"I'm not sure. Just give that not to… to… I forget her name. If she doesn't come back give it to… to… hmm. I don't remember his name either. The guy who did the program. Damn," the voice said.

The voice went on, attempting to relay information to someone, but Bill didn't know who.

"It must be some new medical device, but I hear others around me, so I asked if you were in the apartment. They should be there too," it said.

"I've tried crying, screaming, kicking, fist-pumping and more ways of getting attention, but none of them have worked. After the crash, they must have placed me in this experimental cocoon-like machine. It seems to be helping me out of this coma, but there are problems," the voice explained.

Bill wanted to transmit something but thought it would just confuse things, so he kept his mind silent.

Then he thought, "Do schizophrenics hear voices in such detail and did they have conversations with their voices?" Grabbing his ballpoint pen, he scribbled down the date, time, and conditions that he'd heard the voice. He wrote the reference to something called an iBoard, whatever the heck that was. This whole thing could be just an auditory hallucination. Having the notes would help him when he talked to Sara or a shrink if necessary.

The voice went on.

"It is so frustrating that I don't just have a call button or tara-phone. You'd think with all the technology, they could have installed a simple wireless device. Of course, maybe they did and I just don't know how to use it. Or maybe they knew that in this state, I'd have no means of communicating and they're just monitoring me. At any rate, you can be an enormous help," the voice suggested.

"Tara-phone?" Bill wondered but kept his mind silent. Bill considered what kind of help the voice was going to request. Too often, the defense in murder cases was, 'The voice told me to do it.' But he was relatively sure he wouldn't go off the deep end and kill someone just because this voice told him to.

"Even if I had a call button or tara-phone, I'm not sure I could use one. I haven't been able to coordinate my hands with my brain. I can move them all right, but they seem just to go wherever they want. I poked myself in the eye the other day. Hurt like hell," the voice said.

"Since the accident, things like hearing, sight, and coordination are improving, but my memory is getting worse, not better," it explained.

"You were in an accident?" Bill asked.

"Yes. They transmitted to the car just before the crash. I yelled out just as I saw something fall off the truck but couldn't avoid it smashing through the windshield. I'm sure I've been in a coma for an extended period. Anyway, it must have hit me, and the next thing I knew, I was here in this experimental machine," it explained.

"They must have some new technology for coma recovery. There's no window in this thing, and my eyesight isn't good enough yet to see much more than a little light, but this sure isn't your standard four-walled room. It's more like a body bag in a water bed. I've been sloshing around forever.

"Anyway, I do hear voices around me, but not talking directly to me. But this shroud seems to dampen all sounds anyway. In fact, people are talking around me right now. One of them has a voice that's quite soothing, though a bit loud. Since I've heard it often over the past few months, I'm guessing it's probably my nurse. It's a woman's voice, and she speaks to others in the room, but her voice is so deep and resonating that it's hard to understand. I catch a few words now and then but then again..." the voice trailed off.

"My memory seems to be slipping, so I've forgotten what she's said in the past. I just heard her say Bay View Memorial Hospital, so that's where I must be. You should make a note of that," the voice said.

"Anyway, since I can't get anyone's attention, I tried telepathy because it normally works, but I guess this thing I'm in somehow blocks it. I stumbled onto this combination of thoughts and mind forcefulness and got through to you," the voice said.

"I can't believe I'm having this conversation. I must be going crazy," Bill thought. Then he realized his thoughts were like having an open microphone to this voice.

"What? I assure you, you are not crazy. I desperately need some help. Please hang with me," it said.

Despite being a toneless voice inside his head, Bill could sense a feeling of anxious desperation. Had he met some strange guy who espoused such nonsense on the streets of San Francisco, he'd have briskly walked away, just as he and Sara had discussed. But this was different. He decided to stay with it until, or if, it started getting too bizarre.

"Go, on," Bill thought.

The voice paused for a few moments, and there was only silence. Then it continued.

"I don't remember when they first placed me in here or when I got to this state. I feel stronger and have better hearing than before, coordination is better, and I see some light once in a while, so some things are coming back, but here's my problem.

"From the time I regained consciousness, I've been able to think clearly, remembering everything without a problem. I know about the earbuds and the i.. ah…"

"iBoard?" Bill thought.

"What's that?" the voice asked.

"I don't know; you're the one who said it."

"I forgot. Anyway, I can't recall a thing I should know. That sounds strange, I know. You're probably asking, 'How could someone know they once knew something? If you forgot it, you wouldn't even know you once knew it,' right?" the voice asked.

"That makes sense, yes," Bill thought.

"Let me see if I can explain. We all know that if we had grandparents or didn't have grandparents, we'd know that too, right?" the voice asked.

"Yes, I suppose so," Bill thought.

"Well, I know I had grandparents. You know sometimes there's always a lattice password security question that asks, 'What was your mother's maiden name?' Right?" the voice inquired.

"Lattice? If you mean the internet, yes, I even use that sometimes," Bill replied

He wasn't a techie and didn't know all of their jargon.

"Well, I can't answer that question. I don't remember her maiden name nor my grandparents' first or last names, and that recollection slipped out of my consciousness one name at a time. First, I couldn't remember my mother's mother's name. Then it was my mother's father. Then it was my father's mother. Up until now, when I can't recall any of their names, I've gone through the alphabet, recited names of people I know, every trick I can think of, and I still come up with nothing," the voice explained.

Bill had never heard of such a condition. He wished he could ask Dr. Bonetti, the lecturer on the cruise ship who discussed psychology, if he had.

"If I'm losing those memories, how many more have I lost that I can't recall? More importantly, how will I find my... damn. I know I'm supposed to go someplace and find something, but now I don't even know where it was or what it is," the voice said.

It paused briefly as if it was referring to notes then went on.

"iBoard?" Bill suggested.

"What's that?" the voice asked again.

Bill still wasn't sure what the voice wanted, so he just stayed quiet and waited for it to come back to him. Not only did he hear voices, well a voice, he was also having a conversation with it! It didn't seem like a dream; it seemed as if he was talking to someone on the telephone.

In a few minutes the voice came back.

"If I could communicate with the doctors, I'd be able to tell them that I think it has something to do with the coldness I'm feeling on the top of my head. Maybe they're thinking it will help me come out of the coma or they're numbing me there to perform some sort of medical procedure on my brain. I don't know. Whatever it is, my memory is rapidly leaking out."

There was a pause and silence, then the voice continued.

"Make a note of the time. I'm feeling coldness now, and they might be able to equate it to their procedure and make adjustments, depending on how I come out of this," the voice said.

Bill looked down at his watch and recorded 9:56 AM then took another sip of coffee before going into the kitchen for a refill. By the time he sat back down, the voice was coming back into his head.

"Damn, now I forget my father's name! My brain feels like the sand in the upper half of an hourglass slowly draining out a little at a time. I better get on with my story quickly," the voice said as it faded away.

As he waited for the voice's return, he began working one of those diabolical Sudoku puzzles that are virtually impossible to solve without atomic concentration. As he dug into it, his brain, struggling to find the exact numbers that fit in the proper square and not duplicated in any row or column, he could feel his mind running out of steam, and his concentration slowly beginning to wane. Then it came jumping back into his head.

"ARE YOU THERE?" the voice beamed across just as loudly and clearly as before.

Bill hated to admit it, but he was almost relieved he'd re-established contact.

The voice kept repeating things it had already transmitted as if it had never told him anything at all. Finally, it got onto something different. It told Bill about his experiences before being knocked unconscious that were confusing.

"This guy had these things to wear and something attached to the iThing but the girl -- damn I love her but can't remember her name. It was that damn kid who convinced me he could send things in," the voice said.

"Huh? Send things in where? What does that mean? What happened to you?" Bill asked.

"As I said, I'm not exactly sure. I was there in my apartment. The kid, damn, I can't remember his name. Anyway, when he left the equipment there, and I tried it on and… damn, I don't remember what happened."

There? Here? Kid? Equipment?

None of it made sense. The words were a mixture of science fiction and fact. iBoards, lattices, nothing added up, but still, the voice hadn't asked him to do anything. What did it want?

"I feel cold on the top of my head," it said again.

"Maybe your head is just outside that thing you're in, did you think about that?" Bill asked.

There was a long pause and the voice came back, saying, "You might be onto something there. Maybe I just kicked the covers off with my head and it's cold out there. Good point, friend," the voice responded.

"Well, whatever they're doing to my brain is causing me to lose memory. Damn it. Now I forget my mother's name!" it said.

Bill was about to ask if it felt any pain when the voice jumped into his head in what must have been a yell.

"My God! What was that? I heard a woman scream just as I was trying to get out of this thing! It was a strong piercing scream like someone in pain or agony. I'm not sure, but I think it was my nurse who screamed. Forget about sending e-mails or calling this place. You better get here quick. Please, something's going wrong. Wait, I just heard someone call out the name Mrs. Morgan. She might be the voice I've heard before so many times, the closest one. Hold on… she just called for a Dr. Chopra. I heard those things pretty clear. I hope she's all right. I wonder if she fell or something?" the voice cried.

"Who's all right? Who fell?" Bill asked frantically.

"I think Mrs. Morgan, is she helping me? She screamed in pain, so she may have been hurt!"

There was another pause in his transmission, and Bill began wondering if he should make his way over to Bay View Memorial Hospital and get this thing resolved. After all, the voice wasn't asking him to kill anyone or do anything bizarre; he was asking for help in a medical emergency. He felt morally obligated to do something. If this was real, it could save lives.

The voice's transmission jumped into his mind again.

"Damn. I thought I knew her name, but now I can't recall it," the voice said.

"Whose name?" Bill asked.

Then without answering, the voice asked a bizarre question.

"Oh, no. Did I tell you my name earlier? Why can't I come up with my own name?"

The voice seemed to be asking nobody in particular as if they'd never been communicating.

"No. You haven't given me your name," Bill thought.

The voice went on as if it hadn't heard or received his question.

"My head is so cold now. Sand is leaking out of my mind. I hear sounds but don't know what they mean. People's voices are making noises. Wass going on whif me? Bright lights…cold. Wahs this? Ah! Augghh! Oh my God! Some…" the voice stopped abruptly. "It's some SSara," Bill heard it say.

"It's who? It's what?" Bill asked, hoping for some clarification.

"Some Sara, some Sara, some Sara, some Sara," it repeated.

Then it gave an agonizing cry and abruptly ended its transitions as if it had just fallen off a cliff. Yet, he heard the sound of someone wailing. It was someone in severe agony. The voice was dead, and it had transmitted a message across. But, across what?

Quickly he dressed then headed for his car, key in hand. He started it, and as he pulled out of his driveway, he was thinking, "I must really be crazy.   What   the   hell   am   I   doing?"

50

THE BABY

The smells of cleanliness,
Calms and rests us.
Masking those demons,
Respiring the sepsis.

Perched on the side of the Oakland East Bay hills, Bay View Memorial Hospital overlooked San Francisco Bay. Bill Delgado parked his car in the small parking lot below the hospital. Walking up the stairs, he turned and looked back at the view. In the distance he could see the sunset igniting a yellow-orange glow through a cloud scampering past the soaring towers of the Golden Gate Bridge. Closer in, the support cable lights of the Bay Bridge seemed to point the way to The City where, according to Tony Bennett, "...little cable cars climb halfway to the stars." And, though Mr. Bennett didn't sing it, the Transamerica Pyramid building appeared to be pointing the way to those Tony Bennett stars.

Reminiscent of a Calder design, the hospital's majestic brass doors revealed the opulence encompassed in this exclusive medical facility. Piedmont, and its surrounding wealthy neighbors, didn't need or want a public hospital. Like their country club, the residents in this upper one-percent income area owned the hospital. As a 501(c)(3) institution, they could only operate at break even and pay no taxes. To keep it in operation, members were assessed a monthly fee for its operation based on actual expenses. This way, it could operate to cover costs without inflated markups of public hospitals. Those are required so they can negotiation with insurance companies, Medicare and the State's Medicaid program called Medi-Cal in California. Because it was a private institution, patient information and expenses were closely guarded against public scrutiny, but carefully audited by their Community Board of Trustees.

The massive doors swung open automatically as Bill approached. Entering the atrium, he noticed the pleasant smell more like a library than a chemically clean hospital. Overstuffed leather chairs, complete with matching hassocks, were bathed in light from custom-designed Schonbek table lamps sitting scattered about the lobby. The ceiling suggested a somewhat gothic-like one he'd seen in an old Charlton Heston movie rich

51

with relief and featuring the same vault soffits of Pompeian baths. Original art with little spotlights decorated most of the area accenting the luxurious furnishings around the entry. Nearby, a stuffed magazine rack with the newest periodicals contained none with torn off portions of their front page to remove address labels.

A mahogany reception desk staffed by smartly uniformed volunteers sat in the foyer's center.

Bill walked up to it and was greeted by a stately gray-haired woman whose appearance resembled a model from Worth magazine. She wore a lapel pin that proudly reported her name as Mrs. J.B. Folger, who Bill assumed must have been one of the San Francisco Folger's Coffee heirs.

"What can I do for you, sir?" she asked.

He'd been considering what he'd say to that question all the way from home, but now he stumbled. He wasn't sure who to ask for or what information to divulge. He couldn't tell Mrs. J.B. Folger he'd heard a voice in distress and was coming to save them or he'd quickly become a patient in their psychiatric ward... if they had one. As he stood there thinking of what to ask, Mrs. Folger spoke again with a slight tone of irritation.

"May I help you?"

"Ah, yes. Do you have a nurse named Mrs. Morgan or a Dr. Chopra that works here?"

"I'm not sure about Mrs. Morgan. We don't keep a full list of employees, but I do know that Dr. Chopra is on staff. In fact, I think she's here now."

"Where would I find her? This is kind of important," Bill said, trying to retain calmness with his tone.

"Why don't you just go down that hall and you'll find a nurse's station close to the nursery. They should be able to find Dr. Chopra for you," she said, pointing with her well-manicured and opulently jeweled finger.

Following the pointed finger, Bill made a right turn and headed toward an opening next to the hanging tapestry. Approaching the desk, he noted that there were very few people around. Seeing a solo nurse dressed in blue pajama-like pants with a matching v-necked top, he asked, "Is Dr. Chopra around?"

She looked up from her computer screen, a little startled by the intrusion.

"I'm sorry?" the nurse asked.

Bill realized his approach was a little aggressive and recomposed himself.

"I'm sorry I was a little abrupt. I'm Bill Delgado and would like to ask Dr. Chopra a question. Is he or she around?" he asked with a soft smile.

"Give me a second to finish this report, and I'll see if she's back there," the nurse said.

Bill paced back and forth, trying to remain calm until the nurse finished typing. Finally, she stood and said, "I think she just finished up a few minutes ago and is doing some paperwork. I'll see if she has a minute. Are you the father, uncle or something?"

"No, I just need to talk to her. It's kind of important," Bill replied, paying no attention to her question.

Without much hesitation, the friendly, plumpish, middle-aged nurse shuffled her pajamas toward the rear of the station.

"I'll go see if she has time to talk to you," she said, looking over her shoulder.

Moments later, an attractive, young, dark-complected woman, he assumed of Indian descent, came through the doorway. She was wearing the identical blue pajamas as the nurse, but hers were covered by a white lab coat. With tails streaming behind, she briskly walked toward him.

She was tall and slender with dark eyes and no makeup. Her stethoscope necklace was nicely accessorized, with a chromed ophthalmoscope dangling from her lab coat's right side pocket. Over her pen-stuffed left breast pocket, blue stitched letters revealed her name: Durga Chopra, M.D. Then, directly under her name, the letters OB-GYN.

"You're looking for me?" she asked. "I'm Dr. Chopra."

Seeing the OB-GYN immediately, he thought this couldn't be the Dr. Chopra he was looking for. No Obstetrics/Gynecologist he'd ever heard of worked on brain injuries. Her pleasant and inviting smile signaled she was more of a patient care individual than a medical scientist interested in experimental methods of treating brain trauma.

"I'm sorry. I must have made a mistake," Bill apologized. "I was looking for a physician who might deal with brain damage or working on something experimental. Is there another Dr. Chopra here?" he asked.

"No, I'm the only one. We seldom do neurological work here. Those cases would be transferred over to Stanford or UCSF. But if I can help, I'm happy to try," she answered in a helpful tone. "What is it you need?

He wasn't sure how much he wanted to reveal his conversation with the voice. He didn't know this person, and as lovely as she seemed, if he told her he heard a voice, she may just call security and have him escorted from the hospital.

"Hmm… okay. Well, do you have a nurse working for you named Mrs. Morgan?"

"No. There may have been a temp at some point with that name, but I don't remember one in this department, do you, Martha?" she said, looking down at the nurse.

Martha shook her head signaling "no."

"So, I'm not your doctor, and I don't have a nurse named Mrs. Morgan, and I don't think the hospital has any nurses named Mrs. Morgan. What is it you want with these people, Mr... I'm sorry I didn't get your name," she said haltingly.

"Bill. Bill Delgado," Bill replied before thinking about what he was saying.

"Well, Mr. Delgado, is there some reason you're looking for this particular doctor, at this particular hospital, in this particular department?" she asked, getting very specific.

"I was kind of sent here to look for them," he said.

"Kind of sent here? What do you mean? Who sent you? Maybe I know them and we can figure this thing out?" she wondered, seeming very interested in why he was there. She began unbuttoning that top button of her white lab coat and walked around the corner of the station into the hallway.

Nurse Martha, gnawing on the eraser end of a pencil, was now staring at Bill with a puzzled look on her face. Bill could imagine her on the phone as soon as he mentioned anything about a voice and suppressed supplying any details about how he'd gotten the names, Dr. Chopra and Mrs. Morgan.

"What about a Sam or Sara?" he said, dragging out the R sound in Sara. "Is there someone here by that name?" Bill asked, still searching for any of the names the voice mentioned.

"Or maybe it's Sam Sara or a Sum SARRRRah. Anyone with that name working here?" he again asked.

Dr. Chopra's eyes widened with the mention of that name. Now, standing next to him with her lab coat fully unbuttoned, she looked every bit like a serious physician.

She moved closer and said, "Say that again. What did you just say?"

"Some Sara or something like that. It could be Sam Sara; I'm not sure. Anyway, do you know someone by that name?" he asked.

Dr. Chopra's face displayed a mysterious expression that looked at him quizzically, but now obviously with increased interest. She came even closer. Close enough that Bill could smell the scent of the hospital's antiseptic soap.

She said in a whispered tone, "Would you mind joining me in the cafeteria for a cup of coffee? I've been here since before breakfast and missed lunch, so I could use one."

Turning to the nurse, she said, "Martha, can you get me that bilirubin count for our baby, please? I'm not comfortable with his coloring; let's make sure he's not jaundiced."

"Right away, Dr. Chopra," the nurse said, heading toward the nursery.

Turning to Bill, Dr. Chopra said, "Okay, let's go."

Bill didn't get the feeling this was a social invitation. Yet, it definitely was a request he wouldn't pass up. She was a stunning woman and a contrast to his physician, the plump, balding Dr. Jolly. Bill tried not to show emotion and turned the subject back to the business at hand.

"You think you know someone with those names?" he asked.

"I'm not sure, but I'd like to hear a little more about why you are asking for these people," she said reassuringly.

The hospital coffee shop appeared more like a swank Beverly Hills restaurant than a hospital room for coffee. They offered a series of various boutique coffees along with an assortment of pastries and fruits.

There was no charge for anything in the help-yourself café, so each chose their coffee, Dr. Chopa taking hers and a banana, and they made their way to a booth. The two sipped coffee in uncomfortable silence for a few moments. Finally, the doctor finished the banana, set her coffee down, and looked over at Bill with her dark eyes and pearly teeth that seemed to flash as she talked.

"Mr. Delgado, I have your name correct; right?"

Bill nodded his head.

"I can tell something is bothering you. It isn't every day I have a stranger come up to me asking the kinds of questions you've been asking. How did you get my name?"

Bill thought for a moment about how he could express to this stranger what had been happening.

Rather than answering her question, he asked again for the umpteenth time, "Are you sure there's no other Dr. Chopra here?"

"Not here. There may be other Dr. Chopras around the Bay Area, but I don't know them. Chopra is a relatively common Indian name and several Chopras I've read about practice in a variety of specialties."

"Any neurologists that you know of?"

"No. I've heard of one Dr. Chopra who lectures on mind-body interventions, but that's about as close to neurology that I know of, and I think he's down in Los Angeles. Where did you get those other names you mentioned?" she asked.

"Someone told me that there was a nurse named Mrs. Morgan caring for a patient with a brain injury in this hospital. That same person, who I guess was pretty sick, also mentioned a Dr. Chopra, and what sounded like Some Sara. As I said earlier, I didn't quite catch that name, and I'm not sure if it is two names, Sum and Sara or one. This person said it a few times, but then we lost our connection," he explained.

"It said? Connection? Someone? Are you saying an 'it' phoned you? That's not being very clear, Mr. Delgado," she said.

"I know. It's confusing, but it's something like that."

"What's your reluctance to be more specific? Are you frightened of me or something?" she asked with a quizzical smile.

"Trust me, I studied psychology and psychiatry before my focus on OB-GYN, so I've read some things that might seem very strange to you," she said.

Her mention of psychology caught Bill's attention. Should he introduce the subject of hearing voices? She's a professional, so maybe she can shed some light on the subject. He thought he might bring up the subject discreetly... to test the waters.

Finally, he asked, "What do you know about inner voices?"

Dr. Chopra calmly picked up her coffee and took a sip.

Finally, she asked, "I'm not sure what you mean. Do you mean what can cause people to hear voices with nobody there, something called auditory hallucinations? I know a bit about that subject, and I'm interested in what's going on here. You had my name, and you knew I was at this hospital, but the other things don't make sense. I think you're trying to tell me you had one of those hallucinations. Is that right?" she said as calmly as if we were friends casually discussing the differences between Gloria Jean's and Peet's Columbian roast.

"If you heard something you don't understand, it may not be a hallucination at all. That phenomenon isn't unusual, and your reference to Some Sara may have some meaning," she added.

"I don't want to be rude, but can I make a quick phone call to ask my friend Sara a question?" Bill asked.

"It's okay. Go ahead and call. Is she the one hearing voices?"

Bill pretended he didn't hear her. Excused himself, and walked out to the payphone just outside the door. He dug into his pockets making sure he had enough change for a short call then plunked in a quarter and dialed. He wanted Sara to reconfirm she'd heard nothing but there was no answer. After seven or eight rings the phone went to voice mail.

"Hi... this is Sara. Leave a message, and I'll get back to you as soon as I can."

Bill hung up disappointed, but her voice and the pronouncing of her name with the long R sparked a thought.

Most Sara's were simply Sara, not SaRah like his friend, something he may want to offer up to Dr. Chopra. After laying the receiver in its black cradle, he walked back into the café and sat across the table from Dr. Chopra.

"The pronunciation of Sara that I heard was the same as my friend's pronunciation. Sara, with a long R, I'm not sure if I'm saying it correctly, but it sounded like that," he explained.

"Well, it sounds like you're saying Samsara, a term that has some significance in our family," she explained.

"That might be what it was. What does it mean?" Bill asked.

"It's a term from the Buddhist and Hindu religions that generally refers to their belief in reincarnation. It describes when an individual is between lives in sort of a limbo moving from one existence to the next. It's really much deeper than that, but that's the general idea of the meaning.

"Was it someone from one of those religions who gave you these names?" she again asked, pressing him to explain where he'd gotten the information.

Bill could sense she was becoming impatient with this dragged-out discussion. Her mannerisms and communications transmitted a sense of safety, so he decided he'd discuss this directly with her.

"Dr. Chopra, it wasn't a person who gave me the names. You'll think I'm crazy, and maybe I am. I'm just not sure anymore," Bill said.

"Go ahead. Tell me. I promise I won't think you're crazy. And anyway, if you are maybe I can even help you with that too, but you seem perfectly normal to me," she said, smiling softly.

Finally, he just blurted it out. "It's a voice in my head," he finally said.

She didn't blink or change expression.

"Go on," she prompted.

Bill gave her the history of hearing strange things, not just the voice.

He told her about hearing one on the cruise and how he and Sara heard sloshing of water inside one of the bars on the ship.

"How long ago did this start?" she asked.

"About a year ago," Bill said.

"When?"

"October last year, so that's nine months ago to be exact," Bill said.

"So when you finally heard the voice, it said it needed you right away?" she asked.

"Yes, it said something was going wrong with an experiment, and someone needed to warn the doctors."

"What kind of experiment? Did it say?" she wanted to know.

"He…well, I'm not sure if it was a he or a she, though he or she had been knocked unconscious in an automobile accident and was recovering from a coma in an experimental chamber or something. The voice said it thought it was trapped in something and was losing its memory."

"How did this voice give you my name?"

"It heard what it assumed was its nurse saying your name. But it was losing its memory it told me, so when I asked it to repeat a name after just a short period, it couldn't even remember it gave me one. Then again, maybe this was all just something in my head, I don't know."

"But it gave you my name and the name of a nurse, what nurse?"

"It told me it had been hearing a voice that others were calling Mrs. Morgan so assumed that was the name of the nurse attending him, or her. It'd also heard the name of this hospital, Bay View Memorial. I'd never even heard of this hospital before, so it makes me think this couldn't be something I simply conjured up in my own mind."

Dr. Chopra brought her hand up to her cheek, stroking it in deep thought. Bill could see her mind searching for answers as her eyes slowly shifted from one spot in space to another.

"This can't be," she said finally.

"What 'can't be?'" Bill asked.

"Mrs. Morgan isn't a nurse here."

"She's not?"

"No. This voice didn't say it was absolutely certain that Mrs. Morgan was a nurse, did it?"

"No. It said it thought it must be the nurse because it was so close," Bill clarified.

"Mrs. Morgan is, I should say she was, a patient in the hospital. I just delivered her ten-pound baby boy."

"What do you mean 'was' a patient. Isn't she still?" Bill asked

"I'm sorry to say she died this morning during delivery. She was brought to us last night in an emergency situation by the people she worked for. She was an illegal so they gave the name Mrs. Morgan. That wasn't her real name. During delivery, her heart stopped and we were unable to resuscitate her. She has no known relatives and the family she worked for are prominent figures in the area, so can't get involved other than to pay for our services. Sadly, the baby will be placed up for adoption, something the staff is working on now."

Bill had been at the hospital for almost an hour without noticing the quietness. In larger hospitals, it seemed routine that their intercom system was always calling for something. But not here. In this place it seemed more like a splendid, stately manor than a hospital. He was shocked when he heard, "Code Pink, Code Pink to the nursery."

"What's that?" he asked Dr. Chopra, who was sliding out of their booth.

"It's for an emergency in the nursery. That baby was the only one there, and so that code is saying something has happened with him. It's the first time I've ever heard that code here. We've never had anything like that happen to my memory. Come with me, quickly," she said.

Motioning to Bill, Dr. Chopra slid out of her seat and headed out toward the nursery.

When they arrived, several other nurses and physicians were standing around Martha, who was sitting on the floor dazed. Dr. Chopra kneeled beside her and helped her up.

"What happened, Martha?" She asked.

"I don't know. I was just dictating the bilirubin results to you, and the next thing I knew, I was lying on the floor. Someone must have hit me from behind," she said, holding her hand to request a lift up from the floor.

"You should stay down," someone said.

"No, get me up. I'm okay," Martha responded with a tone of annoyance. "Damn it, I'm a nurse; I know if I'm all right or not."

"Where's the baby?" Dr. Chopra asked.

Several conversations started taking place and after a few discussions, they learned one of the nursing assistants found Martha lying on the floor, and the baby was missing. When Dr. Chopra left with Bill for coffee, there was a baby boy in the nursery who needed a minor test completed and reported. Now the room was empty, and a newborn doesn't just get up and leave the hospital because it doesn't like the food. Someone had taken him.

"Someone call the Piedmont police and report this. Apparently, someone abducted the child," Martha said.

THE SCHOOL CAFETERIA

What is love?
But a desperate plea?
If I loved you,
Would you love me?

The bustling school cafeteria reverberated with a myriad of sounds. Chairs shuffled, and metal meal containers clanged around on tables or slid along the food processing line. Students talked, laughed, and complained about their latest grade in some required subject as they grabbed a snack or something to drink between classes. Small groups of girls congregated around the room, discussing various things that typically had nothing to do with school, mostly relationships, and the cutest guys or professors.

The guys were in huddles talking sports and the ongoing war and where they'd be assigned in the battle after graduation. They knew that all of them would be military at some point.

Mark scanned the extensive room searching for them when he spotted Sue and Duncan sitting toward the back wall. He began making his way toward them, nodding to some of the students he recognized. He then stopped to speak to someone who had a question. Walking over to the table, the guy showed him his iBoard, saying, "Do you see what I'm doing wrong?"

Mark took the tool in his hands, scanned the coding for a few moments then handed it back.

"Yes, I see what you did wrong. Read through it again and you'll see it too," he said.

"You're not going to tell me?"

"If you'd used wrong codes, I would tell you, but it's only your syntax that's wrong. Clean up that mess, and you'll have it. Take your time and reread through your coding. It's a straightforward switch. You'll find it," Mark said then walked away.

The corner where they met was away from the chatter so they could go over their notes with as little disruption as possible. Sue seemed to always arrive at their meeting first, so it was she who would tidy up a table and save a place for the others.

Just behind a pillar near their location, Mark spotted the same guy he'd seen at the café watching Sue. Mark didn't redirect his eyes as they met, and neither did the stranger in the letterman jacket. Their glares stopped only when Mark walked past a post and blocked their view. Instead of continuing on toward the students, Mark stepped back to have another look. As he did, the stranger gathered his things. He stood, glanced back toward Mark, who couldn't tell if he was looking at him or just in his direction. As he continued to push chairs aside and walk toward the letterman, the guy turned and walked   out   a   door.

THE INFATUATION

Some guys are suave;
Some debonair.
Some filled with charm;
Some lack all flair.

Routinely the three met in the cafeteria to plan and discuss strategies, programming and to go over questions they may have. Mark's office at school was too small, and this place, even with the background din, it seemed to work for them. They'd met twice before and things were beginning to come together.

On this occasion, he spotted that same guy he'd seen before sitting again in the same location as last time. Mark mentally scratched his head. In itself, that wasn't unusual since the school wasn't that big and he'd seen several other students that caught his eye, but this one was different. There was some sort of signal the guy sent out that was uncomfortable. It was a similar signal he'd picked up when the enemy was getting close. He didn't have the same orange national tattoo of the enemy on his forehead, yet he emitted that same vibe. Mark decided to let it drop and instead of walking over to meet this guy, he changed directions and headed to the table where Sue and Duncan sat. Sue was reading something on her iBoard in apparent deep concentration. Duncan's chin was in his palms, propping up his head that seemed to outweigh his body. With puppy dog eyes he was watching her. It was like watching a romantic tragedy about to unfold. With eyebrows raised and his brow wrinkled, his puppy dog eyes resembled a scolded dog. He hardly noticed Mark's arrival, he was so infatuated with Sue. Mark marveled at how such a young face could have eyes that seemed to droop and cheeks sag as if devoid of any underlying muscular structure. He even pictured Duncan with his tongue hanging out, panting like some cartoon character in the movies. He was just a boy with a look of love for sure.

Duncan wasn't the same enthusiastic student as Sue, who used her spare time to study. She seemed above the "cute" conversations going on with the other girls and seemed more interested in grades, graduation, and a degree than with gossip. She went about her business without even noticing Duncan's stare.

"How's it going, folks," Mark asked as he squeaked out a chair.

Startled, Duncan jerked his head around and instantaneously reverted back to his nerdy programmer facial expression, "Great! We're doing great," he spouted.

Sue, still concentrating, hardly noticed them, instead looked up and offered a curt, "Hello," then quickly ran a finger over the iBoard screen.

"Here it is, Duncan. See," she said, pointing.

"It's right here. This program was written to foil maintenance programming and was designed to find code that violates convention. The program kept timing out because it forced the maintainer to read every line of your code with a magnifying glass, but we found it. They were using creative misspelling within the code, so a quick search didn't work. Once we found it and corrected the spelling, it works. You can't look at code through a toilet paper roll, Duncan," she instructed.

Duncan simply nodded.

Mark noticed Duncan's attraction to Sue on the first day they met. He'd always been more interested in programming than in women, but Sue wasn't just another iBoard banger to him. Duncan feigned having no romantic notions toward her, but Mark could see through that guise. He could see that his feelings toward her were growing. His manner and even his appearance were changing. His speech was guarded and careful. He was in a mode of attempted charm oblivious to his pocket protector or even the rainbow of colored pens that had long ago been depleted of their ink.

Mark fulfilled his part of the agreement by spending some time going over their class assignments and answering a few questions they had. After their meeting at the café, he'd sent them an electronic message about the project he was working on called "FindIt" and asked them to look at its introductory programming and review its objectives. The goal was to find stocks institutions held when a court ruling required a company to pay stockholders back for some tort proven in a class-action lawsuit. Banks and other financial institutions bought and sold stocks often and in large quantities. Those institutions many not be aware that they held a stock at the time there was such a court order. Consequently, they missed the opportunity to collect on those settlements. FindIt could dig into all their files match it to the dates these torts occurred and get them paid.

Sue had written many lines of code and had some questions about the shortest path from source to all vertices while Duncan had done nothing but glance over the preamble to the programming and read the program's objective.

"What do you think?" Mark asked the two.

"I get the idea, I think," Duncan commented.

"Did you program the beginnings of this?" Sue asked.

"Yes. I started putting together the compiling part of it. There's much more work to do," Mark said.

"How long do you think this is going to take?" She asked.

"A long time. I'm not sure. I'm up against a deadline so why don't we divide up the work and see if we can get something done by next week," Mark said.

"What part do you want, Duncan?" Sue asked.

"Huh?" Duncan replied, unaware of the discussions that were taking place.

"Duncan. Where have you been? I said, what part of the program do you want to handle?" Sue repeated.

"I don't know. You just tell me what you want me to do, and I'll handle it."

Mark began feeling doubtful about the ability to complete the program by the deadline. They'd been at it for several weeks, and there was virtually no progress. Things were missing that required decisions be made. Mark couldn't handle everything. He relied on Sue and Duncan to challenge and question how to approach the issue. Mark began thinking he had to find other options for funds while they continued working on the FindIt program. As Sue and Duncan discussed the architecture of the program Mark's mind drifted to other potential options.

While he'd always stayed away from games, the thought of that new game at Forrest Labs came to mind. Sue said it paid out in mega millions if it could be won. She also said it was unbreakable, but Duncan had something his father's company had developed that might help. Maybe that Forrest Labs thing was worth considering. He'd have to give that more thought with an open mind.

Discussions finished, the group filled their backpacks and headed out. Mark walked with Duncan toward the exit as Sue stopped at one of the few groups still there.

"You didn't attempt any streamlining of the program?" Mark asked.

"I glanced at it and have some ideas. I'll have it for you at our next meeting," Duncan said.

"Sure. I'm sure you're pretty busy in your other classes," Mark said.

"Yeah," Duncan said.

"You seem to be pretty attracted to Sue, Duncan. Can I ask you something?

"Sure, Mark. What is it?"

"Have you asked her out?"

Duncan stuttered then after shuffling back and forth like a pony sampling the turf he finally said, "Yeah."

"Go on," Mark said.

"Well, I asked her if she wanted to go see that new movie that just came out. I heard it's a great flick with lots of action. Some of my buddies said some of the scenes are so realistic you almost duck when the rockets get fired toward you. So I want to see it and asked her to go," he said.

Mark stood there with his hands on his hips in apparent disbelief.

"Don't tell me she said no?"

"Well..." he stammered.

Looking up toward the gray ceiling as if he would count the dots in the soundproofing material, Duncan began running his mouth like revved up a two-stroke motorcycle.

"She had some important stuff going on in her life and had to call her girlfriend and get ready for something they were going to do together that night and wash her hair and put on makeup then work on a project from the Lab so was too busy and she couldn't go," he said with a halting gasp for air.

Mark couldn't think of anything to say. He could have told the kid that a war movie isn't every girl's interest and maybe coach him on dating. He almost went into it, but then held back. He couldn't see Sue ever being interested in Duncan, no matter what he said. Maybe in another 10 years, he'd grow up. Some do. So he remained silent, only offering, "That's too bad, but at least you tried."

"Yeah. Well, I'll try again some other time when she isn't so busy," Duncan said.

Mark looked back as Duncan walked away, turned his head back toward the cafeteria. He walked over to the coffee machine, and then spotted Sue coming around the corner.

"Hey. I thought you left," he said.

"I wanted Duncan to think I left because I don't want to continually say no to his requests for a date. He wanted me to go to some stupid movie with him a couple of nights ago. He didn't get a chance to ask me today during classes or at our meeting. When we were finished I wanted to sneak away somehow before he could say anything so I just said I needed to go meet a friend and stepped into the lady's room for a while," Sue explained.

"Yes, he told me about the movie," Mark said. "Want me to get you a cup of coffee?"

"Sure, thanks."

The two found a corner and began talking about FindIt, his need for revenue, and finally, games.

"Duncan knows one heck of a lot about those grid games, Mark. I'd suggest you not totally rule out the option of games. You might be surprised at what's there and the revenue you can win," she said.

"Okay. I won't rule them out, but let's keep cracking on FindIt for now, okay?"

THE NEED

Nothing yet for him to grasp,
Must get on with it so very fast.
Delay would mean he could not stay,
He must find how some other way.

Sitting at his desk Mark pondered his options. Programming "Findit" properly, and making it work correctly, could never be done in time. The team may write the code, but it would have to be tested and retested before it would be worth any money. His deadline was drawing near, and his military transfer papers could be on his desk any day. If that happened, he'd be back in the war. He was becoming desperate to come up with the funding he'd need to get released.

When he first met the students, they mentioned the massive money involved in a grid game. While he'd rejected that idea for both practical and philosophical reasons, he considered reexamining the potential. Mark turned on his iBoard, and navigated to the Forrest Labs website where he searched for their online game, V-World. If the financial payout was as big as Sue and Duncan explained, and he felt that together they could crack the game, it could work. To make that decision he needed to understand how this game functioned before even considering it. Pressing a few keys, the front page of the game appeared.

"Conquer the World and Win Millions," was the headline on the opening page.

Beneath the heading it read, "Discover a new world, meet fascinating and interesting people, join vibrant communities or build your own business and earn real money!"

Scanning down the page, glossing over scenes depicting lifelike avatars dancing, swimming, singing, and generally having fun, Mark quickly read the V-World instructions.

"Users can play V-World and earn real money by deleting other players or by gaining followers. Players enter the world as a bot or an avatar. Bots, a shortened term for robots, may enter the world at three levels as follows:

Category	Function	Entry Fee
ENTRY	Join the fun and wander the wonderful world of excitement and drama	FREE
BOT Category B1	Also a bot, but with higher than average artificial intelligence (A.I.) programed into your character Category 1 bots may earn Foresters that can be banked and converted to your local currency.	{}10.00
BOT Category B2	Receive one level higher A.I. and the opportunity to earn Forresters by both deleting the foes (other bots and avatars) and gaining followers and 1.5 x the standard pay out rate.	{}20.00
AVATAR A.I.	Receives Group A2 A.I. and earns Forresters at 2.0 x the standard rate for deleting foes and gaining followers.	{}50.00
AVATAR AB	Receives Group A1 A.I and earns Forresters at 4.0x the standard rate for deleting foes and gaining followers. AB avatars are born into the game.	{}250.00

Join the fun, drama, and excitement of V-World. Bots may roam the land, make new friends, have babies, build, manage, set up businesses and role play any type of existence they desire. What's unique about V-World is the game will already contain a bot that looks like you! Search the world and find your own bot or avatar and control it! Imagine the fun of directing yourself in a game with the potential of making big money. Join Today!"

Then in fine print, it read, "Free memberships receive the same benefits as Avatars, but receive only 1% of the financial awards based on the top pay rate, AVATAR AB, birthed."

Below that, another paragraph explained the game further.

"Become eligible for real-world financial rewards that are accumulated as the game runs on. Each day Forrest Labs adds revenue to the prize that continues to build. The longer the game goes without a winner, the bigger the prize! To sign up, just click here."

Pressing the "click here" button Mark selected the Free option, and instantaneously his bot appeared in a vacant lot somewhere in a city. On two sides stood windowless buildings swathed with graffiti. At the end of each building stood a tall boarded fence. At the top of the screen, there was a menu with various selections, one titled "advance" provided instructions to move his bot around in the environment.

A message popped up on his screen saying, "For the best experience, wear your VR glasses."

He pulled his VR receptors out of his top desk drawer and slid them on. He could tell only a small difference in the game, so he took them off and played without them. Next, he grabbed his headphones from the top of his desk and wore them. Through his headphones, he could hear traffic rumbling and horns honking in the streets nearby. Experimenting with some of the commands, he figured out how to make the bot move using the arrow keys. Doing so, he walked toward what appeared to be a loose board in the fence. He selected the "camera" option from the menu, and his view panned out, and he saw his bot standing helplessly naked.

Amazingly, the bot looked like him right down to the scar in his head and on his left thigh.

"How the heck did they pull that off?" he mumbled.

"Better not run out into the street without clothes on," he thought to himself.

He played with the camera controls until he became relatively proficient at searching the nearby area. He noticed a pile of trash in one corner that someone must have thrown over the fence. Examining it, he saw there were some discarded shoes, pants, and some old worn, dirty shirts.

After selecting the help option on his iBoard, he learned how to manipulate the pile, pick what he wanted, and wear it. He chose the least dirty shirt, then pointed and clicked on the pants and the shoes, and the bot put them on. Finally dressed, he made his way through the hole in the fence to the sidewalk on the other side.

Using the keystrokes he'd learned, he had his avatar stroll up the street taking in the sites. Obviously, he was in a vast city that looked similar to those where his college was located. In fact, after closer examination, it seemed it was a copy of the college town where he now taught and went to school.

There was the sprinkling of trash along the gutters, a fireplug needing paint, a vacant store across the street with a sign hanging in the window he couldn't make out. A faded advertisement on the side of a brick building for an elixir that probably claimed a cure for anything. But he couldn't be sure, because it contained writing he'd never seen before. It could have been his city except for one thing: none of the signs were readable. Not the obvious "for rent" sign and not the sign with the familiar colors and logo of a world-famous cola. In fact, the street signs were written in that same hieroglyphics.

He wondered how he'd navigate since he couldn't read the writing. He'd have to begin memorizing the streets and buildings. Another mental note was to ask what that was all about.

As he moved along, he saw a little notice at the bottom of his screen reading, "Newbie, you're prone to attack. Make every attempt to evade the deleters who are after you."

"What the heck's a 'deleter?'" he murmured. Mark grabbed a pencil and scratch paper and wrote down some of the questions he had, not realizing there would be so many.

Navigating along, he spotted an opening between two buildings that appeared to be an alley. Turning into it, he spotted a dumpster. He decided to hide behind it and wait as he searched for that deleter, whatever that was. Seeing nothing, he climbed out from behind the dumpster and walked carefully down the alley avoiding the broken bottles that cluttered the area.

As he strolled toward the other end of the alley, he didn't see a similarly dressed male come out from one of the doorways. It made his way up behind him, carrying what appeared to be a wine bottle. The male tapped his bot on the shoulder, and as if his bot had a mind of its own, he saw it turn and face the stranger. The two engaged in some sort of conversation that seemed to take on an air of aggressiveness.

"This must be one of the deleters," he said to himself.

There was some sort of confrontation, and his bot abruptly turned and began walking. The stranger ran up behind his bot and crashed the bottle over its head. A sign popped up when his bot fell to the ground, reading, "You have been deleted by Gordon Starlight. He will receive one Forrester for his deletion. Play again? Y/N"

Mark pressed "Y" and was again in the field where he originally started. This time, instead of putting on those soiled clothes, he simply read one of the menu options that automatically dressed his bot in a more appealing outfit. Again he directed his bot out of the field and into the street. Again the stranger came out of the doorway, engaged in a conversation then deleted him with its wine bottle.

Again a sign popped up reading, "You have been deleted by Gordon Starlight," and again, Mark pressed "Y" to reenter the game. This time, instead of moving directly into the street, he typed a message into his iBoard reading, "Pick up that piece of metal pipe by the building."

His bot walked over to the building, bent over, and picked up the pipe. His bot slid the pipe up the sleeve of his jacket, then went through the fence and into the street as if it knew what to do. As the stranger and his bot engaged in their conversation, Mark typed, "Be alert. That guy is going to hit you with his bottle."

Mark waited to see what would happen. Rather than being hit by the wine bottle, his bot withdrew the pipe from his jacket and crashed it over the bottle toter's head. A message appeared saying, "You've deleted Gordon Starlight and will receive one Forrester credit." Mark sighed, signed off, and closed his iBoard.

"I don't get it," he thought to himself. "How could anyone make millions by hitting other players with a pipe? Using those bots to make any money would take longer than developing the "Findit" program."

Mark made a note to suggest something to Sue. The game was too mundane and needed the avatars and bots to be more robust in their desire to delete each other. Going to the messaging function of her iBoard he wrote, "Sue, that game is boring. Everyone's the same coloring as we are, white, yellow, brown and black. They should make some of the avatars and bots different colors. Maybe some blue and some orange and implant artificial intelligence in them to fear and hate those colors. That might stimulate   more   fighting   and   more   deletions."

THE SNATCH

Grab him quickly before they see,
The dastardly deed that's planned.
Raise him and grow him and he will be,
The master of the land.

Wallace tossed and turned as something inside his head seemed to be shouting and almost nudging him to move. He stubbornly stirred, fighting the daylight glaring through his eyelids and wishing to remain in the warm dream of cans splashed across the beautiful green mountainside. In his dream, he saw them beautifully scattered over the lush Olympic Club manicured golf fairways that rested virtually empty of golfers. In the calmness of his sleeping brain, after loading the cans into his shopping cart, he easily pushed it with a simple fingertip effort as if it was levitating effortlessly over the grass to the clubhouse where he was served a steak and eggs breakfast.

He rolled over and pulled his dank blanket up to his neck. He turned his head away from the brightness and the nagging of his inner voice.

He felt a very loud "NOW," that he couldn't distinguish from the Voice or just his imagination. But since it came with a sense of urgency telling him to get a move on and to get cleaned up, he realized he'd never think of that on his own, so he opened his eye and greeted the day.

The medications the fee clinic gave him were helping him ignore those sounds inside his head. They weren't coming through as clearly as before. Instead, there was more of an urge, a push, or a garbled noise and gnawing feeling that he needed to do something. It was like an itch he simply had to scratch, or it would drive him mad, something some thought he already was.

The Voice had been with him as long as he could remember. At first, it was like a guide or a friend, but later it became more demanding wanting him to work harder at something or strive to be the president of his youth club or run for office in his school. In high school, it seemed to push him toward things he had no interest in.

Not just school subjects, but activities that involved other people even though he had no friends and didn't want any.

Eventually, he found a way to block it out when one of the other loners offered him a small stick with a needle.

Yes, it worked, and as time passed, the Voice helped him find the sellers and where to get the money to purchase that little piece of heaven.

When he left high school up in Roseburg, Oregon, he came to "The City," where he got his funding from collecting those cans. It wasn't a lot, but it kept him in money and helped him live comfortably on the streets. Can money kept him in food and drugs with enough left over for a cup of coffee on some foggy mornings.

The morning he went to the hospital, he stirred and looked out into the morning sunlight.

Making his way up onto his left elbow, he stretched and scratched his oily head.

There was no voice telling him to do anything, but he had the urge to go get cleaned up, which he knew meant something important was about to happen.

The cleanup spot was a hotel South of Market where he'd work his way into the hotel's back door and into the public restroom to bathe and shave.

He always had a clean shirt and pants neatly rolled up in one of his plastic bags stored in his shopping cart for these emergencies.

He stood, rolled his bedroll, and stuffed it into its place in his shopping cart.

Yawning, he pushed the cart onto the sidewalk and made his way to what he called his cart storage facility behind a dumpster in a nearby alley. Grabbing his good clothes bag, he headed over to the hotel, a place that catered to tourists. There was a service entrance he used that away from the lobby. The door was left open for various deliveries, and once inside, just off to his right, was a restroom where he could step into a stall and strip off his old clothes and underwear. He'd listen to make sure nobody was there, fill a basin with warm soapy water, and splash himself somewhat clean.

After quickly shaving and shampooing, he dried with handfuls of paper towels, then stepped back into the stall and changed into his clean clothes. He pulled his hair back into a ponytail and secured it with one of the rubber bands from his collection and pocketed the little money he possessed along with the razor with a few shaves left.

Stuffing everything into his bag, he pushed his way out and passed a well-dressed gentleman entering the bathroom.

"Good morning," Wallace chirped.

"Mornin'," the guy said as he made his way toward a urinal.

Having a regular-looking guy in clean clothes reply with a greeting rather than a rebuff, gave him confidence enough to walk into the hotel lobby.

Wallace headed straight down the hall to the lobby, where he stopped and looked around at the decorative appointments in awe. Then, he stood there to see what would happen. He wondered if one of the polite doormen or a bellman would ask him to leave like they'd done before in other hotel lobbies. After a few minutes of statue-like boredom, he walked out the front door, amazed he wasn't thrown out and satisfied that his appearance was normal.

Before heading over to see Mary, he had to drop his old clothes in his parked shopping cart. He stuffed the plastic bag he kept them in into his hip pocket and headed over to her Powel Street hang out. Mary carried a large leather bag with many of her possessions because she'd said it looked classier than carting around a plastic bag. She'd told him she was going to become too sophisticated for plastic bags and had to get ready for the transformation.

During the day, she hung out at the Powel Street BART station that was always crowded with tourists and street performers who entertained the tourists waiting to board the Powel Street cable car. Sometimes he'd meet her and share stories of the streets, exchange opportunities for income, and talk about the future. She was working on getting off drugs and was encouraging him to follow her lead. He'd considered it, but he worried about life without it.

He spotted her in the place she always sat with her sign reading: "Please help fund my college tuition."

"Hi, Mary," he said.

"Oh, hi. I didn't see you walking up."

"I tippy-toed," he said, smiling.

"What's going on?" Mary asked.

"I've got an assignment today," he said.

"What is it?"

"I'm not sure," he said.

"How can you be not sure of an assignment?" Mary asked.

"I don't know. I just know I have to ask if I can borrow your big leather bag then go get on BART," he told her.

"Is it your voice again?" Mary asked.

"Kind of, but the meds have been blocking it out. Now it's just a feeling of something I have to do, so I have this urge to borrow that beautiful bag of yours even though I don't know why. If you'll loan me that bag and if I'm getting the bag full of money lying behind a dumpster somewhere, I'll share it with you," he said.

"Deal," Mary said.

Mary emptied the contents from her bag and handed it to Wallace, and he gave her his neatly folded plastic bag.

"Doesn't seem like a very good trade to me, Wallace," she said, stuffing her contents in the bag.

Wallace thanked her, waved, and ran down the stairs into the BART station.

Stopping at the bottom, he moved aside from the crowd awaiting an inspiration when it jumped into his mind to invest in a BART ticket, but he wasn't sure how much to spend, and he sure didn't want to waste his can money.

Pacing like an expectant father, he waited for some inspiration or instructions.

Finally, it came to him to put a five-dollar bill in the machine.

Then it occurred to him to type in four dollars and twenty-five cents and press the "H" button. He did, and a blue ticket with a small magnet strip came out along with seventy-five cents in change. He hit the "return" button again just to make sure nothing else was in there. Satisfied the machine delivered all its contents, he made his way to the platform where the overhead sign said a Richmond train arrived in three minutes.

It squealed to a stop, and the automatic doors jumped open, and he got the urge to step inside.

BART trains in the City are underground, and as they travel east, they pass under San Francisco Bay. When the train emerges into the daylight on the Oakland side of the Bay, it arrives at the West Oakland station. From there, it dives back underground to the 12th Street/Civic Center station. There the train doors jumped open, and like a puppet, he walked off and stood motionless on the platform, wondering what to do next. Decisively he walked up into the daylight and stood on a corner where an AC Transit bus pulled up.

As he boarded it, he saw the opportunity to get a free ride, just as he'd done so many times in San Francisco and darted behind a woman who was asking the driver questions about where to get off to go to the Mervyn's store.

He wasn't sure why he got on that particular bus or where it would take him, but he didn't second guess those urges for fear of displeasing the Voice.

The bus made its way higher and higher into the hillside. He could tell by the larger houses they were going into a more expensive area and the thought of the riches that may be coming excited him. Maybe this was where more green hillsides with free cans would reside, but why would he be collecting cans in his good clothes with Mary's classy leather bag? There had to be another reason he was here.

After several more stops, they came close to a large brass door building on the opposite side of the street. Wallace stood, made his way to the front, thanked the driver for making the stop for him, then walked down the three steps to the curbside. He didn't notice the driver scratching his head as he closed the door and drove off.

THE HOSPITAL

Screams and sounds
are people yelling?
Or 'tis it the departed
Souls all wailing?

Gawking at its magnificence, Wallace made his way toward Bay View Memorial Hospital's regal front doors, then stopped. His shoulders sagged in disappointment when he realized he wouldn't be allowed to walk into the beautiful building through the front door like anyone else. Again, he'd be relegated to the back like the homeless bum he'd been for far too long. But he didn't fight the feeling because he knew it would be no use.

Obediently he surrendered to the urge to walk around the corner, down a narrow walkway to a loading dock where he stood waiting for something he felt would happen.

He turned and glanced down the street just to his left and noticed an algae-filled pond at the end. The pond had meaning. He knew he had to discard a package he'd pick up in the hospital in that pond. He also knew that the package was of no value to him, but something that could be harmful to him in the future.

He wondered why he would pick something up just to dispose of it? Why not just throw it away in the dumpster? Why even bother if it was of no use to him or anyone else? It didn't make sense, but as usual, he'd obey.

He sensed that the security guard was making rounds, but before he went in through the loading dock, he absentmindedly picked up a brick and put it in Mary's bag.

"Why'd I do that?" he wondered.

Making his way up the narrow loading dock stairs, he went through a door on the left. Following the hallway through another set of double doors, he immediately sniffed the smell of antiseptics giving him a feeling of healing cleanliness. Having only seen hospitals from emergency room scenes on television, he was surprised that the hallway was empty and quieter than he'd expected. Everything he'd seen on TV made him think all hospitals were a source of chaotic scrambling and bloody patients lying on those funny little beds with shopping cart wheels, but this hospital was different.

He made his way deeper into the building and came to a large picture window that looked into a room with three tiny beds. One had a small bundle wrapped in blankets and was wearing a blue knit cap. A nurse sat alone in the room, facing the wall, typing something in a computer, glancing alternately between the screen and a clipboard on the desk.

Something told him to go around the corner, enter the room quietly, and close the door behind him. He'd hit the nurse with the brick, then place the blue bundle in the bag along with the brick, and leave the hospital the way he came in.

He hesitated and had a sick feeling about another lady whose head he smashed because the voice commanded it to be done. He wouldn't hit this one as hard knowing to just stun her until he could grab the package and get away down to the pond.

Like a cat unable to contain its reaction to a ribbon, he couldn't stop reacting to the urge. Quietly he made his way around the corner and snuck up behind the nurse who seemed to sense someone behind her.

She began swiveling around, saying, "Bilirubin looks good, Dr. Chopra."

At the same time, Wallace swung his bag, knocking the unsuspecting nurse to the floor. He bent over and felt her neck, though he wasn't sure what he'd do if he didn't feel a pulse.

Making his way toward the middle bed, he picked up the blue bundle and put it in the bag with the brick and briskly walked out. Outside, he opened Mary's bag, looked inside, and saw it wasn't a package. It was a little pinkish baby, with eyes closed and its cheeks gyrating on a piece of plastic that hid its lips.

"Don't worry little baby I'm going to take care of you," he said.

Then it dawned on him something told him what to do with this "package." Maybe it meant some different package he'd pick up as he made his way out of the hospital. Surely, this couldn't be the package he was to dispose of in that lake. He searched through the bag looking for some package he was supposed to dispose of. Unwrapping the blanket, he searched around finding only a tiny Pampers, but nothing else. Where was the other one?

As he crossed the dock, the baby began crying.

"No wonder," he thought.

Wallace pulled the brick out and dropped it on the ground making the space more comfortable for the baby, and immediately the whimpering stopped.

As they strolled toward the pond, he could hear cooing and sucking sounds as the baby's lips seemed to smack together, jiggling the rubber thing. It popped out again. Hurriedly, before the baby could snivel again, he placed it close to the baby's mouth, and it instinctively sucked it back in.

"Wow. This little guy already knows how to work his mouth," he thought.

He hadn't heard from the Voice since that night he'd made the big mistake smashing the head of a pretty sleeping lady. Now the Voice wasn't commanding him through innuendo and urges. It came to him clearly.

"He's the package we need to dispose of, stupid. This package must be destroyed before it grows up or it will learn the truth and ruin our chances of winning."

"Stupid?" Wallace thought. The Voice called me stupid? I might be homeless and might not have finished school, but I'm not stupid," he thought with a wave of anger he'd never before felt.

There was a time he'd do whatever the Voice asked of him just to get his needed supply, but after the killing, he realized he couldn't continue down that path. He had no problem with lying or stealing. Nor did he have a problem living in doorways and out of his shopping cart. But after that night he decided he needed to change some things and take control of his mind. The methadone helped quash the need for horse, as the street people called it, and the people at the Buddha temple were training him on dealing with the Voice. They'd overcome the yearnings for drugs, and fought off the urgings over their voice, so decided so could he. He needed to get back to Mary and seek some advice.

For now, the first thing he would do is defy the Voice.

"His name is Billy Ruben, and I'm not throwing him in any algae-filled pond. You can't make me," he said, now speaking out loud as he turned and began walking back toward the hospital.

"Where are you going? If you return the package to the hospital, you will spend the rest of your life in prison. You have committed some very serious crimes that they will discover. They'll put you in the gas chamber and you'll die choking on your own vomit. Besides, the baby's mother died and she had no relatives, so the baby is destined to be in an institution where it will be beaten and used as slave labor. You don't want that to happen to this baby, do you?"

Wallace didn't. He didn't want to go to jail. And the thought of some institution that beat and worked babies didn't seem like a perfect prospect either, but he was determined not to kill a helpless baby.

"I will not kill this baby," he thought.

There was a long silence as he headed back toward the hospital. He walked to the AC transit bus stop just as one pulled up and stopped.

"Get on the bus. We'll figure this out later."

Wallace complied with the Voice, dug into his pocket for coins and dropped them into the collection box. Trudging down the aisle, he clutched Mary's bag like a worried woman walking through a group of gangbangerlooking hooligans. Finding an empty seat at the back, he sat down with the bag on his lap. Looking inside, he saw the baby sucking away contentedly.

Wallace closed his eyes, a serene smile rolled across his face, and something   warm   settled   into   his   heart.

THE MESSIAH

Was it something you can't remember?
Was it something in your head?
What are those voices now a beckoning,
Are they demons from the dead?

The rocking BART train screamed its way through the under-Bay tube on its way to San Francisco. By the time they reached the Powel Street station, he could feel the baby beginning to squirm in its makeshift bed. He needed someone to help him think this through and looked forward to finding Mary to tell her about what happened. Knowing the voice would come back, wanting him to dispose of what it had falsely called a "package," he would stand his ground and not give in no matter what the Voice might threaten him with.

He was through with killing. He'd done it once and everything went wrong. He wasn't sure if he'd get away from the house and after he did it, it made him sick to his stomach. And now the thought of obeying such a command again was disgusting.

While he was grateful that the Voice had helped him through some trying times, he'd already paid for its services and felt he was now even. Of course, there was always the unknown consequence of disobeying the voice. Never before had he tested the Voice's authority, so he began wondering what it could possibly do? Make it more difficult for him to find cans for his money? Make it harder to get drugs? Make it harder to find a safe place to sleep?

Perhaps. It made him reassess what was happening in all of his life.

Mary wanted a different track, so maybe he could get off the drugs and do something also. Now that he was going to be a dad, it was time for him to consider other options. He was sure Mary would help.

When he came up into the sunlight of the Powel BART plaza, he looked around for Mary but didn't see her. He headed south of Market toward her hotel carrying her bag under his arm and supporting the "package" inside with his hand. At her building, he ran up the stairs to her room and rapped on the door.

"Who's there?"

"It's me," he said, knowing she'd recognize his voice.

There was a metallic fumbling at the door just before it swung open.

"You're back. Come on in, Wallace," Mary said, standing aside and sweeping her hand into the room.

"You're done using it?" she asked, looking at her bag in Wallace's hand.

"Yes. I had a package to pick up this afternoon," Wallace said.

Her small room included a bed, a table and two chairs, a sink and drainboard. Next to her bed stood a nightstand with a clock radio playing some soft rock. At the end of the hall, there was a bathroom shared by the four other tenants. Setting down on the bed, she patted a spot beside her and motioned for Wallace to sit.

"Well..." Wallace started then paused. He wasn't sure where to start or how to explain what had just happened.

The baby had been quiet for a little over half an hour and was beginning to stir.

"Yes?" Mary said patiently.

"Well, I had to pick up a package."

"Yes, I know that. You told me, remember? So what was it? Are you just going to sit there and make me guess? Who asked you to do it? Geez. Come on, Wallace tell me," she pleaded.

"You want to see the package?" he finally asked.

"You have it? Is it money?"

"Yes and no," Wallace said.

"What do you mean?" Mary asked.

"Yes, it's in your bag. No, it isn't money," he said, trying to swallow, but finding his mouth absent of saliva.

Mary leaned closer, looking down into her bag carefully balanced on his lap.

Seeing the baby, she jumped up and drew back against the wall knocking over one of the small chairs in the room.

"What the hell! That's a baby in there!" she shouted in a hushed voice. "Where in the hell did you get a baby? Whose is it?"

"Nobody's."

"What are you talking about, nobody's. I suppose it just grew out of the gutter and you found it collecting cans."

"Not exactly."

"Not exactly? What kind of answer is that? Where did this baby come from? Did you take it from someone? You have to return it. The mother must be frantic."

"No, not someone. I took it from someplace though."

"Where?"

"Bay View Memorial Hospital over in the Eastbay."

"What? Then you take it right back!"

"I was going to Mary, but I can't do that. There is no mother or father and no family, so the baby would go to an orphanage and I'd go to jail."

"How do you know that?"

"I heard it when I was over there. I'm told that if I return it, I could go to jail, and it would do the baby no good anyway 'cause it could go to its own jail, an orphanage. I would never do that to an innocent baby, Mary," Wallace said.

They'd known each other for a year, and they had many things in common.

She'd never divulged how she got on the streets, and he never asked.

Likewise, she'd never asked about his background. Mostly, they thought only about obtaining the substances they needed.

"So you just took it? You can't just take a baby from a hospital because you thought you heard something from some imaginary source. In fact, why were you even at that hospital? Did something tell you there was a baby to be snatched?"

Wallace paused, looked down at the baby, then back at Mary.

"If I tell you something personal, something that I've never really told anyone before, can I trust you to keep it a secret?" he asked.

"Yes, sure. I promise to keep it a secret unless it is something completely outrageous and would threaten someone's life," she said.

"I want to get clean and go to school and make something of myself. When I saw this helpless little guy who'd lost his little plastic sucker..."

"It's called a Binky," Mary told him.

"Okay, lost his Binky. Anyway, I realized that there are more important things in life than simply following a nagging voice telling me to do things that I'd be ashamed of. I'm not ashamed of taking this baby. It is an orphan, and it has no family so it needed my help."

"But how do you know that? You didn't answer me on why you were sent to that hospital to get this particular baby?" she asked again.

A whimper came from inside Mary's bag that quickly turned from a minor displeasure into a very intense lung exercise. Mary instinctively reached over and plucked the baby from her handbag, and it almost immediately stopped crying.

"Run down to the pharmacy and pick up some formula and disposable bottles. This baby will have to be fed. While you're at it, pick up some small Pampers," Mary ordered.

She reached for her purse with her free hand.

"Here, take some money. It's a loan. You are going to owe me big time! When you get back, I want a full explanation and a detailed plan on what your intentions are for this child."

As Wallace turned to leave, Mary said, "Wait. Does this baby have a name?"

He thought for a moment then said, "Yes. It's Billy. Billy Ruben."

Mary looked at him puzzled.

"I understand the Billy part, but why Ruben? Why not give him your last name, Granger? Mary asked.

"He already had a name at the hospital. I didn't give it to him," Wallace said.

"Who told you that?" Mary asked.

"She didn't tell me, she was talking to a doctor and told her Billy Ruben was okay," Wallace explained.

"Bilirubin was okay? I've heard that term before, Wallace. I think it's a test they do on babies for something," Mary said.

"Whatever. His name is Billy Ruben, Mary."

THE BOY BILLY

It changed his life,
though not aware.
This baby's love,
'twas no cross to bear.

Wallace Granger's life slowly changed when he became more involved with caring for Billy Ruben. Responsibility had never before been a word in his vocabulary or a condition for his existence. Most of his life was about pleasing himself because nobody, not his mother, his absent father, nor anyone else, cared about him. From a very early age, he learned that if he was to feel the love he longed for, it had to come from within. Then and only then would his deepest needs be satisfied. Billy Ruben satisfied one of those needs.

Seeing that little baby smiling laughing and cooing made him think for the first time more about the sweet little creature than himself. That baby had no way of surviving if he couldn't come through and care for it. His mindset shifted from self to Billy. He became even more determined to get free of the magnetism of drugs that ensnared him and was the force that kept him living on the streets.

Mary was working at freeing herself. She tried to stop cold turkey and then found a rehab clinic and tried again. Right now, she was clean. If she could do it, so could he. Maybe hers would stick this time, maybe it wouldn't, but he vowed he would try.

It wasn't long before he moved from wanting that substance to hating it. Stopping wouldn't be easy, but he understood that and knew it was his only option. Without it, he realized he'd have a desperate craving that would cause his body to ache for its touch and warmth. But, with the encouragement of Mary and the needs of the baby, he would overcome.

Billy wasn't the kind of baby to cry and throw tantrums like he'd seen in other children when he stood in front of the drug store panhandling. When he was hungry or needed changing, he'd just jabber some baby talk and seemed smarter -- and even intelligent, if that could be something to describe a newborn -- than other babies. Though Billy couldn't talk, he actually pointed at things he wanted or needed. He couldn't walk, but he knew how to get Wallace to take him where he wanted to go.

It wasn't long after Billy's eyes began focusing Wallace noticed he somehow seemed interested in newspapers. Wallace picked up a Chronicle off the messy McDonald's counters while holding Billy on his lap. He noticed the baby seemed interested. It wasn't the same kind of interest a baby would have like slapping it with his hands, but he seemed to be concentrating on the words and images. He'd try his best to grab and turn the pages.

Mary asked him how did he expect to ever raise a child on his own and he admitted he couldn't do it alone. He asked if she could help just a little.

"A very little, but yes, I'll help until you can get your stuff together and he's at least old enough to go with you on the street," she said.

Because Billy was more a small child than an infant, it allowed Wallace to work the streets with Billy hidden in his bedroll. He raised enough money to pay Mary for using her small room. She'd care for Billy while Wallace worked for both of them holding a sign reading, "Baby needs a new pair of shoes."

One day when Mary wasn't available, Wallace learned that carrying Billy with the "Baby needs a new pair of shoes" sign generated much more revenue than usual. But that too created some issues. One of the other street people said, "You can't take care of a baby. You're on drugs and live on the street."

"I'm not doing drugs anymore, so I can take care of him fine," Wallace said.

"Oh, yeah? What about church and stuff like that? You going to take him to church?" he asked.

"Of course I will just like I used to do when I was a kid. We'd always go to church on Easter," Wallace said.

"Yeah? You don't even go to church."

"I do too. I been to Grace Cathedral a couple of times," Wallace said.

"Sure. For food, not church. If you go to church, tell me when Easter Sunday is," the man asked.

Wallace began digging deep into his brain to come up with something.

"It depends on what year you're talking about. I can't dig back that far in my past," Wallace said.

"Well, when's it going to be next year?" he asked.

Again, Wallace was stumped. All he knew was that it appeared on the calendar each year, but never on the same date. How that date was determined, he wasn't sure. Then it dawned on him and without thinking it through he answered with a voice of authority.

"Everyone knows that," Wallace said.

"So, when is it?"

"It's when the Pope sees his shadow," Wallace answered.

"Yeah, yeah, that's right. I forgot about that," the man said as he walked away, scratching his graying beard.

Wallace realized that if he was going to hang onto the kid, he'd have to have some sort of documentation to prove Billy was his. Through his contacts on the streets, Wallace was able to secure forged birth certificates using the name of Billy Ruben Granger. With his savings from his tax-free can money, his panhandled money, and his savings for having no overhead housing in a discarded refrigerator box, he raised enough money for a bus ticket to Roseburg, Oregon. There, he quickly found a job in a lumber mill that paid enough for a babysitter for Billy. Life for Wallace had changed; life for Billy had just begun.

THE HATRED

If God is good,
and God is great.
Why make so many,
so full of hate?

I didn't really know Wallace Granger. I was too young when he was killed in an accident at the sawmill, but I do remember the feeling of security and love during my early years. I don't recall fear or hatred or anything negative. Wallace was a very loving man.

Then things changed when I was older and living with my foster parents. I'll tell you about them later, but for now, let me just explain something. I didn't always hate -- with a couple of exceptions. I hated Brussels sprouts and spinach, but I could clean my plate with a little salt and a smothering of mayonnaise. My foster parents were different. Until them, I had never hated anyone. Not even Hebert Thurston, who was much bigger than me and once chased me around the gym and punched me in the nose when he caught me. I had that one coming for teasing him that he was fat and slow. I wasn't afraid of him or any other kid even if they were a couple of years older and bigger. A little sock in the nose was nothing compared to what I was getting at home.

For some reason, I picked on guys larger and older than me, not even thinking I could kick their ass. Something inside me gave me the impression I was a tough guy and knew all kinds of moves that would allow me to inflict some hurt on them. I have no idea where that came from. It was just some feeling that I was some sort of champion even though I was way too young to be the champion of anything. Still, I always figured I had nothing to lose and everything to gain.

They could beat a little guy and there was no glory in that. But if I beat them, I'd be the hero. But even in beating another boy, there was never any hate in those after-school fights.

No, the hate began with my foster father, Jafar. Until him, I'd never felt the emotions that jumped into my brain and lingered there like a sizzling pot of boiling acid.

Wallace and another woman raised me for my first few years. She was

88

very warm and loving. I kind of remember leaving one crowded city and moving to the next one where I stayed with another woman during the day. Sometimes Wallace would take me along with a few friends he'd meet at a tavern. He'd sit me on a shelf, get me a soda, and I'd watch them play cards. They laughed and drank their beers and would sometimes give me some dice to play with. I don't remember having any other kids to play with or even what town I was in, but one day Wallace didn't come to pick me up at the babysitter's house. I remember a man in a suit went to the house and whispered something to the babysitter, a nice plump lady who seemed to smoke too much, and she started crying.

A day later, the babysitter's boyfriend took me on a long car ride and let me out on the front porch of a police station in Portland, Oregon. I was old enough to get out of the rain, so I walked in and sat down on one of the wooden chairs inside. The policemen were friendly and even let me wear a hat with a gold shield on the front. A lady came by and took me to a place with a bed and some other kids until they finally told me they had a family for me to live with.

Even with the smoking plump babysitter and her boyfriend and the tavern card games, I'd had a pretty healthy life. Normal, except for those pesky voices that kept popping up in my head and those feelings that I knew more than I actually did. Somehow I had a feeling that I should know things kids would never have known: How to shoot a gun, drive a car, operate a machine that hadn't even been invented yet, strange things like that.

At school, I couldn't understand why they were teaching simple math. I could already add, subtract, multiply, divide and work fractions, so why they'd put a simple $2 + 2 = ?$ on the board then show pictures of four apples was beyond me. Pretty soon, the teacher stopped calling on me when I raised my hand.

Even though I was a star at math, the other subjects were pretty much a mystery, particularly reading. I picked it up relatively fast, but somehow something inside was telling me this wasn't my first language. I learned to read, but the letters I saw were totally foreign.

The only parent I knew was Wallace, who once told me he rescued me from an orphanage in California. So when someone asked about my parents, I had no idea what to say to them. I told them Wallace was the only parent I remember, and they decided to reach into the hat and pull out a couple of new ones. They said my new family would be with Jafar and Malakeh Raad, and I should feel lucky to have a family.

When I first saw Jafar, it sent shivers along my spine. He had black hair with a Bela Lugosi Dracula devil shaped vee hairline pointing toward the middle of his forehead. The coal-black hair matched the unshaved stubble on his face, and his eyebrows arched angrily downward toward his nose. His dark eyes seemed almost pupil-less. One was a blue so dark it almost looked black, the other a catlike yellowish brown. The whites of both eyes featured a tint of reddishness, giving them the appearance of death. The perpetual grin on his face seemed more a sneer than a joy, and as I would later learn, that is precisely what it was.

Jafar was active in the local Portland mosque when one day a stranger asked to speak to the group. Because I was well behaved, he used to take me. The Imam granted permission for a stranger to talk to the men. The stranger told the congregation his group was seeking an operative in Portland. That individual would help in the planning of a strategy to protect Islam from foreign powers. I heard Jafar call the man after the meeting and agree to meet him. I was in my room when he came home, but overheard him telling Malakeh he was offered a position with their group called "The Base." The English translation for this newly formed group was called Al Qaeda. He said the group's long- term plan was to gain the return of their land that the United States stole from them and gave to Israel. They would educate about the need for unification of all Muslims by strict enforcement of Sharia, the Islamic laws. I'm sure he didn't think I was old enough to understand what he was telling Malakeh, but I remember it clearly.

The stranger pointed out that though Muslims customarily used the phrase "Peace be upon you," The Base maintained that true peace only dwelled with the powerful. For example, the United States Air Force's Strategic Air Command (SAC) had bombers that carried powerful atomic weapons. One of them, the B-36, had a nickname the "Peacemaker," and the entirety of SAC has the motto proclaiming, "Peace is our Profession." They determined who had the peace because they dominated the oppressed with their powerful airplanes and their atomic bombs. Jafar said once Al Qaeda acquired powerful bombs, and secretly planted them in strategic locations in major United States cities. The Base would dictate who had the peace. And they'd do it on their terms, not the oppressors'. The process would take several years, but there would be a major attack on the United States that they will not soon forget.

"They will be brought to their knees when Al Qaeda takes down their symbols of capitalism. Then it will be followed with the obliteration of thousands more throughout the country," he told Malakeh.

She looked at him but remained silent just as she always did when he was speaking.

"The planning will take time, but it will happen," he added.

So Jafar had hate in his heart from the beginning, and it seemed to grow even more profound over time.

When I was brought into their home, my name was Billy. But Jafar wouldn't call me that and officially changed it to Rasheed so that I appeared more Persian. For some reason, I didn't feel either was my real name. I didn't know why or what my name should be, so I just let it go and played along.

Malakeh, my foster mother, seemed perpetually angry. That anger was obviously brought on from a pent-up fear of her husband's volatile demeanor. He was someone she both feared and surrendered to. When they were together in public, she could present the image of a confident Princess Diana, but at home, she was a slave to his demands.

My life with the violent Jafar was far worse than with Malakeh's shouting and broom handle threats. Jafar could mete out his interpretation of just punishment much more sinisterly and far more brutally than anything his wife did.

This couple tried to teach me respect, discipline, and the love of Allah, and after entering school, I was required to pray five times a day, so I was made to go to school with my prayer rug.

"Do you have to take your noontime nap like the kindergarteners?" the kids would taunt.

I confided in one of the kids that it wasn't for a nap, but for prayers. He must have told someone else because I was ridiculed by the other kids, most of them Christian or Jewish. I wasn't afraid of fighting them, but after several times of being caught, I began hiding the rug in bushes then retrieving it on my way home.

There was no hatred toward the guys I fought at school, even if they beat me. A punch in the nose might cause a nosebleed, but I feared Jafar. I felt I couldn't deceive him after he told me Allah would tell him if I was lying.

When I got home from school one day he must have been in a foul mood. He bent over and looked directly into my eyes and asked, "Did you pray to Allah at midday?"

The question struck a fear in me like a sudden jolt of electricity. My mind darted around, searching for the right answer. I didn't want to withstand another beating, but I feared that Jafar might actually talk with Allah and know that I was lying.

Finally, after quickly considering my two options, but unsure that either was correct, my lying eyes shifted, my fibbing feet shuffled, and my head dropped to the floor. I was an awful liar, so my ability to deceive lacked conviction. I answered, "Ya... ya... yesss, sir. I, ah, I prayed at, at, at noon."

"Again, you are lying to me, Rasheed. I know you are lying," he said. The sting of his belt across my bare arms served as a reminder that he dominated me and I would have to follow his orders.

Another thing I hated was that name, Rasheed. But they demanded that be my name so that I would be presented as a good Muslim. They refused to call me Billy and demanded I accept Rasheed. When he gave it to me, he twisted my head upward and looked into my eyes with that scornful stare that would scare even Chuck Norris. Then he grabbed me by the throat.

"You are now Rasheed, and you will use no other name. Do you understand?" he scowled.

"Yes, sir," I said.

"If I find you using your old name, you will be beaten, and I know when you are untruthful. You didn't think I'd know when you lied, did you? You lied to me again about noonday prayer, didn't you?" he asked.

I couldn't bring myself to utter even a single word in my own defense.

"Pull down your pants and bend over that chair," Jafar commanded loosening his belt he pointing at the sturdy oak kitchen chair.

He'd beaten me this way before and I knew the pain all too well, and I felt my body beginning to shake. I sensed what was about to happen and couldn't hold back the sobs no matter how hard I tried. My chest heaved convulsively as I fought to hold things in, then with a final release, the cry escaped with a screaming, howling exhale.

"Don't be a baby. Take Allah's punishment like a man," Jafar screamed.

Even though sometimes something inside me said I was a man, logically, at twelve I was obviously a boy. That feeling was there when I fought with other boys too. Why? Why was there this burning feeling I knew how to fight? Jafar was much more powerful than I and there was this memory of deeper pain than the pain that he created and I seemed to feel like I couldn't let myself simply lie there and be beaten again.

Instinctively I tried to escape. To where? To whom? I wasn't sure. No place or person would provide protection. I couldn't run to a mother like kids do when they need something. My foster mother was Jafar's accomplice, and she would only hold me in place and even help tie me to the chair with her nasty witch's cackle.

Though I thought I was strong, I also knew struggling was fruitless. But I needed to get somewhere, anywhere, away from the sting of the belt, and the fear and pain. Hence, I bolted and sprinted toward the hallway, hoping I could make the bathroom and lock myself in. Taking the steep turn in the hall, I slid on the bare oak floor, jamming my stockinged foot into the baseboard. The pain shot through my leg, but I continued running, ignoring the pain. Behind me, I could hear the laughing Jafar just as I got to the house's only bathroom.

Inside I locked the door and pressed against it with my body.

"Coward!" Jafar screamed.

I'm not sure why I thought my small body against the door could hold him out, but I held a shoulder against it. I could hear Jafar's slow but solid footsteps coming down the short hallway patiently following him like a cat stalking prey. Then, with the force of a dump truck, Jafar crashed the door once, but I held it. Again, he crashed against it, and still I held him out. Just as I sensed he was about to hit it again, something inside whispered, "open it now!" and I did. Jafar came screaming through the opened door and tripped over the toilet bowl and fell face first into the bathtub.

I don't know what made me laugh, but I did. Bad mistake.

Jafar pulled himself out of the tub, brushed the blood off his porcelain-damaged nose, grabbed my wrist, and dragged me back to the living room.

He slammed my stomach down over the chair then forced his knee into my back driving rushing air out of my lungs, making it impossible to grab a breath. It was as if I was slowly squeezed by a boa constrictor.

"Get the leather straps," Jafar yelled to his wife.

Obediently, she shuffled to the kitchen and pulled out the kitchen drawer that contained some shop scraps of leather from Jafar's leather bag shop. Grabbing a handful, she walked back, head down, and handed them to Jafar.

He looked at the straps and shouted, "Are you that stupid? Get the thicker ones!" he shouted.

She scampered back to the kitchen, and I could hear her digging through the drawers. She returned and handed him something I couldn't see, but heard Jafar yell to her, "You tie him down and this time tie him securely, or you'll be on this chair next."

I struggled on my stomach, but his strength wouldn't let me move. I screamed when I felt first one arm, then the other being secured to the legs of the chair. Next, I felt Jafar reach around and unfasten my belt and unbutton my pants, then yank them and my underpants down my legs and off, leaving me naked below the waist.

I looked over and saw him shove his wife to her knees and told her, "Tie his legs too, you stupid dumb woman. Can't you see I'm holding him in place?"

I could feel the coldness and vulnerability of my spread exposure as the fear began to heighten. The more I twisted and pulled on the straps, the more it seemed to delight Jafar.

"Look at the little liar, squirm. He's so pathetic," Jafar laughed to his wife.

Only my chest area was on the chair's seat. Malakeh tied my legs at the thighs to each chair leg. I tried digging toes into the floor in a fruitless effort to push my legs together. The thought of the stinging blows on my butt and bare legs sent another shock of fright through my body. Finally, I realized escape was impossible and surrendered the struggle.

"Would you like the honors, Malakeh?" Jafar casually asked his wife as if they were opening a birthday present. "I'll steady the chair as you give him a few whips."

"Make him a believer, Jafar. Bring the pain with a force only a man can deliver," she said.

Blinding tears filled my eyes and ran down my nose until dripping on the floor below. Without sight, my other senses seemed to become more acute. I tasted the acrid bitterness of fear in my dry mouth, smelled the stinking scent of shoe polish on Jafar's clothes, felt the coldness of the room on my exposed naked body. I heard the belt swirling in the air as it arched out, seeking its target.

CRACK! An electric shock of pain seared through my body.

Again and again and again, the pain overwhelmed me, then after several strikes, the stinging of the belt began to numb, and my cries slowed from screams to continued sobs.

Malakeh must have sensed the numbness I had acquired, so suggested Jafar change targets.

"Hit the back of his legs," Malakeh urged. "He is not feeling it."

The next stroke landed across the back of my right leg with a piercing pain more acute than the others I'd felt. When I let out a cry, I heard Malakeh laugh with an I-told-you-so tone.

"A little higher, Jafar. You'll get his boyhood!" she encouraged.

That strike caused a searing lightning bolt of pain far more severe than any I'd felt before. My body convulsed and recoiled in an electrifying jolt of agony that seared my brain and slashed through my gut. It was a pain far worse than anything I'd ever felt and more unimaginable than anything I'd ever considered. It was the worst beating I'd ever received; worse than the heavy wooden mop handle, worse than the belt; worse than the many punches to my stomach, placed there so my bruises wouldn't show. Death would be a love compared to the hell of this pain.

The intense pain waned to a sort of stabbing numbness. Now there was only a deadening hurt that, as it went on longer, it transformed my fear into another emotion. I no longer was screaming as I had with the first few strikes. For the first time in my life, I felt that new emotion, the one that became a constant companion. There was no fear, there was no sorrow, there was no fright and no pain. No, but there was revenge, and there was hatred.

Then   there   was   nothing.

THE VOICE

The days of dreams be gone,
The days of fear forever fled,
The days of peace will be won,
The days of fraud must join the dead!

A man who beats you is a liar,
You must feed his funeral pyre.

Time passed since that brutal beating. Others followed, but most weren't as extreme as that one. Still, I refused to call him "father" or "dad." He would take off his belt and strike me when I called him Jafar. I have no idea how these things pop into my mind, but once I attempted a martial arts move. I knew it was called a leg whip, and though I landed it perfectly to the hamstring, my size and strength were not enough to do any damage. He just kept coming at me madder than before. All I accomplished is another sting of his belt. I would never submit to him no matter how much I was punished.

I learned that blackness wasn't a void; it was an escape. Though I'd been sent to the dark side, eventually, the light will come back and in that darkness and the nightmarish dreams dim as new light filters in.

After another evening's darkness, my awakening dream wasn't of soothing voices or green hills and sailing ships silently gilding through a tranquil sea. It was of that first beating almost three years before. Awakening slowly, I rolled over and fluffed the pillow. The rhythm of my heart beating slowly and evenly soothed and calmed me as I searched for a soft female voice somewhere in my mind. Stretching my neck, I began thinking about things in the past and trying to understand my life thus far. The voice was something that seemed to come up from deep inside in a different tone and inflection from the others I'd heard. Though I couldn't distinguish if that previous voice was male or female, it seemed supportive, and now it was saying something strange.

"You must feed his funeral pyre."

The sensation of sound was so genuine it could have been coming from an elf sitting on my bedpost. Or from a radio or television set, even though the home had neither. I thought maybe Jafar was playing a trick on me and that he'd planted some device in my mattress that transmitted the message. Hopefully, I wondered if perhaps it was my savior, the answer to my prayers. I thought it had to be a Jafar trick, but I had to explore this voice, but do it slowly and carefully.

Vigilant not to move my lips or utter any vocal sound, I thought, "You are the liar, not my foster father. He is wise and helps guide me in Allah's ways as taught to us by Muhammad, peace be upon him."

I immediately heard, *"We know you're trying to communicate with us, but we do not hear your message. We only observe your anguish. Just know this: His wisdom is unfounded and untrue, and he knows nothing. He is a liar with a disease in his heart, so he shall have a painful chastisement because he lied. Allah requires punishment to those who lie; therefore, he must be penalized."*

I waited, but the voice said nothing. Like invisible tentacles probing all corners and crevasses of my brain, searching, feeling around for answers. My psyche poked every fold, exploring, whirling in images rather than words. Pictures of devils, gargoyles, werewolves, lions, tigers, and other animals that Jafar released filled my imagination. They scampered through my mind chasing me like a rabbit.

Then I let myself calm down, I slowed my breathing and thought to myself, "I wonder what that was?"

"You must be thinking who I am. You must trust me and know that I am the truth, your friend and companion. It is you and I who will succeed."

I was jolted as if the voice had responded to my thought. I'd never heard of anything or anyone who could see someone and know their thoughts. There was something I'd heard of called ESP, but thoughts were transferred between people, not someone observing another person's thoughts. I decided to test further to see what would happen.

"He communicates with Allah and knows when I lie," I thought.

"You should understand this also: He probably claims he communicates with some God so has supreme knowledge. That is not true.

"He is a lying thief, lower than the lowest being. A snake stands taller than he."

What was happening? Was it Allah who was responding to me? Was it a guardian angel? Why was it only entering my thoughts now? I wondered.

"Who are you?" I thought.

"He cannot avert death because he has spoken falsehoods and stolen your youth. I know these things because I'm everywhere and omnipresent. I'm around you and within you. I taste your tastes, hear your sounds, smell your smells, feel your pain and pleasure, and see the world through your eyes," the voice continued again, not answering my questions directly, almost as if it didn't hear me.

"Why? How?" I wondered.

"We will give him his reward, his justice, and you and I will be together again, and we will win. We have important things to accomplish later on as you grow into adulthood but to do that, we must remove this obstacle and move you into a better position. It is time."

I didn't understand what that meant, but the voice didn't push for me to accept what it was saying, it was more of a comment than a command. It didn't demand to be accepted; it merely transmitted a message of support. There was no badgering, menacing, threatening, or even persistence; it simply sat in the background silently like a hawk watching, waiting, and observing, ready to respond to opportunity or threat.

"It is written 'As for those who swallow the property of the orphans unjustly, surely they only swallow fire into their bellies, and they shall enter burning fire.' Because the only property of childhood is peace and happiness, these people have disobeyed their maker. You are that orphan and your joy and your peace is your property, and they have stolen it. Go back to sleep now, and I will awaken you when the time is right to administer justice."

The moment the voice spoke, I was blanketed with a calmness I hadn't felt in a long time. I was soothed and comforted as I lay, letting the serenity rock me quietly and peacefully back to a restful, comforting sleep.

THE PYRE

Beyond the secret dark celestial,
Wrapped up in a starry birth;
Wonderment of the murky bestial,
Are they murmurs beyond the earth?

The majestic green Douglas firs were bathed by a warm summer sun. A cool, sparkling brook meandered gracefully along in and out of the trees. Standing on the bank, I began taking in the view when I spotted movement among the trees. Squinting, I looked closer and saw a beautiful woman in a flowing gown walking barefoot toward me. She stopped at the other side of the stream and waited. As I watched, she looked down then gradually slid one foot, then the next, into the ankle-deep water. She slowly looked up and our eyes met, causing my heart to jump. I recognized the face, but couldn't remember where we'd met. Slowly she began making her way toward me, and I could see her whispering something, but the splashing of the water drowned out her words. Listening more carefully, I thought she was saying my name. Or was it? We were the only ones there. She was looking directly at me with her beautiful, radiant eyes, but the name she was saying wasn't Rasheed or Billy, it was someone else. I reached out to take her hand when the voice broke the peaceful scene with a jolt, saying something to me.

"It's time."

Now awake, in a state of full awareness, the shimmering brook's sounds changed to a vacant silence. With the corner streetlight partially illuminating the room I raised my head and began searching for someone or something that would have brought me out of my sound sleep, but just as before, there was nothing. My bedroom door was fully closed, but I didn't trust Jafar, and he could have snuck into my room. I rolled over and scanned under my bed to see if he was hiding there. Nothing. There was nowhere else for someone to hide with no closet and only a chest of drawers for the few clothes I possessed.

It had to have been my guiding force instructing me.

Without any clear instructions, just a hunch and a feeling, I began operating robot-like. I rose from my bed, dressed in my jeans, t-shirt, and

Converse All-Stars. Then I began stuffing clean clothes into the duffle bag I kept in the dresser's bottom drawer. Some strange urge drove me, making me think of the baby robins with their mouths held open. I wondered if my actions were like theirs, knowing what to do but not why they were doing it.

Quietly, I opened my bedroom door and stood listening. Jafar's annoying snoring that had in the past awakened me, tonight gave me the solace he was sound asleep. Slowly, taking one soft step at a time, I made my way toward the home's back door located off the kitchen. It fed onto a screened porch where Malakeh stored household goods, garden tools, and some canned green beans from last year's small backyard harvest. The screen door hinges had never been oiled causing a notorious squeak. So rather than pressing the door opened and potentially alerting the sleeping giant, I returned to the kitchen and removed a butcher knife from its drawer. Then I had a spark of imagination. The next drawer down held his leather straps that Jafar and Malakeh used to tie me down in the beatings. I removed the knife and grabbed the straps, and stuffed them into my back pocket. Seeing the cookie jar sitting on the kitchen counter, I remembered that's where Jafar had his savings. He didn't trust American banks, so he hid his money in the jar and more in the cabinet just above. I took everything I could find and stuffed the cash in my duffle bag before dropping it at the screen door. There, I carefully cut away the screen and let it fall into the yard.

The chilly, dewy night, blanketed the back yard leaving a humid sheen on the grass. I could feel the wetness through my canvas basketball shoes as I made my way to the side of the house. Adjacent to the house, a fifty-five-gallon drum was laid on its side on a raised platform. Elevating the drum allowed the fuel oil to gravity-feed the heater in the home's living room. On cold winter mornings, it was my job to set my alarm and do my chores. I'd go outside and open the valve on the oil drum, then go back inside quickly and open the other valve by the heater allowing the fuel oil to flow into the sump inside the cast iron stove. Once the sump was saturated, I'd take a wooden match and light it to start a fire warming the house for when they arose. I had to make sure I didn't let that sump overflow as I did once when I couldn't find the matches. Fuel oil overflowed onto the floor, and I had to quickly turn it off, get some rags and get it cleaned up before they awoke. A mistake like that would inevitably result in an additional beating.

That experience taught me something I could use tonight.

I made my way back to the porch and dug out some pliers Jafar kept in a toolbox, then picked up Malakeh's mop bucket she kept by the door. I also tucked a pair of Jafar's overalls under my arm and pulled some leather straps from the drawer, and went back inside. Using the pliers, I removed the line that fed the heater's sump and placed it in the bucket. Soon, the fuel oil was overflowing the bucket, and oil began spilling over the linoleum floor. As it slowly began to spread, I used the time to work other magic.

I retrieved Malakeh's favorite weapon, the wooden mop handle. I made my way into the hallway leading to their bedroom door. There I stopped outside and listened. There were no sounds of movement, just Jafar's annoying snoring. Setting the full bucket of fuel oil down, I made a small horseshoe type dam around the base of their door. Next, using the leather straps, I tied the mop handle to the doorknob and across the doorframe of the inward-swinging door. When they tried to open the door, the mop handle would prevent it. Slowly, I poured most of the bucket's contents into the horseshoe dam and watched as it seeped under the door and into the bedroom. Finally, I spilled the rest along the short hallway to the living room and the heater.

Rather than pricy security window bars, cheap-ass Jafar bought wrought iron gates at Fred Meyer that were slightly larger than the window casing's width. He drilled holes in their frame, then secured them to the house using quarter-inch lag bolts. Even though they didn't reach the top of the windows all the way, they prevented someone from easily opening a window and crawling in. Unfortunately, as he would learn, they also would make it difficult for anyone to crawl out.

By now, the heater fuel oil was leaving a shallow pool on the living room floor. Reaching in my pocket to make sure I had several wooden match sticks, I poured the remaining oil from the mop bucket along the floor as I backed my way toward the kitchen and onto the back porch. There I set the bucket down and pulled out a match.

Before striking it, a verse from the Qur'an I'd learned at the Mosque jumped into my head:

"And whoever disobeys Allah and His Apostle and goes beyond His limits, He will cause him to enter fire to abide in it…"

As I held the matchbox in my hand, poised, ready to light it, I felt just one emotion. It wasn't sorrow, or guilt, or joy, or fear. The only feeling I felt was love. I had a responsibility bestowed upon me, and I knew that I could not disobey a command from Allah, if that was the voice I'd heard. Even Jafar had emphasized that one cannot deny Allah, so by doing this, I felt the love of the voice that would take the place of the hatred I felt for Jafar.

With that, I slid the match across the striking surface and watched the small wooden object jump into a ballet of flame. Bending over, I touched it to the trail of fuel oil. I saw it snake its way through the kitchen into the living room, and as it rounded the stove, there was a quiet swooshing followed by a bright flare of light shooting a hint of heat toward me. Turning, I ducked my way through the screen door and walked across the back yard into the street and began slowly sauntering along.

Passing the small metal cover plate in the street, I recalled how I'd learned it was the shutoff valve for the fire hydrants. One of my friends said he'd watched city workers stick a pole down inside after removing the cover. He asked them what they were doing and was told they were replacing the fire hydrant and had to shut off the water first. For some reason, the day before, I was urged to do something to that valve.

As I walked along the deserted street, I could hear the far-off wail of a siren. They were coming, but by the time they found the fire hydrant shutoff valve was filled with dirt, the house would not be saved. A sense of calmness filled me, and I could almost feel an invisible hand patting me on my back.

"Good   job,"   I   thought   to   myself.

THE LOVE

With lips so soft, so sweet and warm.
With eyes that sparkle, so brightly charmed.
Project the passion, of love's sweet form.
Fight off the demons,
That'd bring her harm.

After several cafeteria meetings, reviewing class notes, and coding ideas for FindIt, Mark concluded that Duncan and Sue write excellent, uncluttered script. Still, progress was painfully slow. He had just a short time before the government offer ended.

The more Mark sat with them, the more impressed he was with both their intellects and imaginations. Duncan would fight with Sue when she'd find a coding error, and several times he stomped off mad. He seemed defeated that she was so smart and cool to his advances. Still, he continually tried to impress the obviously bright student by putting her down and showing what he knew.

Several days later, after one of their sessions, Mark headed back to his office to score some tests. His workplace was situated in a dark corner of the building behind the much roomier office of his professor. He thought maybe it was stuck out of the way so nobody would steal the toilet paper it had housed before converting it into a peanut-sized office. Walking down a narrow passageway in a short, windowless hall to an opening on the right led into the small makeshift office.

As he sat glancing over some of the test scores, he heard a slight shuffling in the hallway. He rose out of his chair, knocked some papers to the floor, and saw Sue standing there looking back and forth.

"Hi, Sue," he said, startling her.

"Oh... I didn't know this is where your office was," she said.

A telltale smile of a white lie crossed her face. Slowly she strolled toward him.

"I wanted to talk about some things with you, Mark. Do you have a minute?"

"Sure, I always have time for you. Where's Duncan?" Mark asked.

"That's what I wanted to talk to you about and why I came alone."

"How did you know how to get here?" Mark asked.

"I have my ways," she said, smiling.

"Not very many people even know this is here, so you're a pretty good detective. Come in and sit down," he offered.

Mark looked at the chair he'd offered and saw the pile of papers sitting on it. Quickly he picked them up and lay them on top of another collection of documents next to his iBoard. He pulled the chair away from the wall then patted the seat, motioning her to sit.

"You're a pretty typical iBoard nerd, aren't you? Messy," she laughed.

"You should see my apartment!" Mark told her.

Sue almost blurted out, 'I'd like to,' but kept that thought suppressed profoundly in some warm place in her mind. Instead, she just said, "I'm sure one of these days you'll have us over, and your apartment will be as clean as the code you write."

The two had never spent time together without Duncan and began talking about things other than school. Mark wanted to know more about Sue, the woman. She wanted to know about Mark, his life so far and just what kind of person he was. She asked him about family, likes, dislikes, his job, things of general interest. She talked about her dreams and the extent to which she was prepared to reveal them, her desires. She didn't let on that she was developing a magical feeling for him. Doing that would be embarrassing if he didn't feel the same about her. Instead, beyond the attraction she had for him, something was bothering her, and he might be able to help.

"I guess you wonder why I came exploring for your office," she said.

"I'm not really wondering, I'm just happy you're here," he said.

"I need some help, Mark. I was wondering if you could help me with something kind of personal?"

"Sure. Anything I can do to help you would be an honor. What's up?"

"Well, I was checking my grades and saw one of mine had been changed. When I talked to administration, they just said there wasn't anything they could do about it, and whatever grade is in the system is the grade I'd get. Still, Mark, I know I should have better than a D in Calgenic computations. I got an A on all my tests, so why I have D on my record is just wrong, so I thought maybe you could help," she said.

Mark opened his iBoard. With the board sensing his touch and recognizing his face, it immediately came to life. Sensing the shift of his eyes, it navigated to the section containing classes, instructors, then students. He looked at the grade assigned to Sue then checked deeper to see the date it was entered.

"This grade was entered yesterday," he told her.

"Yes, I know, and there weren't any tests for the past two weeks. The professor was called away to Ricron and has no access to the school system, so it surely wasn't him," she said.

"I know Professor Wilson quite well, so let's give him a call."

Mark ran his hand over his iBoard, brought up the telephone feature, and pointed his eyes at Professor Wilson's personal line. Soon his image appeared above the iBoard as a hologram. Mark asked about the grade, how it would get in there, and what his records showed for Sue.

"She's a straight-A student, Mark. I have no idea why the system is showing D. I sure didn't do that. In fact, I haven't put any grades in there for quite a while. Must be some sort of computer glitch or someone hacked in. I'll change it back to an A when I do grades again."

Mark thanked him and turned off the image transfer option of the iBoard then ran a small program he'd developed that showed all grades changed in the system over the past three days. The list showed only one, Sue's.

"Someone changed your grade Sue, so it appears someone cracked the system and did it. Do you have any computer savvy-enemies out there?"

She ran through the list of people she knew at work who had the capability of doing it but couldn't think of anyone who would have the motivation. She had no enemies there, and nobody she considered malicious. Her ex-boyfriend would want to do it, but he had no computation skills and didn't associate with any nerd students. In fact, he hated most of them.

"Is there a way to trace who did it?" she asked Mark.

"That depends on how good they were at covering their tracks. There's a possibility I could find out, but it would take quite a bit of work. We could go through all of that to find out it was just some random kid out there in gridland, seeing if they could crack into the system. It could just be your name came up as a top student, and they wanted to bring you down a notch. If they did it from one of those iBoard cafés, we'd never know who did it without a warrant or something. What about Duncan? I understand he has asked you to go out with him," Mark said.

"Yes, and that's another reason I wanted to see you. I'm worried that it was him and it really bothers me. He's a nice guy and a friend, but I don't want to go out with him and give him the impression we're more than just friends. That might complicate things on this little business arrangement we have. I thought he was just being nice when he asked me out, but I'm beginning to think differently," Sue told him.

She stood, collected her things, and began to turn when Mark saw her wipe a tear from the corner of her eye. He sensed the feeling of despair she hid inside.

"What's going on, Sue?"

Mark put a hand on her shoulder. Sue stopped, turned, and faced him. She looked up into his eyes with tears now flowing down both cheeks. Finally, Mark put his hands around her waist and brought her in close, feeling her head nestled against his chest.

"We don't know it was Duncan, Sue. It could have been a random thing. Keep positive and we'll watch out for any grade changes. I'm sure Duncan isn't a dangerous person."

Feeling his strong arms holding her and the warmth of his body so close soothed her nerves, but the tears flowed still. This time it was more from happiness than sorrow. As she looked up into Mark's eyes, she slowly reverted to another feeling that was beginning to sink in. If it was Duncan, she was pissed. She stepped back, and Mark reluctantly released the arms that wanted to hang on. He reached out and took her hand and pulled her back to him.

Holding her tight again, he whispered in her ear, "Don't worry, Sue. I'm not going to let anything or anyone harm you."

Standing on her tiptoes, she kissed his cheek, saying, "Thank you. You make me feel so much better."

He released his hold then, with one hand beneath her chin, tipped her face up to his lips and softly kissed her. He felt her response and sensed her passions beginning to grow. Feeling aroused, he released his hold, but she grabbed him and pulled up closer, threw her arms around his neck and passionately kissed him. Feeling her warm, loving fervor, Mark held back the urge to respond. Instead, he took her shoulders and held her back, looking into the beauty of her face. His senses told him this wasn't the time or place, so he took a deep breath and smiled down at her.

"I'm not like this with a student, Sue," Mark said.

"I'll try to restrain myself, Mark," Sue smiled.

"It was me, not you. I'm the one that needs to be restrained, but I liked it," he said with a smile.

"When do we meet again?" Sue said.

"Do you mean like this? Come by any time," Mark said.

"No," she laughed. "I mean for our tutoring and programming."

"Tomorrow afternoon," he said.

"Oh. I was hoping it would be this evening," Sue said, smiling up at him.

"For some extra study time?" Mark asked.

"I wish I could, really. But I have to work tonight...maybe another time?" Sue said, hopefully.

"We'll have to think carefully about becoming too friendly, okay?" Mark asked.

"I understand. I'll try to keep my cool, Mark" Sue said

She slowly turned and strolled up the short hallway. At the end, she glanced back and smiled. She was trying to figure out a way to go back without seeming forward. Coming up with nothing, she slowly turned and left.

Mark watched her walk away and couldn't help noticing the sway of her hips and the graceful dance of her stride. The smell of her fresh hair still hung in the air, and her smile was photographed permanently in his memory. If he wanted to get closer to Sue, he'd have to figure out a way to grab that gold ring and buy his freedom.

The slow progress of the programming flashed into his mind. Could he finish in time? That moment with her inspired him even more on making the quick cash that he needed to get his release. If he did, he could live a life of pleasure, something he hoped could include Sue.

THE GETAWAY

You sent them off to God's sweet rest
The best you could for your relief.
No mourning now you did your best,
No pearly tears brought on by grief.
Be happy you regained your own.

You'll dwell in peace;
You're not alone.

It was 4:00 AM as I casually strolled several blocks to the Safeway store. I heard the sound of sirens in the far distance and thought about the long pole with a U shaped end, called a curb key, that I could use to shut off the water to the fire hydrant. I bought mine at the hardware store down the street and put it in the trash when I finished. I couldn't be sure how I figured it out, but I knew that if I filled the hole with dirt, nobody could quickly turn the water back on.

After deciding to rest until daylight, I climbed in the dumpster at the back of the store and looked back to see a glow in the sky as the sirens got closer. Flashing lights lit the buildings, and fire engines came flying past full of firefighters, probably thinking they were going to save some lives.

Ha. They wouldn't.

Closing the lid, I spread out on the flattened cardboard boxes, closed my eyes, and contemplated a future filled with excitement and safety.

The sound of traffic rumbling along Fessenden Street seemed to reverberate off the steel sides like a giant alarm clock. I rolled over and threw some of the cardboard boxes off as I stirred. In my half slumber, I thought back to the funeral pyre and smiled, feeling sure it had done its work. I made my way out of the dumpster and to the nearby sidewalk, where I instinctively made a left turn and began walking north. As I strolled happily along, the voice came to me with a congratulatory, surprising announcement:

"*Excellent work. That's two points for us plus a bonus for the type of kill.*"
"Huh?"

As usual, the voice didn't respond, and I began realizing that the voice came on its own schedule, not at my beckoning. It was like having an absent pen pal who sent you letters with no return address or way to contact them. I'd keep trying, but for now, I was content with this strange one-way relationship. Something startled me to an abrupt stop. Something struck me as the truth. That voice that I sometimes heard wasn't at all absent. It was with me and had guided me without any seemingly verbal instructions. My life seemed now channeled by someone or something along some obscure roadmap I didn't understand. It wanted me to achieve some unknown goal and though I didn't see that map, I trusted it and things would be all right.

Walking again, I headed north the few blocks to Columbia Boulevard, the route out of north Portland's industrial area where loaded trucks connected to Interstate 5. At this time of day, it was busy with departing trucks heading toward places far away from Portland. The cash I'd taken from my foster father's savings was enough to buy a bus ticket. But I remembered a teacher discuss how stupid criminals were to try to escape by buying a bus, train, or plane tickets. Authorities would be checking there as one of the first places they looked for a suspect, so none of those options would be a smart move for getting out of town. I'd try to hitch a ride anywhere with a trucker.

I'd never tried hitching a ride on a truck, or even a car for that matter. I'd seen older guys walking along Lombard Street, sticking out their thumb and get picked up by other students who were fortunate enough to have a car. I guessed the same thing would work with a truck, so I stuck up my thumb and waited. It didn't take long before the hissing air breaks brought a massive truck to a stop.

"That was easy," I thought as I ran ahead toward the slowing semi. Before reaching the running board, I glanced at the license plate of the tractor and noted it was from California. I jumped up, opening the cab door, and saw the enormous cockpit filled with dials, levers, and a huge truck driver behind the massive steering wheel.

"Where you going?" the unshaven trucker asked.

I didn't know how to answer the question. If I would say "Anywhere," it would sound suspicious. If I said "Seattle," and the trucker was heading south, I would miss an opportunity for a ride. It finally dawned on me the license plates said California, so I took a guess.

"San Francisco," I said, hoping it was the right choice.

"I can get you to Sacramento, but I'll have to stop just short of there for a bit because regulations only let me drive so many hours. Will that be okay?" the driver asked.

"Yes. That would be great. Thank you," I said, trying not to sound excited as I pulled myself and my cash-laden duffle bag aboard.

"You can throw your stuff in the back," he said, thumbing backward to an open compartment behind the cab.

"What's in San Francisco?" the driver asked as he let out the clutch and got the rig moving.

"I'm off to visit my father. He's been in the hospital and doesn't have a job to pay medical bills, so I'm going to see if I can get a job and give him some help," I lied.

"What kind of work are you looking for?" the trucker asked as he checked his mirrors and pulled back out onto the roadway.

"I'm not sure, but I'll do anything," I said.

"Oh?" the driver said, then glanced over at me, smiling.

He began shifting gears and gaining speed as he headed toward the exit to I-5 and the trip to the south.

"I might be able to help you earn some money. A long haul trucker always needs special services," he added with a glance and a wink.

I was too young then to understand what that comment meant and had no idea what "special services" he might be referring to. At the time, I wondered if he needed me to wash the windshield, check tire pressure, or fill the tanks with diesel fuel. I'd do it happily. My focus was on getting out of town, so I didn't care.

I was fascinated by the power and size of the rig. I'd never ridden in something that looked down on even high riser 4 x 4 pickups. I watched the trucker methodically run through the gears as he regularly checked his mirrors to see what was around him. When he'd finished the busy process of getting the truck rolling again, he looked over to me and said, "My name's Tennessee. What shall I call you?"

"I'm Rasheed," I instinctively replied.

Before the trucker could respond, I wanted to reach out and grab those words and bring them back. I realized I shouldn't have given my real name and instead provided a more common name like George or even Billy, my first name. Now I hoped the trucker was terrible with names, and he wouldn't even remember what I said.

"Glad to meet you, Rasheed," Tennessee said, reaching across for a handshake between shifting gears.

My shoulders sagged when I realized he remembered.

"It's a lot easier driving once we get away from the city. The traffic around here is awful, and those damn four-wheelers always to want to cut you off," he said.

Pointing to a car that jumped in the space he was leaving between his truck and the vehicle in front, he reached up and pulled a cord that sounded a loud horn. It scared me so badly I almost jumped out of my seat.

"That asshole doesn't realize I've got sixty thousand pounds that would rather keep rolling than come to a quick stop. You see, Rasheed, if the cars ahead came to a sudden stop, I'd roll right over that son of a bitch, kill everyone in the car, and they'd probably blame me," he mused.

Rasheed began to appreciate that driving a big rig like this was far more complicated than driving a car.

"How long have you been a truck driver?" I asked.

"Not long. I was trained as a diesel mechanic but didn't like staying in one place so I switched to driving these rigs," Tennessee said.

"Did you have to go to school to learn to be a mechanic?"

"Yeah," Tennessee said.

"What school did you go to?" I wanted to know, wondering if that might be a skill I could learn.

"Folsom," Tennessee said.

"Folsom? I've heard of that somewhere. Where is it?" I asked.

"It's in California right outside of Sacramento," Tennessee said.

"Wait. Isn't that where Johnny Cash sang about a prison?" I asked.

"Yeah, right. That's where I learned the trade," Tennessee said then after a pause added, "But I didn't shoot a man in Reno just to watch him die," he said, laughing.

"You mean you were in prison?"

"I was, yes."

"If you didn't shoot a man in Reno, what did you do to get put in prison?"

"I pulled a few stick-ups, and someone got hurt. They only got me for doing two even though I'd done many more than that."

"Was it worth it?" I asked.

"Oh, yeah. I bought my mom a new car and had enough stashed away to get myself one when I got out. Plus, I got that mechanic training that leads me to this," Tennessee said.

"What's it like to be in prison?" I asked.

"Hell, my friend, you have to be on guard all the time. You, as small as you are, wouldn't last very long before someone used you as their girlfriend," Tennessee told me.

I thought it wasn't too appealing, but I was sure I could take care of myself. After all, I had that guidance from the voice that was doing well so far.

"I will try hard not to break the law," I told Tennessee.

The miles slipped by as slowly and quietly as the conversation. Then, over the road rumbling white noise, I received a warning.

"There's danger somewhere."

Startled, because I seldom received such clear messages, I checked the sizeable rearview mirror to see what was behind us. I saw nothing out of the ordinary. There was no car directly behind us and the closest looked at least a mile behind.

Over the next few miles, I would glance at the mirror every so often to see if anything was following. After about a half-hour, there still were no cars that seemed to hang behind us. Instead, cars that approached just pulled out and passed then disappeared into the distance.

Tennessee reached over and turned on the truck's radio, saying, "Mind if we listen to a little music?"

I didn't care if the cab was filled with music. In fact, I liked music. It was something I never heard at home.

"Happy, joyful things only come from Allah," Jafar would say.

After hearing a little George Strait and a tune from Willie Nelson, the announcer came on.

"It's the top of the hour and time for some headline news. Take it away, Pat," the disc jockey said.

A newscaster with a stern sounding voice reported President Nixon and Brezhnev met in Moscow to discuss arms limitation agreements. Evil Knievel would attempt a jump over the Snake River Canyon. After a few more world and national stories, the newscaster turned to local stories.

"In Portland, a housefire trapped two people in their home by iron bars used to prevent burglaries. The fire is suspicious and police have issued an all-points bulletin for the teenage son, Rasheed Raad, a suspect in the incident…"

Pat, the announcer, said nothing about the condition of the two inside, just that they were trapped by those home-made bars. I wondered if they died or were still alive.

Tennessee slowly moved his hand up to the radio and turned it off.

He looked over at me and asked, "What was your name again?"

I hesitated, trying to think of something quickly. Finally, I replied, "Ray… Ray Mead," hoping to sound convincing.

There was a period of silence before Tennessee spoke up again.

"Yeah, of course. Ray Mead, not Rasheed. I must have misheard what you said when we introduced ourselves.

"Well, anyway Ray, let me explain how truckers work. The law only allows me to drive seventy hours a week before we have to take a break. That's why I have that little sleeping compartment behind us. I can make it just short of Sacramento, and then I'm going to have to stop for a while. You might be able to catch a ride from the rest area to San Francisco, and I'll see what I can do to help you out. Probably be best if you do it first thing in the morning when the other truckers are getting started."

I glanced back over my shoulder and saw the small cavern where I'd thrown my bag with a mattress and sleeping bag. There seemed ample room for two or three people to sleep, but little room for anything else.

"Go ahead and take a look back there if you want, Rasheed. I mean, Ray, but don't ruin any of the porn magazines I have back there," he said with a wink and smile.

I looked over my shoulder into the small compartment, then unfastened my seatbelt and climbed in. There was a mattress that seemed serviceable, but not necessarily bedlike. Shelves with guardrails were built along the sides to keep things from sliding off. On one side, the shelves contained a coffee mug, shaving cream, aspirin, and three cans of sparkling water. On the other side, there was a rack with hooks he presumed was for a rifle but was empty. Instead, a hunting knife hung from one hook within arm's reach of the pillow that lay toward the cab's driver's side.

Also included were two magazine racks, one with Hot Rod Magazine that featured a 1972 Chevy El Camino, and the other a magazine called *Stud* with a photo of two shirtless men, one sitting on the other's lap.

I pulled it out of the rack, thumbed through it, and quickly understood the content. Seeing the pictures inside, I closed it and carefully slid it back into place. I didn't want to leave any indication I'd looked into it, even though the pages seemed somewhat dog-eared already.

Climbing back into the passenger's seat, I slipped into my seatbelt, saying nothing.

"See anything you like back there?" the trucker asked.

"Nice hunting knife and that was a cool El Camino on the cover of that Hot Rod Magazine," I said, not mentioning "Stud."

I then turned to my right, away from the trucker, and watched the green Oregon fields scamper past.

"Yeah, I subscribe to Hot Rod so I carry several issues on the road with me. That other one I pick up at truck stops along the way. You like it? That one with the two guys on the cover, Rasheed?"

"I didn't look at it. They didn't seem to be doing anything but sitting there," I answered, trying to move off the subject.

Tennessee chuckled, saying, "Well, if you checked out the inside, they were doing a lot of fun things."

I began to realize the danger I was in. Earlier, Tennessee mentioned he'd pay me for special services, the magazine, and the realization that Tennessee knew my name, sent a shock of fear along my spine.

Though Tennessee tried to feign he misheard the name Rasheed when we introduced ourselves, he wasn't convincing. He obviously was suspicious of the news broadcast and my name being a part of it. This Tennessee guy had me in a moving trap making escape almost impossible. If the truck stopped, I could jump out and run, but if I did that, where would I run to? Running could simply allow Tennessee to claim he picked up someone in Portland matching Rasheed's description. Running from the truck wasn't an option. I'd have to wait for a different opportunity.

Maybe at the rest area he mentioned might be that opportunity. Perhaps I could sneak out of the truck as he slept and get a ride from another truck parked nearby.

In a few miles, we pulled into a service station designed for trucks. Tennessee pulled in beside a pump, jumped out, and an attendant began filling the tank. Tennessee stuck his head back in the cab and announced quietly, "Stay put. We don't want to bring attention to us now, do we?"

He went inside the store there and bought us lunch. He started the truck and pulled forward into a large parking area. Leaving the truck idling, he handed me a burger and we set our drinks on a convenient flat platform by the truck's dashboard. The idling diesel jiggled my Coke into a fizz as we chomped down on our late afternoon hamburger and fries.

"Rasheed... ah... Ray, let me tell you about the time I was caught in a snowstorm coming over..."

His emphasis on Ray was another signal he knew. Then he probed a little more, saying, "Ray, you sure are a handsome kid. I bet you have a lot of girls after you. Do you like girls, Ray?"

I wished he'd stop calling me by name, any name.

Lunch was in a bag and drinks were in a cup holder Tennessee had by the driver. He shifted the big truck as we headed to the on-ramp and back southbound on Interstate 5. As he worked the struggling truck into its top gear, his CB radio came alive, announcing the Oregon State Police radar trap's location.

"There's a bear in the grass at milepost 199," one of the announcements came. Almost immediately came another transmission saying, "How's the food at Tracy's in Cottage Grove?" To that question came several replies with a variety of answers.

For the next few miles, Tennessee drove and ate with the skill of a professional truck-driving hamburger eater. With one hand, he munched on the burger and with the other shifted gears while steering with his knees.

We traveled further south for several hours without much conversation. I felt he may know I was the person they were looking for. My mind was spinning considering my options. Perhaps he was too concerned with eating, shifting, and steering and hadn't paid attention to the CB, but I couldn't be sure. He'd spent too much energy going between Rasheed and Ray to make me think otherwise.

Several other truckers asked about conditions up and down the highway when another announcement came across: "Breaker, breaker, this is Speedball I-5. Just thought I'd let you guys know papa bear came on back in Eugene to report that they are looking for some guy who they suspect burned down a house that had people inside back in Portland. They think it was a young guy who may be using an alias, but his name is Rasheed Raad. They're requesting we pass it along. I'm at milepost 210, so if you're south of here, pass the message along. Speedball I-5 out."

As the CB radio went silent, Tennessee slowly turned his head looking at me with a glare. I said nothing, but my heart sank. He heard the announcement and now knew who I was.

We traveled in silence for several hours through Roseburg, Oregon up over and through the Siskiyou Mountains, through Redding and Red Bluff, California then down the California Central Valley. It was near sunset when I sensed the truck slowing as we approached a roadside rest area I assumed was the one Tennessee mentioned earlier. As he slowed the truck, I noticed one side of the area was for autos and the other for trucks. The parking space closest to the restrooms contained four large rigs like the one they were in with several open spots next to them. Tennessee drove past those truck parking spots and into a more secluded dirt pullout just off the entrance ramp to the freeway. That placed them in a position that made the noisy freeway mask any sounds coming from the truck. It also had no place for any truck to park on either side. Tennessee had purposely isolated us.

As the big truck stopped with a loud hiss of air breaks, Tennessee flipped a switch, and with a cough and a whir, the big diesel engine died.

"As I told you in Portland, I'm over my log time, so I'm going to have to stop for a while. Tell you what, Rasheed or Ray, whatever you claim your name to be, I'm going to help you out. You need a little work, and you sure don't want me to grab that CB and call the Highway Patrol now, do you?"

My head spun considering his threat: I'd already concluded that running would be futile since there was no place to go. All those other trucks had CBs and probably heard the alert. The rest stop was in the middle of farmland, with no building or houses in sight. If I ran, Tennessee would just call the cops, and they'd be after me before I could get anywhere. Obviously, Tennessee was much bigger and stronger than me. I was at his mercy, if he had any, something I doubted.

"We'll take a little rest here until I can proceed. Later we'll head on down to Sacramento where I'll let you off. But for now, let's just jump in the back and put our heads down and rest awhile," he said.

I wondered why he was he being so nice? Maybe I had his comments about a job wrong. Maybe he'd put me to work at dirt poor wages in return for not calling the police. I hoped that was it, but it was the only hope I had, and I figured my only option was to cooperate and see where this led.

"Go ahead. You get back there first, and I'll follow," Tennessee indicated, pointing toward the sleeper compartment.

"I can just rest in the seat here," I said.

"Now that wouldn't be a good idea, would it? What if the highway patrol came by and saw a kid sitting here in the cab? What if he thought that suspicious and came asking for some identification? That wouldn't be very good now, would it?"

Tennessee was right, but I still didn't know why I shouldn't comply with Tennessee's wishes. Where was that voice that helped me in the past? Nothing came to me, so I'd just have to deal with things as they came.

I surrendered to Tennessee's request by turning and crawling into the back. As I did, I felt Tennessee's hand on my right butt cheek, giving me a too friendly boost into his chamber, his chamber of horrors?

The advances came slowly at first. We lay on our backs in the semi-darkness with just an overhead glow from the compartment light. Tennessee pulled the copy of "Stud" from the rack and paged through it, pausing at some of the pictures before showing them to me.

"Go ahead and check it out, Rasheed. It ain't going to kill you, but someone might if you have to go into prison," Tennessee said, reaching over with his hand touching me.

When I flinched, Tennessee threw a leg over my body, pinning me in place. When I struggled, he just laughed.

"Don't fight me, Rasheed. It will do you no good."

Then the bigger man took both arms over my head and held them in place with one hand as he reached down and began fumbling at my belt with the other.

"You know what the police will do when they get their hands on you, don't you?" Tennessee said softly.

"You'll be in big trouble in prison when someone wants you for their girlfriend, but the police will be worse. They don't just gently handcuff murderers and take them off to jail. No, that's not the way that works. They first give them some punishment in the back of their police car and claim you were resisting arrest. They'll beat you, but they'll also have their way with you because you're so young and cute. Who'd believe a murderer if he claimed he was harmed?

"Now, if you cooperate with me, I'll show you how it works and teach you how to respond, so you're not harmed. You'll need to know how to relax and just accept it, and everything will be fine," Tennessee said with an insincere smile.

Struggle as I might, I couldn't get away from his hold. I felt Tennessee's hands on my zipper, and my pants being dragged down. Twisting, I attempted to fight him off, but Tennessee just laughed.

"That won't do you any good. Just relax. Nobody can hear anything outside this cab with all that freeway noise, so just remain quiet. If you relax, I won't hurt you. If you resist, I'll just tie you up, and it's going to hurt like all hell. Besides, I'm going to give you a hundred dollars for a little job I need to be done, and when we're finished in the morning, I'll take you to Sacramento and drop you at the bus station. There'll be no police involvement, no announcement that you're the fugitive from Portland. How's that sound?" Tennessee asked.

I wished my voice would help, but nothing was there. It was stark clear to me I was trapped.

"What do you want?" I finally asked.

Tennessee looked down at me, smiling.

"I'll have to show you. It's hard to explain. Just don't move a muscle. Relax, and I'll take care of everything."

"Okay," was all I could think to say.

The slap across my head stung, but the sting was nothing as bad as I'd felt before. What did the man have in mind? Would he whip me with his belt? Was that what he wanted to do? Those thoughts crept into my mind, but then I thought about the pictures in the magazine and now understood.

"Oh… now I understand the job you have for me," I told him, turning my head to him, beaming a fake smile.

"I did look at the pictures in that magazine, so I know my job. Let me sit up and take off my shirt, and we can relax a little together," I said.

Tennessee gave me a puzzled look.

"You looked at the Stud magazine yourself?"

"Yeah. I've seen it before and used to look at it all the time with some friends at school," I lied.

"Why don't you just lay down on your back, and I'll give your chest a little massage," I said.

Tennessee's eyes beamed with the excitement of what I'm sure he thought was a young guy being so sexually assertive with him. He complied and quickly rolled to his back as I swung a leg over him.

I began massaging his chest then whispered something soft to him.

"Close your eyes now, and just relax. I'll take care of everything."

As I ran my left hand over Tennessee's chest, I watched his eyes close in a relaxed amorous state. Casually I reached over and pulled the hunting knife from its sheath and held it behind my back. Then, with a quick sudden motion, I grabbed Tennessee's hair pinning his head to the mattress.

"You like it rough, Tennessee?" I asked.

Shocked, Tennessee stammered as if wondering what was happening then said, "Oh, baby. You bet."

"Good. You'll never have another guy who will give it to you as rough as I will," I said.

With a quick, sudden movement, I slid the razor-sharp knife across his throat. As a final "rough" gesture, I plunged it straight down into Tennessee's heaving chest.

Tennessee's eyes bulged in surprise, but as he tried to yell, his body simply exhaled a rush of air as the blade plunged between ribs and into his heart.

THE DISPOSAL

Listen to those voices;
Listen to their sighs.
Listen now they're with you;
Watching through your eyes.

Moving off the lifeless body beneath me, I grabbed some of the baby wipes Tennessee kept in the back and cleaned my blood soaked knees and the little splattered blood on my arms and face. Fortunately, the knife through the heart stopped its beating and kept the blood flow from Tennessee's opened neck to a minimum. I grabbed my clothes and bag, threw them from the truck's sleeper compartment into the truck's cab, and climbed forward.

"How'd I think of doing that?" I wondered to myself. Then added another thought, "Thank you, my guardian angel."

I slipped into my pants and pulled on my shirt before considering my next steps. My first thought was to drive the truck away. I'd watched Tennessee drive, and I'd taken driver education in school, so maybe I could drive this.

Sliding behind the wheel and adjusting the seat so I could reach the pedals, I glanced down. Instead of a familiar two-pedal layout I was used to in driver's education, there were three. In driver's education, cars shifted themselves, and this thing had to be shifted multiple times by the driver. That extra pedal had something to do with the shifting. If I could just get the truck moving, I'd figure out what the pedal was for.

Recalling Tennessee shut the truck off and restart it when they'd stopped for food in Roseburg, I knew how that worked. I flicked the switch and pressed the starter button just as he had. The truck jumped forward as something in the engine growled. I sensed the engine had to turn by itself, so I moved the transmission lever into what I thought was the neutral position and tried again. This time the truck began idling nicely.

Smiling to myself, I grabbed the shift selector and pressed it forward as Tennessee had done when he got the rig moving.

GRRRIIIINNNNNDDDDDD!

118

The sound caused me to nearly jump out of my seat. The harsh mechanical grinding sounded like the truck was ready to explode or send pieces of machinery all the way back to Portland. I tried again, but this time I moved the gearshift to a different position. Again, there was only grinding and a vibration that shook my hand off the lever. I needed instructions, but Tennessee, whose body lay motionless with the knife standing as erect as another appendage of his body had a few moments ago, was in no condition to drive or answer any questions. I reached into the glove box, thinking I might find a manual that explained how the rig worked, but the only thing there was a pair of gloves, some maps, a book with penciled in times, and cash register receipts.

Unable to get the truck moving, I reached into the back and carefully pulled the trucker's pants toward me and searched the pockets. Finding his wallet, I opened it and liberated the crisp bills. The money wouldn't do me much good for now, but it added to my already abundant stash. I stuffed the cash into my jeans pocket just as the rising sun poked its way through the eucalyptus trees.

I left the truck idling and, opening the passenger door, stepped down, pulling my bag with me into a cool, refreshing breeze. Looking around, I spotted some buildings in the middle of the parking area and headed toward them. As I got closer, I could see it was the restroom area I'd observed as we drove through the stop. My first move was toward the bathroom where I used the stainless steel urinal, washed up and dried my hands under a stream of hot air. Looking at a piece of polished stainless steel that served as a mirror, I checked for any blood on my face. Seeing nothing, I began feeling more comfortable. I left the restroom and walked over to a display with local information and a map that advertised: "You are here."

It appeared we weren't too far from Sacramento, but not close enough to walk and much too far from San Francisco. But I was thankful to be a long way from Portland.

*****

The ride down I-5 from the north was hectic with kids scampering around the bus with little discipline from the two chaperones. Those two seemed to be more interested in each other than with the chaos behind them. They'd left the area around Redding before dawn, and the kids, too excited to sleep, ran around as if they'd all had too much coffee.

It was just past dawn when the yellow school bus pulled off the freeway and parked in the only open spot on the rest area's truck side. It hissed to a stop and kids ran to the front to get off. The driver opened the door, letting the crowd escape their confined quarters.

As the last one stepped down, Mrs. Dixon said to her friend, "Were we supposed to take roll or something?"

119

"They'll know if a friend is missing when they come back aboard," her unconcerned friend said.

I was wondering how I'd make those last few miles to San Francisco when I saw that bus arrive. Walking along the freeway was out of the question, and I didn't know if there were side roads. I was sitting on a cement table when that school bus pulled into the truck side of the rest area. Watching closely as the bus emptied, I spotted kids heading in different directions. Some headed to the restrooms and some came over to the picnic area and formed into groups of six to ten, taking up most of the tables. One, a slender blond male, perhaps a couple years younger than me, stood alone watching the others laugh and talk. Finally, he walked away from the area and stood alone under one of the many eucalyptus trees close to my table.

"Hi. They don't like you either, huh?" the kid said to me.

I wondered what to say. Should I tell him I wasn't with the group or play along?

Finally, I said, "Naw, but that's okay."

"My mom said this would be fun, but I was the only one from my church who could come on the trip. All the others are from the same churches, so I don't have any friends," the towheaded kid said.

"I didn't see where they picked you up. Are you the only one from your church?" he asked.

"Yeah. I don't know anyone here either," I said, going along with the story.

"My name's Ray," I said, sticking out my hand.

"I'm Joey. Nice to meet you," he said, then asked, "Have you ever been to San Francisco? I'm really looking forward to the trip out to Alcatraz. Are you?"

"For sure. That will be a neat place to see," I said.

"The heck with the others. You and I can be friends if you want. Want to sit in the back of the bus with me?" Joey asked.

"That would be great. I've been sitting alone, so I'd like to join you," I offered.

We walked together toward the bus talking and as we approached, I felt a sense of apprehensiveness. I wondered if they'd call the police if they found a stranger on the bus. I stopped and kept talking with the guy and learned he was a sophomore in high school, and all the other kids were juniors and seniors.

"I wonder if they counted who got off the bus when we got here," I asked Joey.

"I doubt it. The two ladies don't pay much attention to us at all. They didn't do a roll call like other church trips I've been on," he said

120

I decided to take the chance and board the bus with Joey.

After everyone boarded, the driver closed its door, and one of the ladies stood and began a count. Seeing her walk down the aisle pointing fingers at each kid, I knew I was doomed. She'd discover there was an extra person aboard and would need to take roll, even though Joey thought they wouldn't. When all the names were checked off except mine, I'd be caught.

Looking around the bus for a way to either hide or escape, I noted an escape door beside the next row back. I thought I could sneak out that way if she turned and walked back forward. I got up from my seat beside Joey and moved toward it.

"Where you going, Ray?" he asked.

"There's nobody in the back row. Let's go there it'll be more fun," I said.

At my gesturing, Joey took the seat by the window, and I sat by the back escape door. As I laid my hand on the handle to open the door, a big rig pulled in behind us, waiting for the bus to leave. When the woman got to the back of the bus and finished her count, she hurried back to the driver and the other chaperone.

"I didn't get a correct count. I'll need to do it again."

"We've got an impatient trucker behind us," the driver said. "How many are missing? Do you need to do a roll call?"

"Nobody is missing; I've got one too many."

Another big rig pulled in behind the one behind the school bus. The impatient driver behind our bus pulled on the cord and blew his air horn.

"Well, we're not short, so it's not a big deal. I'm going to pull out and let this guy in before he starts pounding on our windows. Go ahead and recount as we move," the driver suggested.

After giving it some consideration, he added, "If we were short, we'd wait, but being over one isn't a big deal. We can figure it out later."

The driver started the engine and the bus pulled out of its parking place and waved back at the rig with a signaled, "Sorry, buddy," then crawled toward the interstate.

As we moved out, I saw Tennessee's rig still idling beside the feeder road to the freeway. Eventually, someone would examine that truck, but by then, both Tennessee and I would be long gone; Tennessee much further than   me.

THE OFFER

Others hear them;
No fretting alone.
They hear their voices;
With hearts of stone.

Gray clouds scampered through San Francisco's Golden Gate Bridge towers as the bus rolled up to Fisherman's Wharf. As I stepped off, I felt a chilling breeze off the Pacific Ocean that seemed to blow through me. Wrapping my arms around myself in the cool, I thought of the slogan I'd heard saying, 'I spent the longest winter of my life one summer in San Francisco.' Shivering, the cold air jogged my memory of something important; I left something behind.

"My jacket? Where's my jacket?" I thought.

I remembered taking it off in the back of Tennessee's truck when I was examining the Hot Rod and Stud magazines. I tried to recall if there was any identification in the jacket. I couldn't remember, but it was too late to worry about now. What was done was done. It dawned on me, even if it was there, and even if my name was in it, all it would tell them is that I'd traveled that way. They still wouldn't know my destination. I could have gone to Sacramento or Los Angeles or any of the smaller cities along the way. Or even over the mountains to places east and could still be in another truck headed to Timbuktu. How could they tell?

I had more immediate needs to handle.

Kids were scampering around donning jackets or sweaters to the barks of sea lions lounging on the piers below. They jabbered, shoved, and laughingly shouted out questions to the chaperones about where to line up for the Alcatraz tour. I had my bag with cash, some clothes, and the cash from Tennessee's wallet, so I had a sense of security. I'd need to get away from the group without being obvious, so I told my new friend I was going to meet up with a cousin and join the group later.

"Don't miss the boat to Alcatraz," Joey warned.

"Don't tell anyone, but I'm not going out there. I was there once before, and I know you'll enjoy it, so don't worry about me. I'll catch up with you later, okay?"

"Okay, but I hope you're here when we check into the hotel."

"If I'm not, I'll meet you later tomorrow. My cousin might have me stay at his place."

"Okay. See you soon, Ray," Joey said, following the group toward the boarding platform.

I walked away and waved then held a finger up to my lips in a "shush" fashion.

Not knowing where I was going, I headed across the street, caring only to get away. I'd seen some travel photos, so I knew San Francisco was geography small and walkable. Looking around the waterfront, I could tell that both left and right directions paralleled the bay, so I decided the best avenue into the more populated city area was up the hill away from the pier. More people, more buildings, and more places where I could melt into the surroundings that offered security.

After several blocks up Kearny Street, I spotted a park with an overpass leading to a Hilton Hotel. The park was filled with people doing what appeared to be Tai Chi. I stopped at the corner and watched before turning up the side street. Looking for a place to blend in, I stopped and stood behind a group of Asian men watching four others playing a game with what looked like dominos. Mixing in there would be a little like the Incredible Hulk trying to blend in at a Little People's convention. No, I'd have to find somewhere else to disappear.

Across the street was something called the Buddha's Universal Church. I might hide in there for a while, so I dodged the slow-moving traffic and crossed the street. Approaching the church, I noticed the barred entrance and another obvious tourist wearing a Golden Gate Bridge decorated sweatshirt.

"This isn't nearly as interesting as the other one," the stranger said.

"What other one?" I asked.

"Guess you're new in town too, huh? You might want to walk up a block and turn right then go see the temple. It's up on the third floor. It's one of the main attractions in Chinatown," he said.

"Thanks. I'll go check it out," I said.

I followed the directions and made a turn up a street as narrow as a Portland alley. When I got to the destination the tourist had described, I walked into a nondescript doorway. Arms folded to ward of some of the cold, I ascended three narrow flights and stepped into the first and oldest Buddhist temple in the United States. Noticing some of the writings, I learned it was the Tien Hau Temple. The place contained an intricately carved gilded wooden shrine and ornate Buddha statues where some of the local Buddhists were burning a pungent incense. A man standing beside me whispered, "They are leaving offerings to the goddess Tien Hau in return for the promise of happiness and long life."

Startled, I turned and looked at the man. "Huh?" was all I could say.

"I can tell by the look in your eyes that you are new here. Am I correct?"

"Yes. I just arrived here in San Francisco," I told the man dressed in a plain brown tunic, brown pants and wearing leather sandals.

"Without a jacket or sweater?" the man asked.

"I left it on the bus," I told him.

"Maybe we can find you something warm to wear in the office. What is your fascination with Buddha?" the stranger asked.

I was not able to think of anything but getting away with the murder of three people, so I couldn't respond immediately. I just stood silently. Finally, I recalled something I learned in a history class.

"I understand that it has something to do with suffering and peace. Is that right?"

"Yes. That is correct. At the end of his life, Siddhartha Gautama, who we now refer to as the Buddha or The Enlightened One, taught four essential truths I won't bore you with. Generally, it has to do with suffering, what causes it, and how we stop it. Indeed, his emphasis upon the suffering is inherent in samsara.

"Samsara?" I asked.

"It has several ancient meanings that generally refer to cyclical, wandering, things like that. With us, it relates to the continuation of life through a rebirth. You're correct that the Buddha preached a doctrine of an analysis of suffering and its causes. This would bring about its end, and therefore usher in a feeling of new and lasting peace. So yes, in that sense, peace is part of our tradition. Does that answer your question?

"Yes, thank you," I said, not knowing enough to ask anything more.

After some small talk about the weather, the City, local transportation, and a touch of history, the man gave me a curious look saying, "You're one of them, aren't you?"

"One of them? What do you mean?" I asked, wondering if the man was referring to the school bus now parked a half-mile away down by the pier.

"You hear voices," he said.

I tried not to widen my eyes, but the stranger picked up the hint of my surprised expression. I said nothing, I simply stared at the man who seemed to be reading the thoughts that were buried inside of my skull.

"Ah, I'm not crazy or anything like that, if that's what you mean. I'm just looking around enjoying the City and its wonderful views. I only came into this temple because I was walking along the street and saw the grand stairway leading up to it, not because of any guidance or voice," I said.

"I don't mean to insult you, I didn't mean it that way. I just want you to know there are more of us than you think. In fact, we have a support group that meets right here the first Wednesday of every month. Because I've been here so long, after a while, I can recognize those who have the blessing. There's something in their eyes or the way they hold their head while talking that gives the keen observer the signal. I hope it hasn't told you to kill someone," he said.

I almost ran down the stairs, skipping two at a time, to escape but held on, curious why he knew so much about my inner thinking. I hoped those killings didn't project in the way I held my head or by the cut in my eyebrow. After all, they all deserved to die, even if the voice hadn't prompted my actions. Based on what I just learned, it would seem to comply with the teachings of Buddha. All the voice did was explain why they had to be punished according to God's laws.

"No. I couldn't kill someone because of something in my head," I said, knowing that was only partially true.

"Well, don't worry about it for now, but eventually, you will be given a target. Everyone here has or will have one or more. Here we try to help people cope with that urge, but for so many, it is like trying to deny scratching an itch. The more you focus on the itch, the more you need to scratch it. So if you get that itch, we might be able to help scratch it without violence. One of the things we learn in Buddhism is the power of meditation. It broadens our senses and increases our awareness of things that ordinary humans do not hear or see. I can only sense that you are someone special who is receiving the signals from beyond. It means you have a special mission here, and you are an important person to something mortals cannot comprehend. I do not mean to intrude; I'm simply offering you the support you may need at some point in the future and forewarning you of the things that others like you have discussed in our sessions," he said.

My comment that I couldn't kill someone because of a voice wasn't true. But I wasn't going to go into any discussions about my voice.

"Would you like me to show you around?" the man asked.

"Sure. I've never been around anything Buddhist," I said.

The stranger walked me around the temple and explained rituals of worship being performed by a few. He also showed me into a room with a statue of a large fat man, I assumed was the Buddha. It sat surrounded by bouquets of flowers, candles, burning incense and stacks of reading materials that sat off to the side.

In a room across the hall there was a lone reading table with stiff wooden chairs where a man sat reading. He looked up as we walked in.

"Hello, Jimmy. Let me introduce you to a newcomer in these parts. Jimmy, this is... I'm sorry, I didn't get your name," he asked.

I thought for a moment, wondering if I should give my real name or my new name. Rasheed was relatively common, so it shouldn't raise suspicion this far from home. If they wanted to know my last name, I'd tell them Mead instead of Raad.

"I'm Rasheed. Nice to meet both of you," I said.

"I'm Ye, this is Jimmy. Jimmy owns the Jefferson Street Café, the best authentic Chinese food in town. Isn't that right, Jimmy?" Ye said.

Jimmy had no smile on his lips or in his eyes and instead simply nodded his head without comment. He appeared to be in deep thought about something that had nothing to do with chow mein and seemed irritated with the disruption. Sensing it, Ye took my arm, and we turned to leave when Jimmy spoke.

"I'm sorry, Ye. I'm not in a very good mood. One of my workers didn't show up last night and I had to do all the dishes and clean everything up at the restaurant this morning. I just tracked him down and he said he has a friend visiting, so he couldn't come to work. That was the third time he didn't show up without notice, so I fired him and now I'll have the same problem tonight," he said.

He looked over at me and asked, "Rasheed, was that your name?"

"Yes, Rasheed. Rasheed Mead," I emphasized.

"You live around here?"

"No. I just arrived in town by bus. Came over from Reno," I lied.

"Ye likes to show newcomers around, so I thought you might be new to the area. You plan on staying around or are you going to head back soon?"

"I'm not sure yet. I don't have anything going on in Reno, so I thought I'd see about living here for a while," I said.

"Interesting. Here I am in a pinch and you come along. I'm looking for someone to help out at the restaurant. The pay isn't great, but I pay cash, so nothing is taken out of a paycheck. It would give you some spending money while you're here," Jimmy said.

"I don't know. I've got to figure out a place to stay too. I've got some money, but I'd guess rooms aren't cheap here."

"No problem. I've got a room you can stay in if you're working for me. Consider it a bonus and part of your pay during your probation period. We're not talking about the St. Francis, but there's a bathroom just down the hall, and the mattress is pretty new; got it three years ago as I recall," Jimmy said.

"When would I go to work?" I asked.

"Well, as I was saying, I hate to get so far behind, so I could use someone this evening. You'd be working in the kitchen, washing dishes and pans, sweeping and mopping, cleaning tables, and then getting everything cleaned and set up for lunch the next day. We don't do breakfast, so after that, you're free to roam the City to check out the nightlife and stay out late like you young people do because you don't start the next day again until noon. The job is yours if you want it. I'd put you on a thirty-day internship, and if I like your work, keep you on permanently."

It didn't take me long to think about it since I wasn't sure how long my cash would last, so I needed both income and a place to stay. A Chinese restaurant in the heart of Chinatown seemed like an excellent place to lay low without raising suspicion. Probably few people around here had even heard of Portland, Oregon. Those who had surely didn't follow their local news.

After making arrangements with Jimmy to see his establishment and the room, Ye showed me around and told me he'd be happy to answer any other questions about Buddhism.

For now, I could look around parts of Chinatown and familiarize myself with the neighborhood.

"Jimmy can sometimes be very intense when trying to understand his voice. He probably heard from it when we interrupted him, so he's like us and not a bot," Ye said.

"Bot?" I asked.

"It's just a term I've heard some of the blessed use to describe the others who don't hear voices. We think of ourselves as the gifted and everyone else, just robots or bots for short. There are millions of bots who hear nothing, some do, but they're the minority. There are only a few of the blessed ones like us," Ye said.

*****

The room Jimmy showed me was around the corner from his restaurant. It was just one flight up a dark stairway in a building as ancient as the city itself. The bare wood stairs reported a resonating squeak on the second and third step as we walked up to view the room he had there. At the top, the dimly lit hall emitted the odor of garlic and the sound of hollow vacancy. I caught the flushing of the toilet down the hall, but other than the background sound of Broadway traffic a few blocks away, the place was surrounded by an eerie silence.

Jimmy stopped at a first door with a faded Chinese character above it. I assumed the character was the room number. He removed a key from his pocket, unlocked it and pushed the door open. A familiar starkness that was similar to my bedroom in Portland gave me a strange sense of comfort.

The room was basic with a small bed topped by a bare mattress, a straight back wooden chair next to a chest of drawers. On top of the chest of draws sat a black rotary dial phone next to a small brown-stained dripping sink. Across the room was an open-air closet with some wire hangers and a pulled-back curtain for someone wealthier than me to hang their extra clothes. At the far side of the room, without curtains, was a double-hung window that looked out over the black tarpaper roof of the building next door.

"There's a pillow and some sheets and blankets on the shelf in the closet, and I'll give you a couple of towels and a washcloth tonight that work. As I told you, this isn't the St. Francis," Jimmy said, handing me the key and something else; a small address book with his home and restaurant's phone number.

"The phone in this room has an answering machine. I'll pay for the phone, but don't abuse it. No long-distance calls. And communicate with me if something happens like you just died, or something just as catastrophic, and you can't make it to work," Jimmy said with a smirk.

I looked at the phone and acknowledged I wouldn't be calling Paris and certainly wouldn't be calling Portland.

When Jimmy headed toward the stairs, a message beamed in: *"Be careful. Be very careful. There is a danger here."*

I jumped as the communication filtered into my brain. I hadn't felt or heard anything from the voice since the warning about the danger in Tennessee's truck. Then I didn't realize the threat was the guy driving the truck. Was this because there's a danger with Jimmy or was it just this place? Recalling how I didn't get specific instructions to that danger made me realized I needed to fend for myself. The thought caused a surge of confidence to flow into my mind.

"Am I the only one with a key?" I asked.

"No. I have a key, but it's my room, so you'll just have to trust me. Now, why don't we go on over to the restaurant and I'll show you your duties," Jimmy said.

He gave me my key and placed his own on the long key chain that hung from his belt. Could I trust him with that key? I'd trusted several people in my life, like Jafar and Tennessee, and wondered if I could ever trust anyone again. In my current situation, I couldn't reject this offer of a place to stay and a job. Besides, it made no difference if Jimmy had a key since I could easily secure the room by propping the wooden chair under the doorknob when I was inside.

We went down the squeaking stairs, out the door, and around the corner to Jackson Street and into the restaurant where Jimmy showed me the chores I'd perform. It was a simple job that included washing the dishes then stacking them back under the dining counter in the main dining area. My last task of the evening would be to scrub the pots and pans, put them back in the cooking area, and sweep and mop the floor. When he finished showing me, he flipped the Chinese character sign on the door from what I assumed meant "Closed" to "Open."

Within a few minutes, a small group of customers came in and took a seat at one of the tables. Jimmy greeted them in Chinese and handed them a menu as they talked back and forth in what I assumed was Chinese. Then, after some high-pitched talk of what I believed were disagreements, they gave Jimmy their order. Jimmy then went back into the kitchen to prepare the food.

I put on my apron, took a damp towel, and began wiping down the countertop then looked back at four empty tables behind me when a lone man came in and sat at the counter. He was more round than tall but not in a plump way. He appeared muscular enough to play guard for the 49ers but too old for sports. There was a scar running across his eye from his forehead to his cheek. The eye was now just a white marble without an iris or pupil. I couldn't help noticing the man as he turned his head sideways, watching me with his good eye. His hair, dark with streaks of gray, was as shiny as a newly waxed Ferrari, something that befitted his image that was more Humvee-like than racy. He turned his back to me as Jimmy served him what must have been his standard fare because he'd placed no order. He ate it, laid cash on the counter, then quietly rose and left, saying nothing.

That same strange man came each night and as time passed, the next, and the next. There were so many next nights I lost track of how long I'd worked for Jimmy. He had never demonstrated anything that suggested danger. Despite this, the voice always warned me walking up the squeaky stairs. That's why I always put my wooden chair up under the doorknob.

Time passed quickly without anyone questioning me about my past. I'd grown older, stronger, and bigger thanks to the excellent meals I got at work. There had been no police looking for a young man from Portland, and there was never anything in the Chronicle, the local San Francisco paper, about the incident in Portland.

One typical San Francisco cool summer evening, the restaurant was reserved by a group from corporate giant Procter and Gamble, who were staying at the nearby Hilton. The smartly dressed group of mostly young recent college graduates was escorted in by one of their Chinese-speaking coworkers. The guide interpreted the menu for the gathering, and soon overloaded plates of calamari, shrimp, Peking style roast duck, and stir-fried vegetables filled their table. I acted as a server and busboy for the group that ate quickly then left to attend one of their late-night meetings.

Jimmy twisted the sign on the door and announced, "It's probably too late for anyone to come to dinner, so let's make it an early evening, Rasheed. I have some things to attend to, so please lock up," he said after handing me the key.

Locking the door, I was headed back to my room when I saw a flier nailed up on the telephone pole. The leaflet described a meeting at the Buddha Center with a guest speaker, Dr. Douglas Bonetti, an expert in auditory hallucinations. The meeting was scheduled to start in just a few minutes, so I decided to make my way over and catch the end of it.

THE PROFESSOR

Taking in the peaceful scene;
No worries now those winds did sing;
Of starry skies and moonlit views;
No concept of what horror ensues.

Shielding my neck from the cold, I pulled my sweater up higher as I made my way to the Buddhist temple meeting. The meeting room was full of participants who seemed to be from all walks of life, all sexes, races, and probably, though I didn't take a poll, all religions. By a group mingling outside, it appeared the program was in a break, an opportune time to find a seat. It wasn't a big auditorium and I found a vacant chair in the almost-empty front row. The only other unoccupied seat, without a paper or jacket saving it, was on the aisle end next to an attractive mature woman.

Sitting down, I said, "You must have been late, too. Late people always have to sit closest to the teacher."

She turned her head toward me and smiled.

"Yes, but not as late as you," she said.

"I'm Rasheed," I said, sticking out my hand.

I tend to be a little reserved, so I don't usually strike up conversations with strangers, but this was different. Somehow I was immediately attracted to this woman with the striking blue eyes that sparkled in the reflection of the lighted stage. Yes, she wasn't my age, but her smiling lips, as red as the columns that contained the gold Chinese characters, seemed inviting and friendly.

Her fresh dark hair tumbled over her shoulder, reminding me of a painting I'd seen by the Ukrainian painter Taras Loboda in a Geary Street gallery. She gleamed intelligence and was attractive even with the tiny, almost undetectable, small lines smiling from the sides of her eyes. Yes, she was mature but carried her beauty more radiantly than women far younger.

"Hello, Rasheed. Nice to meet you. I'm Mary. Mary White," she said, shaking my hand.

As I shook her hand, I felt a grip that wasn't the soft feminine grip I expected. It wasn't masculine, but it wasn't dainty either. It was firm yet warm and inviting.

Shaking off some of my embarrassing carnal feelings, I could finally speak.

"What brings you here?" I asked.

She looked away without a reply with seemingly little interest in me that I supposed was natural. After all, I was a young nobody dishwasher and she was a goddess. There was a tense silence as she looked back. She was scanning the room behind us then turned back to me, saying, "I saw a poster for it on a pole down south of Market, and it reminded me he was coming," she said.

"He?" I asked.

"Dr. Bonetti," she replied without further comment.

"Oh, yes. I saw that same poster," I said.

I knew about "South of Market" but couldn't imagine she'd live there. Of course there we some new condos, new and quite expensive condos, going in so perhaps she was in that area and not the south where all the drug deals took place.

"South of Market? So you deal drugs with this Dr. Bonetti?" I said, smiling.

"Not that South of Market," Mary laughed.

Before any further conversation, Ye walked to the front of the room and approached the podium.

"I'm in one of the new condos down there," she whispered just as Ye grabbed the microphone, tapped it to make sure it was on, and tipped it up to his lips.

"So let's continue with our program and let me welcome you late arrivals to the Buddhist Temple. It's nice to see you here this evening for our enrichment lecture. We promise this will be an exciting session because we've invited Professor Douglas Bonetti as our guest speaker. You all know he's a prominent medical doctor and psychiatrist at the University of San Francisco Healthcare Center. Dr. Bonetti has published several papers in the New England Journal of Medicine on the subject of auditory hallucinations and will be discussing it this evening. So let's give a warm welcome to Dr. Bonetti."

Soft applause greeted Dr. Bonetti as he made his way forward from the rear of the hall. Ye stepped down from the small stage and looked out at the audience. His face changed from a toothy smile to a sunken frown as he looked toward the back of the room, eyeing one of the late-arriving members. The man appeared to be making his way to the stage but then diverted at the front row toward his right and took a seat at the far end of the same front row as Mary and I.

I glanced up at him as the man walked by and saw the scar and the large white pupil-less eye I'd seen so many nights before at the restaurant. Taking his seat, the man slowly turned his head towards me, giving that familiar stark stare.

I turned to Mary and asked, "Do you know that guy?"

She tipped her head forward and looked past me at the big man.

"He's been to a couple of meetings, but I don't know him," she said. "He's a little weird, even taking the stage one time and grabbing the microphone to curse what he called "bots" for attending their meeting. Other than that, he never says anything, just seems to stare at people."

"He is a little strange, for sure. I've seen him a couple of times at the place I work," I told her.

After thanking Ye for the kind introduction, Dr. Bonetti began his talk giving a brief introduction to basic psychology. He then moved into a discussion about schizophrenia and, in general terms, about the abnormal perceptions of reality, disorganized speech and thinking. Using an overhead projector, he outlined some general things about psychology, explaining the differences in various psychiatric illnesses, symptoms, and treatments. Finally, he got down to why everyone was there: hearing voices.

He related that it wasn't uncommon, and many famous people claimed to have heard voices, including Joan of Arc, Gandhi, Freud, and Phillip K. Dick, the author.

"There are other famous examples. Did you know Robert Schumann, the famous composer, had auditory hallucinations? He wrote in his diary that for most of his life, he'd been hearing the note A5 sounding in his head. His musical hallucinations became more complex as he grew older. He claimed to have been visited by the ghost of Schubert one evening and wrote down the music he was hearing. What's more interesting is that later he began hearing an angelic choir singing," Dr. Bonetti said.

Dr. Bonetti went on to cite statistical information about the condition along with types of treatments prescribed for those that voices or sounds bothered. When he'd concluded, he asked for questions.

"I have a question," someone asked.

"Sure, go ahead."

"Do inner voices mean someone is tormented, agitated, driven crazy, things like that?"

"It could be, but only one out of every three individuals who hear voices requires psychiatric help. The other two don't consider the voices, or sounds if you prefer, annoying, troubling, or distracting. In fact, they may consider them supportive or inspirational. Some have reported that their voices alert them to potential dangers or suspicious people and provide them with encouragement in stressful times. I'm sure that, initially, Schumann enjoyed the angelic choir, and if things went on for his entire life, it would have been a great source of comfort," he stated.

"Was it?" Mary, sitting up front, asked.

"Sadly, it wasn't. Later, the beautiful choir he was hearing turned into demonic voices, and he warned his wife, Clare, that he was afraid he would kill her. Soon after that, he attempted suicide by jumping off a bridge into the Rhine but was saved by a boatman. At his own request, he was admitted to an insane asylum, as they called them in those days, where he died just two years later. As I recall, he was only about forty-five at the time.

Mary raised her hand and was called on.

"So, it's not just voices people hear. It's sounds?"

"That's correct. Like Schumann, it's all kinds of things. For example, on the positive side is the twelve-year-old musical savant, Alma, who said in an interview with the New York Times, 'When I was four, I just had these melodies and ideas in my head, and I would play them at the piano. And sometimes my parents would think that I just remembered music that I'd already heard before. But they weren't. I wrote them on my own.'

"Then in her interview, she was asked where these melodies in her head came from and she replied that she had lots of imaginary composers even naming one Albert Cogwheel. She said he and other imaginary composing friends lived in a country where imaginary composers write, each in his own style of emotion, so she can develop melodies that are either joyful or stark. She said, 'I have lots of composers. And sometimes when I'm stuck with something when I'm composing, I go to them and ask them for advice. And quite often, they come up with exciting things.'

"She's young now, and let's hope that those composers in her head help her the rest of her life and don't do to her what Schumman's did to him," Dr. Bonetti concluded, then asked if anyone had other questions.

A man on the other side of the room raised his hand, and Dr. Bonetti pointed at him.

"You said four percent of the population admit to hearing voices. How many out there hear them, but say nothing?"

I looked down at the floor, doing a guilt-like twist in my chair.

"Good question. Who knows? It could be double or triple that estimate. It might be as many as half the population. As I was saying, if something is soothing, helpful, or simply a part of someone's personality, something they accept as normal, they'd never be counted. The four percent number is based on people who have issues with these sounds. For example, I saw an open letter one of my colleagues wrote in a paper called 'The Seven-Year-Old Schizophrenic.' He pointed out that you can't simply call someone, particularly a child, schizophrenic because they hear voices. Treating someone who hears voices with powerful psychotic medications could do more harm than good and must be carefully considered. In fact, they claim more children got better taking nothing compared to children who were treated."

There was a collective sigh in the audience. Mary looked over at me and gave a head nod signaling that she too may be hearing something. She whispered to me, "The subject is so fascinating, and I like that the idea of this place where people learn to deal with the voices rather than having a doctor putting them on those darn drugs."

"To just build on something we discussed, there was a broad study in Holland that found a significant number of people hearing voices didn't seek psychiatric services. They either described themselves as being able to cope with their voices and/or described their voices as life-enhancing," he said, then paused for a follow-up question.

Not hearing one, the psychiatrist shuffled some papers on his podium and announced, "I'm sorry, but our time is up. If you see me in the foyer after the meeting, feel free to ask your questions, and I'll see if I can answer them for you."

With that, Dr. Bonetti turned, stepped off the stage, and walked up the aisle seeing everyone beaming with smiles except for White Eye who was still sitting staring straight ahead emotionless. Slowly, his head turned, and his huge white eye became visible.

By the look in the other eye, I could see he was again focused on me, and maybe Mary, who'd turned to tell me goodbye. She saw the strange single-eyed man looking toward us and tapped me on the shoulder, "Why is he looking at us like that?"

"I have no idea. As I said, he comes into the place I work every so often and does the same thing. Once I even asked him why he was looking at me, but he didn't respond," I said.

"He sure gives me the creeps. Would you mind grabbing a cup of coffee with me? I don't want to leave this place alone, and I don't think you should either," Mary said.

"Sure. We can walk over to the Hilton and grab a cup there."

As people stood, I noticed Mary had a book on her lap so leaned over and asked, "What are you reading?"

She turned the book over showing me the cover and read it, "Muses, Madmen, and Prophets: Rethinking the History, Science, and Meaning of Auditory Hallucination By Daniel B. Smith."

"Is that why you asked him the question about hearing sounds?" I asked.

"Kind of, yes. I guess this has piqued my interest," she said.

The audience was thinning out, filing their way out of the auditorium. A few hung around, asking the speaker some questions.

Mary stopped as if she wanted to ask a few herself, but instead turned to me.

"He's too busy, so why don't we just head over," she said.

We left together and walked through the safety of the crowded streets over to the Hilton just a few blocks away. As we walked and talked, we both continued to glance behind us to see if White Eye was following. Though we saw nothing, we walked around the block for a diversion, checking again behind us before going into the hotel's main entrance. The restaurant was now closed, so we walked into the busy bar, found a seat facing the door, and sat.

A uniformed waitress took our order of two coffees, and we leaned back in our chair, keeping a good eye on the entrance.

"I guess we're not being followed," Mary offered.

"I can walk you home if you'd like," I suggested.

"That's kind of you. I can just grab a cab, but thanks anyway. Will you be at the next meeting?" she asked.

"When is it?"

"They have them every month, but normally just support group stuff without a famous speaker," she told me.

"I'll try. I normally work late, so don't know if I can make it," I said.

"I don't go all the time, either. It's supportive, but I don't think I need it. I've learned to control it. I think pretty soon, after a year or so of not following its prompts, it just gave up on me probably thinking I was a lost cause," Mary said.

"You've heard a voice too?" I asked.

"Of course, silly. Why else would I have come to that meeting?" she teased.

"Yeah. Guess that was a dumb question," I said.

"Not so dumb. Some go there because someone they know or love is troubled by a voice and they don't know what to do to help. So I guess you have one too, right," Mary asked.

I hesitated but finally responded with a simple, "Yes."

"Does it bother you?" Mary asked.

"Not at all. I have no control over it; it gives me pointers or tells me about danger, kind of like a car coming that I don't see."

"Well, if it ever starts pushing you to do something you're uncomfortable with, let me know. Mine did that, and I went along with its request. Well, it was more than a request. It was like a demand and I later rejected almost everything it said to me. Heck, it wanted me to take off with a guy and a baby one time, and I refused," she said but offered no explanation.

I didn't press the subject, but I did want a confidant, someone I might be able to explore this thing with.

"Hey, if we're not able to make the meetings together, why don't we exchange phone numbers and maybe we can have coffee again sometime."

"Sure," Mary said.

I handed her my little phone book with just two numbers; the store and my room phone number.

"You don't have a lot of friends or family, Rasheed," Mary said.

"No. I'm kind of new to the area, and my parents are dead, and I have no other family, so I don't know many people," I told her.

She scribbled her number in the book and handed it back to me. I tore off a page of the book, wrote down my number and gave it to her.

As we finished our coffee, we shared the typical life stories. I lied about most of mine but learned that Mary was alone with few friends. She'd been married to an abusive husband who was mayor of their city. She was told to kill him by her inner voice, but decided instead to move away and hide amongst many. She'd been in San Francisco about the same length of time as I and was making pretty good money holding a "Homeless" sign by the BART station down on Market Street.

Getting a job would have left an identity, something she wanted to hide.

Finishing our coffee, I motioned to the waitress for the bill. "I hope we can get together again soon," I said.

"You can find me almost every day at the foot of Powel and Market Street with my sign, my coffee can, and my grungy clothes," she smiled. "I make more money doing that than I did in my white-collar job before I came to San Francisco," she added.

"I don't mean to be nosey, Rasheed, but can I ask you something personal?" Mary said.

"Sure. We've explored some pretty personal things already, so ask away."

"I'm not trying to hit on you. For goodness sake, I'm old enough to be your mother, but I was wondering if you have a girlfriend or someone else close to confide in? I know it's easier to fight off these voices if you do," she said.

"Yessss... Wait, no. I mean, it feels like I do have a girlfriend, but now I'm not sure if I do or don't. I thought I did, but I don't remember now. Damn, that's confusing isn't it," I asked.

"Very confusing, but if you feel like it, maybe you'll figure it out sometime and let me know?" Mary said.

"Darn, Mary. I'm not trying to hide something, but I honestly don't understand so many things. When I was younger, I'd pick fights with guys bigger than me because I thought I was a karate expert. I'm sure I could strip down a military weapon and put it back together with my eyes blindfolded, but I have no idea where those feelings come from," I told her.

"Maybe it's something like Dr. Bonetti discussed in his talk. You know, those famous people who heard sounds and voices from somewhere," Mary suggested.

"Maybe, but it's never said anything about any of those subjects, including a girl," I told here.

"These voices work in strange ways," Mary said.

"I've got an early class tomorrow, so I need to get home and to bed. It was nice meeting you, Rasheed," Mary said, holding out her hand.

I took her warm hand, softly shook it, then paid the bill. The doorman held up his finger, and a cab pulled up to the curb. Mary jumped in and rolled down the window.

"Be careful. Give me a call sometime and we'll talk," she said as the cab pulled away.

I looked back and forth along Kearny Street, checking for anything suspicious. I was pretty sure that White Eye, with his bulk, couldn't hide very easily. I rode the escalator up to the hotel's second floor, where a bridge spanned the street to the park on the other side. Once across, I turned right then walked up the street toward my room, checking every few yards to see if anyone was following. When I approached my building, I heard a subtle, *"Careful."*

My eyes squinted as I scanned the street, looking up and down before inserting my key into the building's door. Opening it, I glanced up the dark stairway and saw nothing.

Slowly, taking one step at a time, I began my climb up, and as usual, the third step announced my coming as it let out its usual squeak. Just as my head cleared the landing, I stopped.

The narrow hall, illuminated only by a naked bulb hanging from an exposed black cord, cast shadows in each doorway, making it difficult to see someone hiding there.

Haltingly, looking carefully into each shadow, I finished my climb, approached my door, and waited. If there was danger inside, hopefully my voice would give me a warning.

Nothing.

Twisting the knob, I pushed the door inward while remaining in the hallway. As it swung around, it hit the inside wall, letting me know nobody was hiding behind it. There was enough light in the small room that I could tell it was vacant unless someone was under the bed or in the small door-less closet disguised as a pair of jeans. I entered my room and closed the door, locked it, then double-checked the lock and finally let out a sigh of relief.

After placing the rugged wooden chair under the doorknob, I turned on the small lamp beside my bed and sat down with Mary on my mind. Hoping

I wouldn't sound overly assertive, I opened my address book, sorted through all three numbers in it, and found hers. Holding my breath, I dialed.

"Hello?"

"Mary? This is Rasheed. I just wanted to make sure you got home okay," I told her.

"Yes, thank you, Rasheed. I made it just fine and assume you did too?

"Yeah, I'm fine. Just got to my room."

"That was sure a creepy experience, wasn't it?"

"Sure was. He's a strange looking dude," I replied, but something else was on my mind that I'd considered on my walk home.

"I hope I'm not out of line asking you this, but would you get a warning if that husband of yours came close?" I asked.

"I'm not sure. Perhaps. It's warned me about other things. Why do you ask?" Mary said.

"I'm getting a warning and have been for a while. Not sure if it's because of White Eye or something else. I don't know," I told her.

"I've got a personal question for you, Rasheed. Hope I'm not coming across as a nosy old lady," Mary said, then without waiting for my response, said, "Has your voice told you to kill anyone?"

I gulped. She'd confessed hers had. I wondered if she discovered something from my past, or was she just curious? I couldn't be sure, but I was certain I wasn't going to tell her about the fire or about Tennessee. I didn't know her well enough to go into any of it, and if I did, it could scare her away.

My hesitation allowed her to jump in.

"I'm sorry. You don't have to answer that, I just wanted to suggest that if it hasn't, it will. A lot of people in that group have had that experience. Their voice wants them to kill someone for some reason, and they're not sure why," she said.

"Yes, I know. You told me yours did," I said.

"Yes, but we'll discuss it some other time, perhaps the next time we meet, okay?"

"Sure. We can share experiences and maybe help each other," I told her.

"Maybe for coffee some evening?" Mary asked.

"Remember, I work late," I reminded her.

"How about breakfast then?" Mary suggested.

"Sure. Isn't there a Micky D's right there by Powel and Market?" I asked.

"Yes, there is. How about eight? Will that be too early for you?" Mary asked.

"Not at all. I look forward to buying you a coffee at eight. Good night, Mary.

It was really nice to meet you."

I placed the phone on the receiver, and reluctantly ended the conversation.

Maybe in the future I could explain things, and it would be okay.

I kicked off my shoes, threw my jeans on the floor, then reached over and turned out the light, and closed my eyes.

Tomorrow would be a new day and a meeting with a new friend. My eyes slid shut, the sounds of the city dimmed, and in a few minutes, a song began to play lulling me into a soft, mellow place.

"I open my mouth to the Lord and I won't turn back..."

THE LINEBACKER

Are you the meanest in the room;
Beat 'em whip'em make 'em swoon.
Beware my friend though you are tough;
Someone's out there much more rough.

Packing up his things, Mark turned off the office light and made his way to the ground floor.

At the bottom of the stairs, he saw Sue at the bulletin board pointing at something and talking with another student. When the two finished their conversation, Mark walked over. Sue caught his approach from the corner of her eye. She turned her head and offered a warm smile.

"Hi! It's nice to see you again," she said

"Hi. You're still here. Where are you off to?" Mark asked.

"I was going to grab something to drink, why?"

"Mind if I walk along with you. I have some questions about that game," Mark said.

"Not at all, I'd enjoy the company," she said.

"You checked out our game? I thought you didn't want to deal with games. Are you giving it some thought?" Sue asked.

"Was that 22 billion for the top prize?" he asked.

"Is it that high now? It grows all the time, so I haven't kept track." Sue said.

"I'm not sure we can get this FindIt program done in time. I'm grasping at straws, Sue."

As the two strolled across campus, Mark noticed that same guy he'd seen the day they met in the cafeteria. He seemed slightly bigger and more muscular standing in that doorway than he had when sitting behind a table, but still had that same athletic look. He wore an expression of dejection with a sprinkle of anger painted on his face. Mark turned away and began talking with Sue paying little attention to Mr. Hulk. He didn't notice as the guy walked down the steps and started following them as they headed toward the small campus café.

Once inside, Mark purchased their drinks then made his way to the table where Sue sat near the back of the room. He handed Sue her drink then explained his brief adventure into the Forrest Labs game.

"What's a 'Forrester'?" he asked.

"That's the artificial currency in the game that can be converted into our dollars easily. The game has its own internal economic system, and the currency can fluctuate just like in the real world. When you accumulate Forresters, you can sell them off each week, and the real-world currency is transferred to your bank," Sue explained.

Unnoticed, the guy watching them from the doorway walked in and purchased his obligatory drink. He walked to the opposite corner and sat watching them. The wave machine cascading its colors synchronized with the music sent an eerie shade of colors over the scowl on his face. Sue hadn't seen him come in, and she didn't see anyone else except Mark. Her eyes, ears, and all other senses were fixed on him and nothing else, particularly not her ex, Jake.

Like small kindling, the fire burned slowly at first, but the more Jake looked at them, the more wood was added. Now a virtual inferno blazed within him, and he could feel a fueled rage build by her undeniable attraction to her new male friend.

He watched her as she smiled up at Mark, sipping his drink as if he was her fucking Prince Charming. It made Jake wonder if they'd slept together and were now grabbing a little energy after their nooner. He wanted to pounce on both of them now but held back. He'd watch for a while to see what other lover moves they'd make. His blood pressure rose and his heart began to race as she scooted closer to her prince. He felt the same sensation he had with the anticipation of the kick-off before a big game. His tension and the excitement of an anticipated violent collision between foes flooded his mind with the desire to strike. As they sat there chatting and smilingly back-and-forth, Jake could no longer contain himself.

Trembling with anger, he got up and briskly walked toward their table.

Sue saw him immediately. She elbowed Mark and whispered, "Oh, oh."

Mark glanced over at Sue and saw her eyes staring toward the figure walking toward them. Mark recognized him immediately remembering he'd caught him watching them on other occasions, but then paid little attention to him. Mark could tell now that his first hunch was correct that this was the guy with hate in his mind and fury in his heart. He knew he was about to meet the worst possible enemy, worse than the enemy he'd fought in any of the wars. This guy emitted hate that was fueled by a high octane fuel... Jealousy.

"A friend of yours?" Mark asked, sounding unconcerned.

"It's my ex-boyfriend," she said.

The message on the front of the guys snugly fitted t-shirt read "Ripped," which was about as necessary as a sign reading, "Danger! Steep slope!" on the side of a cliff. The guy obviously spent most of his waking hours pumping iron at the school gym and was definitely ripped, just as the shirt read.

Jake boldly walked up to them with a twisted look on his face. Laying his palms flat on the table, he bent over and looked squarely at Sue, ignoring Mark.

"Who's this guy?" he asked, using his thumb to point in Mark's direction.

"What business is that of yours?" Sue said.

"Everything you do is my business."

"You are so wrong about that, everything I do is my business. If your brain were as large as your muscles, you would have understood that it was over when I said it's over. Now please, move away from our table and let us talk."

A command by her was like a challenge to his manhood. Instead of backing away, he stood taller and began pressing his body against the table, pushing it back towards them. He glanced at Sue then turned his attention toward Mark.

"You," he said, pointing the finger at Mark. "Come on outside, and we'll settle this."

Mark glanced over at Sue, whose mouth had dropped open as she stared at Jake.

She held back from screaming at him. She knew it would just send a signal that he'd upset her. Instead, she whispered, "Jake! What do you think you're doing? This isn't a boyfriend, he's an instructor at school."

Others in the room could sense the tension and a strange quietness settled in the café. The only sound was the whirling of the beverage machine and the soft background music. Eyes were now up from iBoards and fixed on the table that Jake hovered over.

"You think I give a shit about him or this school," he snapped back loud enough for everyone to hear.

"You'll get kicked out of school and off the team," she tried to reason.

"Too late for that. I've already been kicked off the team, so I don't give a shit about this fucked up school or its instructors. Particularly this piece of shit instructor," he said with his index finger pointing directly at Mark.

Mark tried to calm things.

"Wait a minute. I don't know what your problem is and I have nothing to do with the athletic department or the operation of this school. I'm just an assistant here and provide some tutoring for students. I don't know you and I don't have a beef with you so why don't you just go back and enjoy your drink. I think in the long run that would be better for both of us."

Jake stared at Mark with the sneer of a Hulkamania combatant.

"Fuck you. I said I was gonna take you outside and kicked the shit out of you just to prove what a worthless fuck you are, and that's exactly what I intend to do," Jake said.

"I know you're pissed and jealous, but you're taking your frustrations out on the wrong guy. First, as I said, this is not my girlfriend; she's a student. Second, and probably more importantly, despite having that muscle-bound body, you couldn't kick my ass without the help of your barbell and your defensive line," Mark said, looking Jake squarely in the eye.

Sue's head whipped around, looking at Mark with her mouth open. Then it shot back over to Jake.

"What? Hell, I wouldn't even need our skinny field goal kicker to whip your ass. You're nothing but a fucking nerdy geek with his head up someone's ass sniffing for goodies. Get your chicken shit ass out from behind that table, and we'll see how tough you are," Jake said, now standing straight with his hands on his hips.

Mark pushed the table back away from him, forcing Jake to back up.

"Okay, if you insist," Mark told him as he calmly stood.

Sue was dumbfounded. She looked at Mark then Jake and couldn't understand why Mark would possibly fight him. She feared he could be seriously injured or maybe even killed. Jake's violent temper had created other fights during their short courtship, and his beating of another student was why he was no longer on the football team.

She thought back to the hug in Mark's office. Hugging him shocked her. It wasn't the soft hug she'd experienced with her girlfriends or even the men in her family. Hugging him was like hugging a piece of granite. He wasn't muscle-bound like Jake, he was lean, trim, and very, very firm.

She knew Jake was big, mean and unrelenting, and Mark, as solid as he was, wouldn't have a chance.

"Wait!" she pleaded. "This is stupid," she said, standing up.

Mark reached out his hand, causing Sue to sit back down.

"Jake, is that your name?" Mark asked.

"Yeah, asshole. And you'll never forget it when I'm through with you," Jake snarled.

"If you want a piece of me, take your best shot right now," Mark said, pointing at his chin.

Jake looked at him, puzzled. Why someone would allow him to take a swing? The comment gave Jake pause to wonder why anyone would ask him to hit them. But he wouldn't throw a punch in the café, that could get him arrested. He'd have to get him outside and out of sight. He'd have him walk in front of him, tap him on the shoulder, and as he turned, deck him. He didn't fight fair; he fought to win.

"We need to take it outside. This place knows me, and I could get arrested for starting something here again. Outside!" Jake said, pointing toward the door.

"Okay," Mark said.

"Don't do this Mark," Sue insisted.

"Do it chicken shit," Jake said.

"I will. Don't worry, Sue. We'll get this settled once and for all, but we must take care of a little business first. You don't mind do you... what's your name? Was it Jake?" Mark said calmly.

"Huh? What business? I'm not payin' for your fuckin' drinks, if that's what you mean," Jake said.

Mark said nothing as he reached into his rear pocket and pulled out his wallet.

Opening it, he took out what looked like a small business card and slowly slid it across the table to Jake.

"Please read the front of this card and then sign the back. When you're finished, give it to Sue so she can sign it as a witness. If you had thrown a punch when I asked, we wouldn't have to go through this. I'm allowed to defend myself. That's why I invited you to take a swing at me. You didn't or can't, I understand that, but since you're asking for a confrontation, it's required that I provide full disclosure. So, read and sign it, and we can go outside, and as you said, 'settle this,'" Mark said as he pulled a pen from his jacket pocket and held it out to him.

Sue looked up shockingly at Mark then turned her gaze to her ex-boyfriend. She saw his eyes darting back and forth as he read. His eyes stopped then went back to the top of the card as he reread it. By the time he finished, his expression had changed from anger to surprise. He threw the card violently back on the table, then turned and stomped toward the door of the café. Before opening it, he turned and looked back at the two.

"We'll settle this another time," he said.

Mark sat back down as Jake left the café and casually took a sip of his brew as if nothing had happened.

"What was that all about?" Sue asked, picking up the card from the table.

"Sue, let me have that," Mark said, reaching for the card.

She pulled it away, then turning her back to him read the small type on the card:

> "By signing this card I understand that
> the bearer, Lt. Mark Gorman, is a ninth
> degree Black Belt and holds the All

Military Heavyweight Mixed Martial
Arts Championship.
I initiated this confrontation and
thereby waive my rights to civil
litigation and relieve Lt. Gorman, and
the Government, of any legal
responsibility.
Further, I agree my opponent is acting
in self-defense and has fully disclosed
that I could be harmed, receive
permanent disability, or lose my life
during this combat.
I hereby stipulate that I was under no
duress to sign."

"Oh," was all Sue said as she slowly turned around looking at Mark.

"Okay, give it to me, please," he said.

"All Military Champion? You beat up everyone in the military?" she
asked.

Laughing, seeing that she knew nothing about an elimination
tournament Mark explained, "No, after a few elimination bouts, I only had
to beat about sixteen. Now, let's talk about that game."

"Talk about the game? You can talk about V-World after that? I don't
think I'm ready. Aren't you too upset to talk about that thing?" Sue asked.

"Upset? No. Why would I be upset? In training, you practice staying
calm in situations like that, and even in a major fight, you don't get upset. If
you do, you lose. You have to stay calm. Anger makes mistakes; calm
focuses on technique and training. He was upset, not me," Mark told her.

Sue saw Duncan coming through the door. She stood and motioned
him over.

"You should have been here sooner, Duncan," Sue said.

"Why. What did I miss? Did you solve the riddle of V-World or
something?"

"No. Mark made my ex back down. It was amazing," Sue said.

"That football guy? Mark made him…"

"Yeah."

Duncan looked at Mark then back at Sue.

"He's the biggest bully at school. What did you do Mark?"

Sue jumped in and explained what happened.

"And now he wants to know more about V-World," Sue said.

"Don't know if we can tell you everything, but I'm beginning to think you should strongly consider that game. Time is running short," Duncan said.

Mark had the feeling that he was right

THE ESCAPE

Go, now go,
Make it fast.
Save yourself,
This life must last.

"They're here," the voice said urgently.

Awakened by the sharp call, I sat up surprised. Was it a dream, or did I hear a warning? Sleepily I glanced around the dark room wondering if the sign was for something in the building or my room. What did the voice mean by "they?" If it was they, it sure wasn't in my room. It had to be from outside, so I knew I had some time to prepare. Quickly, I threw my feet off the bed and tipped my head to the side, listening carefully for something… anything.

Nothing was there. Not any sound of movement.

"They are here. Danger," the voice said again this time more insistently.

Trying to catch a hint of movement, I placed my ear against the door squinting my eyes as if that would help me hear. I flipped on the light to neutralize any advantage someone might have had while waiting in the darkness. Checking the closet, I saw nothing. Slowly I lowered myself to the floor and looked under the bed to find only dust mites and a Milky Way candy bar wrapper. With the minor exception of a lone cockroach that jumped down the sink drain when the light came on, I realized I was the room's only occupant. But then I heard the squeak of that noisy third step. Someone was coming.

If whoever was coming up those stairs found an empty room, maybe they'd think I was out on the town and leave to come back another time. It would give me time to consider what to do next. I reached over and turned off the light, smoothed the blanket, grabbed my clothes and shoes, then nudged opened my door, and tiptoed my way down the hall to the bathroom. Stepping inside, I dressed and watched through the cracked door to observe who was coming.

The bare lightbulb in the hallway revealed movement at the stairs. Taking one ginger step at a time, I saw a head begin to appear. When it cleared the last step, I saw Jimmy coming up over the stair landing. At first,

I was relieved, but then wondered why he would be so cautious coming up the stairs. Behind Jimmy, just a half a step away, a bald head appeared with a familiar face. It was White Eye, the stranger who seemed so interested in me in the restaurant and at the Buddha meeting. The stairs weren't too far away to hear the third step squeak again. Was Jimmy bringing the San Francisco Police Department into the building? When two more heads appeared, my eyes widened. I looked back to be sure. It was them. I couldn't believe what I was seeing. Even though the light was dim, I saw two stooped-over figures standing beside Jimmy and White Eye. Without seeing a full face, I recognized Jafar and his wife, Malakeh.

"Oh, my God!" I thought. How could this be? They were blocked in the house by the fire and his makeshift burglar bars. How did they escape, and how did they know I was working for Jimmy?

The four stopped and faced my room when Jimmy held up a hand, calling for a halt. He turned and placed his ear against the door as White Eye reached behind his back and grabbed for something. The light from the bare bulb reflected off the long shiny blade he held at the ready. Jimmy pulled a string of keys from his pocket and inserted one into the door. He slowly opened it, and the group slid quietly inside. In just a few moments, they all came back into the hall.

"He's not here, and it doesn't look like he's been here for a while. We'll have to separate and search for him. You two scan the streets around Chinatown; it's where he normally hangs out," Jimmy said, pointing at Jafar and Malakeh.

"We'll search this building beginning with the bathroom," he said, pointing towards the crack in the door where I stood watching.

I slowly nursed the door closed, twisted the lock, and slid the security bolt into place. I remembered the high window over the shower, and quickly stood on the edge of the bathtub and unfastened the window's latch. A faint sound caught my attention, and I looked down at the door to see a twisting of the doorknob. Momentarily, I stood frozen, watching the doorknob twist. I could hear someone placing their weight against the door. I knew I had to act or be trapped, so I put one foot on the faucet and grabbed the window sill. As agile as an Olympic gymnast, launching myself upward, I shoved my head through the opening.

With my head outside the window, I forced one elbow through then launched myself through to my waist. My head and torso were now outside and I could see an open trash bin below. There was a resounding bang of the door being kicked in, and before I could get my legs and feet through, I felt someone grab one of my pant legs. I kicked the hand off with my free foot and launched myself headfirst out the second-story window into the cool night air.

Instinctively reverting to something I learned somewhere, I tucked, and just before I landed in the trash bin, my body rotated enough to allow my back to slam into plastic garbage bags. Momentarily I lost my breath and senses but recovered quickly enough to jump up and over the end of the dumpster before my chasers could look out the window. Then I heard someone yell something.

What they yelled made me think of something I'd read about boxing. For some reason, I was fascinated by that violent sport. So when I ran down the back alley, I heard someone yell something boxer Joe Lewis said in 1946. In 1941 he had a championship fight with a lighter Billy Conn who was winning that fight through twelve rounds by outboxing Lewis. Then, in the thirteenth round, Conn changed tactics and started slugging it out with Lewis. Lewis caught him with a right cross and knocked him out, winning the fight. After the war in 1946, Conn got a rematch with the champ. Reporters asked Lewis what he would do if Conn used his hit and run strategy again like he did the first fight?

Lewis's reply: "He can run, but he can't hide."

That same thing was shouted to me by someone from above as I sprinted to the street.

THE EXISTENCE

Running watching
The danger that's alive;
Need to find a place that's safe.
Need to stay alive.

They couldn't be alive. Was I seeing something? Maybe it was someone who looked like Jafar. I couldn't be sure. I knew about his association with "The Base" and thought their network might have helped locate me and, for some reason, felt I needed to be out of the way. Maybe he survived the fire and visited Jafar in the hospital, and he told them I knew about their plan. He looked at me strangely after one of his telephone conversations with them, so maybe that was it. But why someone who looked like Jafar and how did they find me?

Then I remembered the jacket I left in the truck. Maybe it had been recovered by the police. The members of The Base had infiltrated the Highway Patrol and got a message back to Jafar if he survived. Or maybe they called him and said they had the jacket and Jafar told those from The Base. It didn't matter. They found me and I had to do something.

My jump from the window gave me some time to sprint from the area and get a head start over the pursuers. Running zigzag up one block and down another, I continued the stagger for several blocks until getting to Market Street. At the corner, I crouched behind a newspaper stand and watched for any trace of my hunters. Seeing nobody but homeless vagrants and teenagers looking for trouble, it seemed I'd lost them, at least for the moment. Walking further south, I spotted an alley with several blue dumpsters. Opening the lid of the first one, I closed it quickly, gagging on the smell of loose garbage from a restaurant. In the next one I saw mostly cardboard shoe boxes, so I marked it as my new home before heading back to a payphone I'd seen on the corner.

I needed to warn Mary since she too might be in danger. At the phone, I pulled out my two-number phonebook and placed the call.

"Hello?" she said in a sleepy voice.

"It's Rasheed," I whispered.

"Who?"

"Rasheed, the guy from the meeting."

"Oh, what time is it? What's wrong? Is something wrong? Is it that guy?" she said, answering her own question.

"It's that guy and others, Mary. I don't even know how to explain it, but the others were people I knew who'd been burned to death in a house fire a long time ago. They came to my room a few minutes ago, and I think they wanted to kill me. White Eye had a sword Sir Lancelot would have envied, and he had three people with him: the two I knew, and the other was my boss, Jimmy. I don't know what's going on or why they are after me."

"Oh my God, Rasheed, I think they've got you targeted and want to delete you for some reason. You are in a danger that I can't explain in just a few minutes. Come over here right away," she said.

"No. They might follow me there."

"They don't want me. They want you. Where are you?" she asked.

Targeted? Delete me? I was confused wondering who "they" were. Did that mean it was more than just Jafar and Malakeh? Was Mary a part of those "theys?"

I didn't want to believe it but decided I'd need to proceed cautiously.

"I'm at a phone booth right now."

"I know that, I mean are you going to be safe for a while?"

"Yes. I think I found a good hiding place, so I'll be okay," I said.

"I know every hiding place in the South of Market area so you get in one and I'll come get you in the morning. You don't understand, Rasheed. For some reason you are a big prize for them. Trust me, neither they nor anyone else understands why. They just know they have to take you out. They could walk into my place, walk right by me without even noticing me to get to you. I'd be safe because I'm not the target, you are. You can hide here," she said.

I thought about it for a while and still thought it wasn't worth the risk. She must indeed be on my side, but still, I didn't want to be there if they came in with guns blazing. Another death would be on my hands if an innocent lady was killed.

"I'm still not going to come to your place. First, I don't even know where it is. Even if I did and they're after me, I wouldn't put you at risk. I'm going to a safe place for the night and I'll call you tomorrow," I said and quickly placed the receiver on the cradle.

It gave me a good feeling that she was concerned for my safety, but I'd figure something out even if I have to live in hiding until the threat goes away.

I hurried back to the dumpster and jumped in. Just as I was closing the lid, headlights flashed as a car turned into the alley. Quickly I lowered the lid, ducked down, listened carefully to the car stop and four doors open and slam shut.

I was fortunate to find this dumpster behind the Payless Shoe store. In that first one, I would have had to deal with mashed potatoes, coffee grounds, onions, and decaying cabbage. The empty shoeboxes allowed me to dig down through and cover myself. As I finished pulling the boxes over myself, I heard the lid of the dumpster open, and the dull beam of a flashlight began poking around inside.

"Stick it around in here," someone sounding like Jimmy said. I worried if the "it" would be that long sword I'd seen in White Eye's waistband.

Even though I wanted to jump and run, I held perfectly still as the poking began. I tensed in anticipation of the shiny blade savagely slicing through me. The first stab was just to my left, and each thrust came closer and closer. One came within inches of my left arm. I wondered if whoever was stabbing was doing it recklessly or methodically moving inch by inch across the dumpster. If that was the case, I was in trouble. As he stuck again, the blade missed my torso but ran along my right arm. I wanted to scream and had to fight its drive to escape my lungs. I held it back with all my strength.

The shoebox assaulting continued down to the end of the dumpster and the lid finally squeaked close. After waiting several minutes, the car doors slammed closed and the engine started. I worried that one of them might have stayed behind. Slowly, I opened the lid and scanned the area but found it empty. Finally, I released the pent-up scream but I muffled it through my nostrils rather than my vocal cords.

There was a warm trickle of blood dripping from my elbow. In the darkness, I removed my shirt and wrapped it around my arm to stop the bleeding. Exhausted from fear and holding my breath for what seemed hours, I laid my head back on a shoebox and slowly let the darkness enter my mind.

My internal alarm clock told me it must be morning. I pressed open the lid just an inch and saw the daylight. Through the bright glow, I saw the profile of a figure staring at me. Holding up my arm to shield the dagger thrust I was sure was coming from White Eye, the arm blocked the sun. What a relief it was to see not White Eye, but Mary.

"I was so worried about you, Rasheed. Are you okay?"

"Yes. What are you doing here?" I asked.

"I told you I know all the hiding places south of Market. Now tell me, are you okay?" she persisted.

"Do I still have my right arm?" I asked.

"What? Yes, of course." Then she noticed the red shirt wrapped around the arm. "My God. What happened?"

"You know how some people sometimes cut themselves shaving?

"Huh?"

"Whoever did this was a really crappy barber," I said.

"Stop playing around, Rasheed. Tell me what happened," Mary said.

"I was hiding in here and saw a car pull up so I dug deeper into the boxes. Then someone began stabbing around in here and cut me."

"Was it them?"

"Yes. I think so," I told her.

"Let's get you out of here. We need to take care of that wound. They're sure not following you now and you'll be safe with me. I've seen this too many times, Rasheed. I'm not a target, you are. Now don't argue with me," she said, pulling me by the left arm.

Mary lived in an apartment just a little larger than the one Jimmy loaned me. Hers was above some stores just off Market. After climbing the stairs and going inside, she opened a partial first aid kit, poured some red iodine over the wound. The liquid caused an electric shot of pain that I easily handled. Looking into my eyes for any sign of discomfort, she immediately placed a few four by four gauze pads on the wound and wrapped it with a rolled-up bandage.

"I hope it heals okay. You should probably have stitches," she said.

"It'll be okay. Thanks for everything you've done, Mary."

She took my shirt, rinsed it in cold water then let it soak in a bowl of sprinkled-on Tide. She pulled out the other chair at the table and sat across from me.

"You're safe now, for a while anyway," she said.

"What did you mean that I was someone special and that's why they're after me? You sounded like everyone knew what was happening," I asked.

"That group where we met the other night was for people who hear voices," Mary said.

"Yes, I knew that, but what do you mean I'm targeted?" I asked.

"One of the Buddhist monks has been keeping notes on these meetings over many years and they suggest that for some reason, people are given instructions to kill. It could be a message that went out to one person or several. Do you remember what happened to Harvey Milk?" she asked.

"Was that last year?" I asked.

"That's right. Anyway, he was someone who was 'targeted.' Several of the group got that message, and one of them, an infrequent attendee, was the one who deleted him," Mary told him.

"But how do you know I'm targeted? Did someone tell you?" I queried.

"Because I'm one of those in the group getting the message to delete you," she said as casually as asking if I'd have one lump or two.

"You hear a voice?" I stupidly asked.

"Of course. I told you that before, and why do you think I was at that meeting?"

154

"That's right. Guess it just slipped my mind with all of this stuff happening. Wait! Did you get a message to delete me? Is that what you said? What the hell does delete mean?"

"It's the same thing as kill you. Yes, I got that message from my voice," Mary said, straightening the tablecloth.

"You don't have a great big knife and a blank white eye, do you?"

"Rasheed, this is serious, so don't kid around. I get those messages every once in a while and just ignore them, so don't worry about me. I'm your new guardian angel, so let's put our heads together and develop a plan."

"What do you think I should do?"

"You need to go into hiding for a while. Maybe even go back to where you came from and stay away from here," Mary suggested.

"I can't do that."

"Why not?"

"I can't tell you. I don't want you to get involved," I told her.

"Okay. I won't press you on that. Wait. Are you from Portland, Oregon?"

My skin jumped when she asked that question. I didn't want to lie, but I also didn't want her to know what happened in Portland.

"I'm from Reno," I lied.

She looked at me, puzzled in one of those 'I don't believe you' looks a mother might have.

"Okay, then tell me what is Reno's nickname?"

I just stared at her, saying nothing. I had no idea what the nickname of any city, except Portland, was the "City of Roses."

"You don't need to lie to me, Rasheed. I have a feeling I know you, and I can't understand why. Were you in San Francisco sometime in the past?" she asked.

"I think so, when I was very young I was here, yes," I said.

"How long ago was that?" Mary asked.

"I think it was about eighteen years ago, but my dad took me up to Oregon," I told her.

"Your dad? Did you have a mother, too?" she asked.

"No. Dad told me there was a woman who was kind of a mother, but she didn't go with us to Oregon for some reason. He didn't say why."

Mary looked at me strangely. She had a puzzled look on her face, nervously rubbing the side of her face. She stood and walked over to the window looking out on 5th Street. Finally, she turned and came back to the table.

"I've been here in San Francisco for about twenty years, and I knew a man, another street person like me, who had abducted a baby boy named Billy," she said.

My heart skipped a beat... no two beats, and I had to gasp for some air after most of it exploded out of my lungs.

"My first name was Billy," I said.

"Billy Ruben?" she asked.

"I think so, yes."

"Oh my God, Billy, I mean Rasheed. You're the Billy I helped Wallace care for before he left for Oregon," Mary said. She came around the table and gave me the biggest, warmest hug I'd ever received.

THE STREETS

Pavement cold and hard and wet,
Running now with fear and scorn.
Knowing now a man he'd meet,
Knew just why his soul was born.

Mary received the same kill message as the other hunters. The difference was she had learned how to ignore them. When she told me, it gave me more confidence she was on my side. If she was the enemy, I'd be dead now. Another thing that was comforting was that she helped me decide that I needed to become invisible by either leaving town or going into hiding by blending into the city fiber.

"Maybe I should go further south, maybe L.A.," I suggested.

"If you do, the hearers there will get the same message I did and you won't know who is after you. At least here you know who they are and in what part of the city they live and hang out," Mary suggested.

She was right. Leaving town could be more dangerous. Here in San Francisco, I know who's after me and I have a confidante in Mary. My safest bet was to disappear into the city, keep a watchful eye for those I know are after me. Maybe after a time, things would settle down. And as it turned out after in a couple of weeks they did.

I'd become a scraggly looking man with my youth hidden by my full beard. I wore tattered clothes, mostly because that's all I had. It was like a disguise allowing me to openly wander the streets of San Francisco. I toted a rolled-up blanket along with my thin cardboard mattress and pushed a Safeway shopping cart and begged for money, just like the others.

For weeks I never spent the night in the same place, moving from place to place like a cat. I figured being obvious but disguised, the chasers may see me but they wouldn't recognize me. I'd just be one homeless person in a crowd of hundreds. Nobody pays much attention to someone holding out a cup or a coffee can.

I felt safe enough to approach Mary once in a while, but not to such an extreme I'd become obvious. In those casual meetings, she'd update me on the voice's messages about deleting me. Things seemed to be settling down and she wasn't sure why. She just advised me to continue living the way I was.

After a few weeks with no warnings, I decided just to make a seldom-used theater exit my home. It provided some semblance of security, and the small crack below the metal doors leaked a hint of heat and an aura of warmth on the chilly San Francisco evenings. Toward the street, my Safeway shopping cart served as a partial wall and helped shield me from passersby's prying eyes.

Laying in my lair one night, I rolled over thinking back on how Mary took care of me. She'd been on the streets for years. She taught me and made me feel I'd earned a master's degree in street wisdom. I was more worried about other street people who might be more envious of my prized cart than the chasers. I became almost possessed in protecting that cart.

To prevent it from being stolen, I rigged up a security system consisting of some Home Depot plastic twine tied to the cart and secured to my wrist. Doing that would serve two functions. First, a homeless burglar alarm so ingenious I wondered if some home security company would buy it. Beyond security, the cart across the doorway provided a little privacy by blocking off the entrance to my makeshift bedroom.

Mary was taking college classes, so I didn't see her very often, but I knew where to find her during the day if I needed her. She hung at a public place where financial gifts were rewarding. If I came there after dark, she would have disappeared to her South of Market room, preventing the potential of attack and robbery, something she'd experienced before. I came to that area also to panhandle, avoiding Chinatown where Jimmy and White Eye lived. Hopefully, after all this time, their voice had given them another target.

If I wanted to meet Mary, I'd meet her in that area where Powell Street met Market Street in the mornings when she didn't have classes. She'd tell me about school, check to see how I was doing for food. She'd tell me if she'd received any messages to delete, that word for killing me, like she'd received about other targets. Because she'd received other targets and nothing about me, she felt the mark on me had been dropped.

One morning she asked, "Rasheed, have you considered moving on with your life? Take it in a different direction and overcome the urgings you're getting from the voices we hear?" Mary asked.

"I guess so, but I have no idea if I could go back to school or if I could focus on a subject," I said.

"I'll show you how. The college can provide some help too," she said.

"I'm not sure I'd like it or even fit in," I told her.

"Would you like to come to a meeting with me?" Mary asked.

"I don't know. Why would I do that?" I asked.

"Maybe it will pique your interest and you'll want more. Why don't you come with me to a study lab I go to and meet one of the instructors at State. I think you'd find it interesting," she said.

"What class is it?" I asked

"World Religions," Mary told me.

"Religion? I'm not sure. I've had plenty of religion and sure don't want any more."

"It's not a religious class. It's a study and discussion about all the religions of the world, not some sort of particular theological indoctrination or preaching. It's just a discussion. Maybe you'll learn something and get your worries tucked away. If you do that, maybe you can move on with your life," she said.

I thought about it for a minute then wondered why not? I didn't have anything better to do. Besides, I enjoyed Mary, and she might be right. It sure couldn't hurt.

"Sure. Why not? I'll go along with you if that's okay," I told her.

"We'll do it Thursday so you'll need to get cleaned up before that, okay?

"Yes, I know a thrift shop a few blocks away where I can get something clean and I know where I can bathe. I'll be ready," I told her.

"Good. Let's meet here Thursday," Mary said. We nodded in agreement, and I headed back to the theatre.

THE QUANTUM

The world is round, or 'tis it flat?
Filled with matter, and all of that?
Was it made, in days of seven?
From up above,
that place called heaven?

Beams of sunlight poked through the low-hanging clouds scattered along the hills in the East Bay. I rolled over, stretched, and then stood scratching my now oily head. With another night of no warnings or messages, I had a good night's sleep. It had been several weeks without any alerts. I was beginning to feel a little more comfortable and looked forward to going to school with Mary, but I'd need to clean up first. Rolling up my blanket and carefully folding my cardboard mattress, I placed it all in the Safeway shopping cart. Grabbing my corduroy jacket from an old lamp hanging in the doorway, I thrust my arms through the sleeves and searched into the pockets for any coins or folding money. Inside the breast pocket, I felt something papery and looked down at a picture of Abe Lincoln.

"Thanks, Abe. You'll be buying me breakfast."

With excellent advice from Mary, I decided to continue laying low and out of sight as much as possible. Once Mary was my kinda mother. Now she was my best friend and my closest ally in the world. She was smart and the courage to change her life from her days of drugs impressed me. She was the guiding angel I needed and the spirit that kept me going. Still, I couldn't count on her for everything and needed to fend for myself.

Ensuring everything was secure in my cart, I slipped into the hotel's back door, washed up and changed clothes and made my way to Mc Donald's. Mc Donald's wasn't unwelcoming, but you couldn't just hang around. You had to buy something. Instead of the hotel bathroom, I could use Mc Donald's but it was small and busy. The hotel was spacious with more than one stall. I looked forward to having one of their Egg McMuffins before hitting the streets to earn a living.

There was a construction dumpster sitting in front of Mc Donald's, so I parked my cart near it where I could keep watch on it as I ate. I purchased breakfast and a cup of coffee then sat at the only unoccupied table near the door. I removed my jacket, slid in, and unwrapped my McMuffin. Just as I took a bite, someone approached asking, "Is this seat taken?"

I looked up and saw an unshaven, droopy bloodshot-eyed man in wrinkled clothes standing beside me. His shirt and pants were as crinkled as a popcorn kernel, and his shoes, once expensive wingtip Florsheims, were now scuffed and laceless. I couldn't detect any unpleasant body odor but had I not just washed up, my own would have canceled out the stranger's. There was a hint of alcohol that seemed to seep out of his pores like the morning dew off a hot dung pile.

I'd never seen the man before, but then again, I didn't know all the homeless in the city since I tended to keep to myself. I avoided associations with those who were winos or lying about being Vietnam vets. But, still, I had a fondness for anyone on the streets.

There weren't any other tables vacant and there was a chair across from me, so I offered it to him.

"You can sit there if you'd like," I said, pointing across my table.

"Thanks, friend," the man said as he sat.

"You know the difference between a wino and an alcoholic dontcha?" Then, without waiting for me to answer added, "Winos don't have to attend all those damn meetings," he said, coughing and laughing.

I wasn't sure if he needed an emergency room or a sip of whatever was wrapped in that brown paper bag to help him stop the coughing.

Because of this new guy's smell, I assumed he too was a wino but didn't see the harm in letting him sit down and eat. I wouldn't have to be best friends and maybe he'd even have some amusing stories.

"My name's Walter," the man said, sticking out his grungy hand.

I'd just washed my hands, so just waved and said, "Glad to meet you," without offering mine.

"You work this corner?" Walter said.

"Sometimes. You?"

"No. I'm kind of new here. I had some money saved up so don't have to panhandle much. I've been over in Berkeley for the past few years finding places to sleep. Used to work at the University until hard times fell on me. Couldn't get myself to leave."

We talked about life on the streets, where to best panhandle, where to get free meals, places to avoid, places to rest during the day, things that all new homeless people need to know about a new city. One of the things I wouldn't discuss was where the best place to get cans, my primary source of income. I was beginning to like Walter. He was easy to talk to, a non-assuming guy. He seemed genuinely interested in me and spoke little about himself, so I was enjoying the conversation over breakfast. After he told me he'd worked at the University of California in Berkeley, I wasn't sure what kind of work they offered at a school. I assumed he was probably in some low paying position.

"What did you do at Cal?" I asked

"I was an instructor," he said

I was shocked. The guy taught at a University and was now on the street? He went on.

"The booze got to me and I couldn't handle the work. They helped me through some of those programs, but they didn't stick, so because of that, and a few other reasons, I just decided to leave. I guess I like booze more than my work," he said.

"Mind if I ask what those few other things were?" I asked.

"Not at all. I was doing some research and when I'd get to a point where I felt I was making progress, I'd get some interference," he said.

"From the school?"

"No, it was internal. Something in my brain made noises, screeching sounds, loud awful music, things like that. When I started working on the project, I thought it would take my classes into new areas and give them something to think about. As soon as I'd mention it, I'd be disrupted and couldn't continue.

"What subject did you teach, Walter?" I asked.

Walter scratched his head, looked out the window, then said, "Quantum physics."

"Wow! That sounds very interesting," I said as if I understood what it meant. I'd heard the term "physics" but didn't really understand "quantum."

"What the heck is it?" I finally asked.

"A simple explanation is that it's the science of particles."

"Particles?"

"I don't want to bore you. It's not that easy to explain."

"Just tell me what particles are. I won't be bored. Do you mean atoms?"

"Atoms and things even smaller, yes," he said.

"Smaller than atoms? I didn't know there were things smaller."

"Look into your coffee and tell me what you see," Walter said, pointing over at my insulated cup.

I looked down, pulled off the stubborn lid, and then peered inside the cup.

"Coffee," I said simply.

"But you see more than coffee, don't you. Coffee is made up of many things, isn't it?"

I looked back down into the cup, understanding now that Walter was asking me to give him all the ingredients the coffee.

"Right. I see coffee, of course, but it's diluted in the water, and there's also some cream intermingled in the cup," I reported.

"Now imagine you broke apart the coffee, the water, the cream, and looked further into one of them. Let's pick water. If you had supernatural vision and could see all the water elements, what would you see?" Walter prompted.

Thinking back to my chemistry class in high school, I said in a questioning tone, "Hydrogen and oxygen?"

"True, those two elements. What about the minerals in the water? Do you suppose there's some calcium, some iron, and maybe a little chlorine?"

"Yes, those are there too, I suppose."

"How about a touch of fluoride to satisfy the American Dental Association's campaign to prevent cavities? Could it be in there too?" Walter asked.

"I guess so, yes," I answered.

"Then, if you could break down all of those components, you'd get things even smaller, right?"

I nodded my head. "I guess…"

"You said hydrogen was in there, yes? It's the most abundant atom in the universe with just a proton and neutron, so doesn't that tell you there are things smaller than an atom?" he asked.

"Oh, now I remember. Those protons, neutrons, and electrons, right?"

"Now, wouldn't you think those are the smallest things in the universe?" he asked.

"Yes, I guess so."

"Well, there are things smaller than that. You mentioned the neutron and protons are in the middle of the atom. Those two things are called hadrons, and those hadrons are made of even smaller particles called quarks and leptons. There may be things even smaller, we just don't know. You don't have to write any of this down, there won't be a test," Walter said with a smile.

"The point I'm making is that there is coffee, but when you start going down deeper into that coffee you find things smaller, and smaller, and smaller, and smaller and maybe even smaller, we just haven't found them yet."

"So quantum physics is about those particles?" I asked.

"On a fundamental level, yes. But it also goes beyond the particles. Now the question science has, is what is in the space between all these particles? In the beginning, we didn't think there was any space between things in water. It was just water. With more advanced research, we found that there was space there, we just couldn't see it. I think the same holds for looking outward. What about the space between planets and galaxies? When we look inward, we find things get smaller and smaller. When we look outward, do they get bigger and bigger? Is our universe just the head of a needle for something larger than we can imagine? Those are questions yet to be answered, and that was something I was working on." Walter said.

"Have you heard of the term 'dark matter?'" he asked.

I nodded, acknowledging I'd heard the term.

"I was beginning to understand those things when the interruptions began happening."

"What was interrupting you?" I asked.

"I found what I thought was the answer, and there is something there... damn," he yelped.

Walter lowered his head and brought both hands up to his ears as if to shield off a high pitched noise.

"I can't talk about it. It won't let me," he said.

"What won't let you?" I asked, now concerned.

"That damn voice that drove me out of the research. It won't let me discuss the subject. Once it gets in my mind, things go all squirrely so I better just shut up and talk about something else," he said.

I took a bite of my McMuffin and sipped some coffee as Walter showed some signs of relaxing. I decided to get off the subject of dark matter. I was sure he was trying not to sound like the weird scientist the people at Berkeley may have labeled him.

"A lot of us on the street hear a voice. In fact, there are group meetings for people who hear them that are crowded. Maybe you could attend one and see if it's for you," I suggested.

"Good idea. I might just do that," Walter said.

"Have you always heard a voice?"

"No. It started happening when I discovered something,"

"What?"

Walter looked around the restaurant as if someone who might steal the world's most precious secret was listening in.

"I was on the verge of a breakthrough and knew I could prove there was something right here as large as our observable universe, but could fit right there on the end of a pinhead, but couldn't get my thoughts together with all its interference," Walter said.

"What do you mean by interference," I asked.

"A voice. I'm not crazy. It just controls things I do, and it wouldn't let me concentrate any longer. It kept insisting that I do not think along those lines and that it gave me a terrible urge for booze. When I finally drank a couple of bottles, it would stay quiet and let me sleep for a while. Of course, when I drank, I was too intoxicated to think straight. Then, when I'd wake in the morning, the voice would be right there, telling me the same thing again. The only way I can get peace in my mind is to drink. Like now, it's telling me to stop discussing this."

"Shut up!" Walter shouted, causing others to turn and look at him.

Even I looked at Walter with astonishment. The others on the street had stories about their voices, but Walter's was the most unusual story I'd heard. His voice didn't want him to discover something about the world's existence. I wondered if my voice was warning me about something I didn't understand. I would have to think this through, but this wasn't the time.

Politely, I excused myself, saying, "I know what you mean, Walter. Damn things won't shut up sometimes. I guess I better get some things done before mine starts ragging on me."

Walter also stood and we shuffled over to the trash to discard our used paper cups and other junk. As we walked out, we bantered back and forth about issues regarding the universe and things around the general subject of science. Walter was impressed that I wasn't the dunce that was the typical street person. Maybe we could carry on a conversation another time before Walter began the daily consumption of his favorite spirits.

As we walked in separate directions, Walter turned his head over his shoulder saying, "Just remember the Law of Conservation of Matter: there is no increase or decrease in matter in an isolated system. There is never any more or any less. Quantum mechanics just tries to understand why that is so."

"Shut up!" Walter yelled then quickly glanced over at me.

"Not you," he said and continued his stroll down Market Street.

Walter had definitely piqued my interest.

THE LESSON

Considering now life's darkened plight;
Thinking about it throughout the night.
Who was the one with golden might?
Are they the one who's really right?

My shopping cart was still where I parked it and not stolen like it had been so many times. I couldn't help wondering why there was static while listening to Walter. I could understand some of what he was saying, but much of it was blocked. I tried to move his discussion to the back of my mind. It was too complicated for me to grasp anyway.

I met Mary at our prearranged time at the corner of Powel and Market. It was a convenient location because across Market Street was the relatively new downtown Campus of the San Francisco State University in the Emporium. We crossed Market and inside found the room where the lab would be held. People were gathering outside the door and Mary introduced me to the ones she knew. She mentioned I was just along for the meeting and was considering going back to school. It was a relatively small group, maybe fifteen young people, made up of mostly women with a sprinkling of males just to keep things interesting I supposed.

Just before start time, a slightly older male Mary's age, maybe his thirties, came down the hall, stopped and greeted the assembly and opened the door. The group followed, walking into the room like sheep following the shepherd. We took seats around the U-shaped table as our shepherd took his place behind a small table at the opening of the U.

The buzzing in the room politely tapered off as the instructor smilingly raised his hand calling things to order.

"I see we have some new people here today, so let me introduce myself. I'm Luther Sturtevant, one of the instructors in World Religions here at San Francisco State. I'm happy to see you all here this evening. For those of you who are new, let me explain what we do at these get-togethers.

"This is the lab for my Religious Studies class that those enrolled come to for extra credit and, more importantly, extra learning. By coming to these, you'll not only learn a little more than you did in class. You'll get a little boost in your final grade. For those not enrolled, maybe we'll get you interested in my regular class and perhaps you'll sign up next semester.

"Now, let's talk about how we go about these sessions. This is a study group, not a religious gathering, so no arguing your particular belief. It's designed to help you consider and discuss some of the concepts lectured in class to help you understand the meaning. Some of you may not even be religious and you're just taking the course as one of your requirements, and that's fine. Hopefully, you'll learn something even if you are atheists or agnostics. If you are of a particular faith, you can compare your beliefs to someone else. Now let me repeat this: No matter where you come from, treat each other with respect. Remember, we seek to understand, not be understood. Do not confront or condemn others, or you'll be asked to leave. No judgments. Understood?"

He looked around the room and saw heads nodding.

Picking up a piece of chalk, he turned to the group.

"At our last meeting we outlined the number of followers of the world's religions and listed them from most followed to least. Christianity was number one with over 2.1 billion or about one-third of the world's population. It is followed by Islam with 1.5 billion, twenty-one percent of the population. Hinduism represents another 1 billion, a unique belief system in that it doesn't profess a specific founder," he said, turning his head to the group.

"The others include Buddhism, Chinese traditional indigenous beliefs, Sikhism, Judaism and a smattering of others which represent about eighteen percent of the population," he said, listing them on the blackboard.

"Then we looked at the prophets from the religions we called the Big Three," Luther said as he began listing them on the blackboard. He wrote:

Christianity: Jesus of Nazareth.

Islam: Muhammad, and spelled out his full name: Abū al-Qāsim Muḥammad ibn Abd Allāh ibn ʿAbd al-Muṭṭalib ibn Hāshim.

Buddhism: Siddhartha Gautama, who is commonly known as the Buddha or the Awaken One.

"You didn't think I could spell Muhammad's full name did you? Anyone have any bets on that?" he asked, laughing.

The group chuckled then nodded, recalling the discussion.

"Do you remember from class that we counted twenty-three prophets listed in the Holy Bible?" he asked again.

Except for me, most of the people nodded in agreement.

"The question we raised was why these people were considered prophets. We know something of their lives as reported in the Bible, Qur'an, or Tipitaka, but what about their deaths? Does anyone want to take a stab at their deaths?" he asked, pointing his chalk at the group.

"Yes?" Luther said, pointing at the young man wearing a red SFU Purple and Gold tee shirt.

"I did some checking this week of the Big Three, as we've called them, and learned they were all either murdered or died a mysterious death. Is that what you mean?" the young student asked.

"Good. Yes, that is exactly what I mean. Not just famous ones, but what about some of the other prophets mentioned in the Bible? How many of them died of old age, and how many were slain? Anyone know?" Luther asked.

Hearing no answer, he replied, "We can't be exactly sure, but about half is a good guess. For the ones who lived, if their death wasn't attributed to someone killing them, only three or four were reported as dying of old age. My namesake, Luther, was one who died at the not-so-old age of sixty-two, but for others, we don't know. I guess you might say that being a prophet in the old days was dangerous work," Luther told the group.

He looked around the room at the students who now had their eyes glued on the blackboard, then glanced down and scribbled some notes. Mary whispered to me that they'd talked about various things in religions: the concept of the hereafter, heaven, hell, and everything in between, but they'd never discussed the prophets from this perspective.

"Let's go back and look at their lives and ask ourselves what made these people considered prophets or carriers of the word of God? Was it because they heard God's voice? If they did, why wouldn't everyone else hear it too?" he proposed.

"Most likely they heard it internally, I'd guess," someone offered.

That comment got my attention. I didn't know prophets heard voices. It was always simply that they'd heard the voice of God. I was taught Muhammad heard a voice from the sky saying he was the messenger of God. They never said it was a voice like mine. I was also taught that God gave Moses the Ten Commandments; it wasn't just some obscure voice like the voice I heard. I'd never considered that the voice I hear was God's, but what was it? The thought of it being God was ludicrous since it had never told me to prophesy anything to anyone or even reveal anything it said.

These discussions made me wonder again, something I'd done many times before, why was this voice in my head?

"Just look along Market Street here and you'll see many people who would report hearing voices. Are they hearing the voice of God?" Luther asked.

Why did he ask that question?

I began to feel exposed, wondering if there was some flashing light over my head blinking on and off spelling out, "Looney Tune."

"No. Most of them are mentally ill," one of the girls said.

I cringed.

"Really?" Luther asked. "How can we be sure? Maybe someone simply said they were mentally ill because they couldn't explain it or weren't very good at relating what they heard. Maybe the ones considered prophets were simply more persuasive orators. What do you think? Makes you wonder, doesn't it?" Luther asked the group.

I sat there in silence, but more attuned to the subject than I ever thought I would be. My exposure to Islam came from two directions; the Iman and Jafar. It was a peace and hell confrontation.

"All of the religions we've studied had leaders we might call prophets and people considered them divine in some way. Just to follow what we were discussing about how they died, what's interesting is that the prophets, the Big Three, as we've said, met their deaths early. They came at the hands of someone else," he said then turned back to the chalkboard. He pointed to the listing of the prophets.

"Okay…Jesus…how did he die?"

"Hung on the Cross," everyone said almost in unison.

"Muhammad, founder of Islam, how did he die?"

The class looked around at each other, and after some time when nobody had raised their hand to answer, Luther spoke up.

"It is conjectured by some Islamic scholars that he was poisoned by his two wives," Luther said.

"Really?" someone asked.

Luther walked over to the folder he'd laid on the table and pulled out a piece of paper.

"Let me read this. A famous scholar from the Bakri sect reported that Abdullah Ibn Massoud, a companion of Muhammad, said, 'I am willing to take an oath nine times that the Prophet was murdered, but I am not willing to take an oath even once that he was not. This is because Allah made him a prophet and a martyr as well.'"

"Gives us pause to think, doesn't it? Those two major prophets were executed or murdered."

"What about the third, Buddha? He had a great following and died right after a meal that some consider was contaminated or included poison mushrooms making some wonder if he too was murdered," he told them.

"Remember we talked about what we called major and minor prophets? Everyone knows or has heard about John the Baptist. I guess we'd consider him major since he is reported as baptizing Christ and was someone Christ followed. He's mentioned in the Canonical gospels and the Qur'an, which would seem to comply with being a major figure in the history of faiths. Well, how did he die?" he asked the group.

A small dark short-haired girl raised her hand, and Luther pointed at her.

"I think he was beheaded by Herod," she answered.

"Correct. The Jewish historian Flavius Josephus also relates in his Antiquities of the Jews that Herod killed John stating that he did so, 'lest the great influence John had over the people might put it into his power and inclination to raise a rebellion'," Luther said reading from a piece of paper on his desk.

"Herod was obviously concerned that he could be overthrown by the followers of John the Baptist so had him done away with," Luther told the group.

"Let's look at something more recent. What about a modern-day prophet, Joseph Smith, founder of the Church of Latter Day Saints; how did he die?" he asked.

Obviously, there were no Mormons in the room or they would have had the answer.

"It was at the hands of a mob," Luther announced. "So he too was murdered just like the others."

"So if we classify prophets, can we conclude that if they were prophets that obtained a significant following, they were murdered? Can anyone take a stab at why?" he asked.

There was a silence in the class as people considered the question. Finally, someone raised their hand and Luther pointed at them.

"Because someone saw them as a threat?" the student replied.

"Good. And why do you think they thought of them as a threat?"

"Maybe because they had followers and those followers were leaving their fold?" someone suggested.

Luther laid his white chalk down, wiped the chalk off his hands, and turned to the room.

"I don't know. Nobody knows, do they? Interestingly, so many of these prophets had their lives taken by other human beings simply because they had a following or a philosophy that might generate the interest of others," Luther said, pointing back at the names he'd written on the blackboard.

"Now those are some of the major prophets in history. Any others we should consider?" he asked.

"Zarquon," someone offered, referring to a prophet in *Hitchhikers Guide to the Galaxy*.

"Very funny. We're talking in the context of religion, folks. Anyone want to add another?"

When there was no response, Luther asked, "Then could we say a prophet would be anyone who others believe has supernatural powers and is delivering a message to us ordinary humans? Do you suppose these prophets are actually hearing the divine, hearing God, or something paranormal?" Luther again asked the group.

"Probably some of them are fake and some sincere," someone said.

"Yes, that's true, of course. Many cultures have had claims of prophets that have said they heard things inside their heads, and these voices guided them and asked them to guide other people. Some were followed, some weren't. The point I made earlier was that those who attained a significant following were often murdered or died young. Is there a causal relationship between their power to gain followers and their early deaths? Why could they do that?" he asked.

"Well, that depends on whether or not they're cute," a dark-haired girl directly across from Mary said, generating a good laugh by everyone.

"Maybe not cute, but they'd have to be someone who attracts your attention, right? None of these prophets can prove the message they relay is directly from a deity, the devil, libis, or someone supernatural or is worshiped by visitors to 'The Restaurant at the End of the Universe,'" Luther said looking over at the short haired boy who'd mentioned the name Zarquon.

He then added, "I know a little about *Hitchhikers Guide to the Galaxy.*"

The discussion went on for most of the meeting with people providing their perspective of prophets. I sat silently considering everything that was discussed. I had questions, many of them, but didn't offer anything. I couldn't help thinking how these prophets had voices in their head, just like I did. Were their voices like mine and like Mary's and like the others' I knew on the street? I hadn't thought about that before, but Luther's discussion about their deaths and the incident with Jimmy and Jafar gave me pause to reconsider this voice I carried.

Why was this voice coming to me and where was it from? Was I being prepared for something? So far, the voice hadn't told me to provide some revelation of things to come or to send people in a particular religious direction. Would it? I didn't know the answer and doubted if anyone in this room could provide one either. Besides, I wasn't even interested in discussing it or thinking about it any further.

The meeting was adjourned after forty-five minutes, just as Mary had promised. We walked across the street to her favorite Pizza place, "1702," a little place down a block from the meeting at, ironically, 1702 Market Street. We grabbed a booth and ordered a small pizza and two beers. Budweisers. Not those trendy strange dark beers so many of the kids drank.

"What did you think?" Mary finally asked.

"About the meeting? It was interesting. Gives you pause to think about some things, doesn't it?" I replied.

We chitchatted back and forth about the people at the meeting, Mr. Sturtevant and that gabby dark-haired girl who kept asking stupid questions. I didn't want to let on how troubled I felt about the voices, even to my best friend, but I wanted her perspective.

When the beers arrived, I took a sip and asked, "What did you think about prophets and hearing voices?"

"I'd always considered Jesus was the only Prophet, or at least the only one I ever thought about. But when you think about it, the Bible talks about many prophets, doesn't it? The most obvious one I hadn't considered was Moses. Heck, God gave him the Ten Commandments," Mary said as if wondering out loud.

"I guess that's what the Bible says, and if you have the faith you believe it too. But if you disregard your faith in what they call 'the word of God,' how do we know it was God Moses heard? Maybe he just heard a voice in his head and it wasn't God at all. Maybe he just had a good idea on ten things we should live by and told everyone it was God who gave them to him so they'd accept them," I said.

Setting my mug down on the paper coaster, I looked closely at Mary saying, "Do you think anyone who hears voices is hearing the voice of God?"

Mary thought for a minute then finally said, "I don't know. Never gave that much thought. I just believe in the word of Jesus Christ and that's what it says in the Bible. I don't think what I've heard is the word of God."

"I'm not sure about that either," I said.

"About what?"

"The word of Jesus Christ."

"What? You're not a Christian?"

"Nah. You knew that, didn't you? I was being raised as a Muslim."

"Yes, of course. I forgot. You only have one prophet to keep track of unlike we Christians," she laughed.

We were hungrier than we thought as we gobbled down pieces of pizza and gabbed about things happening on the streets. We hardly noticed people coming and going when Luther walked up to the table.

"Hi, folks. How are you doing this evening?"

"Oh! Hi, Luther," Mary said, lowering her slice of pizza. "This is my dear friend Rasheed, Luther. He came along with me to the lab this evening."

"Yes, I remember you there, Rasheed. Nice to meet you.

"Nice to meet you, too, Mr. Sturtevant," I said.

"Just call me Luther, please," Luther said.

"Luther, pull up a chair. We were just talking about some things from your lab, but we can change the subject if you would rather talk Giants!" Mary said.

"I don't want to impose. I just wanted to say hello," Luther said.

"You're not imposing at all. We're inviting you; right, Mary?" I said then looked across at Mary's eyes to make sure she wasn't giving me that evil-eye look she had when there was something she didn't like.

"Please. Sit with us, Luther. It's fun to talk with instructors outside of the classroom. I can get some further education for no extra price!" Mary said.

Luther smiled and reached for the cane-backed chair near another booth and slid it up. Before he sat down, he motioned over to the waiter holding up three fingers.

"Have a piece of pizza, Luther," Mary offered. "We always order more than we can eat anyway and I hate pizza for breakfast."

Luther smiled, sat down, threw his elbows up on the table, and then rested his chin on his upright hands.

"You folks had some interesting conversations this afternoon. I enjoyed the input from everyone," Luther commented.

"Yes. We were just expanding on some of the thoughts as you came in. When you discuss religion from an unbiased and pragmatic point of view, it opens your mind. That discussion about the major figures in religion was fascinating," I said.

"Yes. What's your take on why those prophets got a following?" Luther asked.

"Charisma?" I offered.

"I'd agree, but that sure isn't to discredit or challenge anyone's faith. Who knows that a particular belief may be exactly right. But from a historic, theosophy, and practical view, charisma, charm, personality, presence, magnetism, appeal, may have drawn people to them. I'm sure if you're a Catholic, you may believe Muhammad had those traits rather than being given anything from God. And, on the other hand, if you're Muslim, you may perceive Jesus as just some charismatic Jew.

"Theosophy? I hope that wasn't on the test because I'm not familiar with the term," Mary said.

"No, it wasn't. Theosophy isn't a religion. The theosophist seeks to understand the mysteries of the universe and what bonds it with humanity and a deity. They consider that the universe and everything in it are expressions of the ultimate reality, not creations out of nothing by a personal creator. They try to blend religion and science and consider that everything is evolving with more and more knowledge. Therefore, religion cannot be static," he told us.

"But that's a whole different subject and one that probably could be an entire course in itself."

There was a pause in the discussion as they enjoyed more pizza and beer. The topic switched to the politics that were going on around campus and The City, the Giants and 49ers, and sports in general then got back to Luther's class.

Luther set his empty pint on the table, wiped the foam from his upper lip, and held up the same three fingers to the waiter who walked by. Feeling in a festive mood, he laughed and told us, "Our conversation here reminds me of something George Carlin said about religion."

"What was that?" Mary asked.

"Let me see if I can find it in my backpack. I always goof up good comedy by trying to remember things," Luther said.

He pulled up his backpack. Digging through some of the files he was carrying, he came up with nothing.

"Darn. I must have left that file on my desk," he said.

"Go ahead, Luther. Just tell us what it was, and we'll laugh even if you don't deliver it like Carlin," Mary laughed.

"Well, it was something like this: He was saying he didn't believe in religion or God. He'd tried, but he saw too many things wrong. War, disease, poverty, torture, crime, corruption, tornados, earthquakes, and the Ice Capades," Luther said, trying to hold back a laugh.

I looked at Mary with a blank expression.

"It's a dance on ice skates, Rasheed," Mary said.

"But anyway, Carlin went on to say that God's work was not so good and that his work shouldn't be on a 'Supreme beings' résumé. If it was, he'd never get the next job.

"Then Carlin said he knows God was a 'he' because no woman would screw things up this bad," Luther laughed.

"You talk about this in your lectures?" I asked.

"Yes. I don't want to get bogged down into debating faiths during a large class, so I often interject some of Carlin's humor to lighten things up. Some people get offended, but my classroom isn't a church, mosque, or synagogue.

"That reminds me of something, Luther. We were talking a while back and discovered that Christians and Muslims had the same thoughts about what happens when we die, but that's not true in Hinduism, is it?" Mary asked.

"What do you think, Mary?" Luther asked.

"I'm not sure. I'm still a believer that we get to Heaven through Jesus Christ. I guess I'm just programmed that way."

"Remember in past labs we've discussed reincarnation. As a Christian, you can't believe in reincarnation, can you? You can't believe we come back in a different form or as a different person," Luther said.

"Isn't that a Hindu belief? Reincarnation, I mean," Mary asked.

"Yes, and there's also some similarity in the Jewish belief system. It's something about a Jewish tradition written in the Zohar. I don't remember the exact quotation, but it goes something like this: 'as long as a person is unsuccessful in his purpose in the world, God replants him over and over again,'" Luther said.

"Who knows? It's all about what you believe, and there's no way to prove what is right or wrong because proof requires logic and logic won't convince anyone to change a belief," I surmised.

"Are you college age? You're drinking a beer, so you must be," Luther said.

"He's close," Mary answered for me.

Luther looked at me, puzzled. I was sure I looked older than my age from merely living on the streets.

Luther went on talking about student comments in class, telling us some funny stories without mentioning any names. Then he went to something else relating back to our subject about prophets.

"I've had students tell me they have a true belief that "X" profit is right and I can't agree or disagree with them. That's their belief," Luther said.

"True belief? Isn't that an oxymoron?" Mary wondered.

We all laughed out loud, causing us to lightheartedly click our beer glasses.

"Amen to that," Luther said, perhaps realizing he was using one of the few agreed-upon terms between Islam, Christianity, and Judaism.

"So when you depart this earth, Luther, who will officiate over your funeral? A Priest, Minister, Imam, or a Rabbi?" Mary asked.

Luther laughed. He took a sip from the new mug the waiter placed in front of him. He sat the chilled mug down and looked at us.

"Here's what I'd do, even though I haven't worked out all the details. Just to be safe, I'd have all of them. A Priest, a Minister, a Rabbi, an Imam, a Bihikku for the Buddha, maybe the Dali Lama, a Swami, and of course, Mary Baker Eddy," Luther told them.

"Mary Baker Eddy? Isn't she the founder of Christian Science, the people that don't believe in doctors?" Mary asked.

"That's a misconception about those who follow that religion. It's not that they don't believe in doctors. They don't believe in sickness and there's a difference. Like most other Christians, they believe we were made in the image and likeness of God, right?" Luther asked.

"Yes, of course," Mary responded.

"So, since Christians all agree God is spiritual and we're made in his likeness we too must also be spiritual and our body is just a physical copy of the real us. I'm not sure what she was thinking, but maybe she assumes the real us is in heaven. This thing we live in is just an avatar. Anyway, that's the general idea," he said.

"Interesting, I'd never thought about that," Mary said. "What's an avatar? I've never heard that term."

"Generally speaking, an avatar is the personification of a person or idea. I like to throw around words nobody knows. It makes me seem smart," Luther laughed.

"Another thing that interests me is that the Bible says in Genesis 1:26 , 'Let us make man in our image, in our likeness,' Luther quoted.

"Does the word 'our' suggest more than one creator? Do we all have our own God? Is that what you mean?" I asked.

"Who knows? You could be right, but only the one up there really knows," Luther said pointing his mug toward the sky.

"Don't you mean the ones up there?" Mary asked laughing.

THE ENCOUNTER

We're here when they clap,
We're here when they yell.
Is this our heaven?
Or is it hell?

Mark Gorman left his office and walked down to the cafeteria with its clatter of metal serving trays and the constant growling of guys and the squeals of freshman girls. The noise made concentration difficult, hampering progress for the project. Then there was the constant interruption of friends coming over to talk to Sue or students asking Mark questions. Since Duncan had few friends, it wasn't a disruption to him. Still, they decided meeting somewhere with fewer distractions and less noise was a good idea. The school library was out because that required silence, so talking out their ideas would be challenging. Sue was in a dorm and Duncan lived with his parents so their places wouldn't work. Sue knew Mark had an apartment so suggested his place. Mark flinched at the suggestion. It was big enough, but it was a typical male cave. No drapes, no lace, no vacuum cleaner, just a broom and a worn-out sponge for cleaning spills. Bright red beer cans were the only accent color in the pale interior.

"I'm not so sure that's a good idea," Mark said.

"Why not? You told us you didn't have a roommate," Sue said.

"I'm not sure my place is ready for company. I hate to admit it, but I'm not the best housekeeper," Mark said.

"We'll help you clean it up," Sue said.

"No. That's okay. I'll get to work on it this afternoon and we can meet there tomorrow," Mark said.

After their meeting, Mark headed directly to his apartment to assess what he needed to do to make the place presentable. The front door fed into the apartment's main living space where one corner seemed to be the catch-all for various sports equipment, including a football, golf clubs, baseball mitt, tennis racket, along with a pile of dirty sport shoes. A 3D receiver perpetually playing the Sports Channel was the only piece of wall décor. It hung on a wall's dirty muted green paint splashed on years ago and now sagged like the sun-damaged skin of a 70-year-old stripper.

His front room furniture consisted of two small, unmatched couches, one plaid and the other with a tropical flower pattern. He'd found them on the sidewalk with a "free" sign taped to them. Additionally, he placed between them a makeshift coffee table made from a dirty piece of plywood screwed securely to twin empty beer kegs. On one side table, a naked nymph lamp sporting a lampshade with a brown stain from a too close light bulb, was decorated with more naked women dancing and prancing around it in merry-go-round fashion.

Pondering the thought of having such a beautiful and fastidious young woman visit caused his mind to flip back to the scolding from his mother about keeping his room clean.

"You never know when someone you like might want to come over," she'd told him. "And always make sure you have on clean underwear when you go out in case you have to go to the hospital," was another warning. The hospital he went to after his war injury didn't count. In battle, soldiers often were in situations where changing anything except ammunition was impractical.

Now that he was in a civilian world, he always wore clean underwear just in case. Keeping the house was a different story. He knew from his military boot camp days how orderly things should be, neither that nor his mother made the clean room policy stick. Even though he dreaded it, he drew a bucket of soapy water, rolled up his sleeves and started on the kitchen floor. Just as he got down on his knees, there was a knock at the door.

Mark opened it and standing there in the moonlight was the girl with golden hair. She'd pulled it back into a ponytail and was wearing a too-big sweatshirt, jeans, and athletic shoes along with the bulky iBoard bag on her back.

"Sue? What are you doing here?" he asked.

"You said you needed to clean up, so I came here to help," she said, pushing her way inside.

"Yeah, sure, but I needed a while to clean it up myself. The place is a bit of a mess," he muttered glancing around behind her.

"Geez. Did you bring Duncan too?"

"No. Duncan hardly cleans his iBoard after he's splattered it with cereal and milk. It seems always to have the dried remnants of his lunch on the keyboard. We don't have time for you to spend cleaning your place yourself, Mark. And Duncan would just be in the way. We need to stay on track if we're to get this Findit project done in time. That, or talk about winning that V-World game," she said.

"But, but..." Mark started to say.

"Don't worry. I have a brother whose room looks like a trash can at the stadium after a big game, so I can't be shocked by a single guy's mess. Let's get it done tonight so we can focus on what Duncan is bringing tomorrow.

"Remember? He said he had something he is sure can help crack a grid game. Stop being a guy and just let me help you get ready for tomorrow," Sue said.

Mark relented and let her in. Together they picked up his dirty clothes, leftover take-out containers, and a few beer cans from the night before. When they'd finished cleaning the bedroom, even changing the sheets and pillowcases, the bathroom, living area, and finally the kitchen, Mark asked if she'd like something to drink.

"Sure. Thanks. I'll have whatever you're having," she said.

Mark opened the refrigerator, pulled out two cool ones, and opened them. He watched Sue sway her way into the living area to sit down. He couldn't help noticing the tightness of the jeans and the curvature of her slender body. Instead of sitting on one of the unmatched stained couches, she tip-toed over to one of the wooden chairs, swiped the seat with her fingers, and sat. She wasn't a neat-nick, but she did practice self-preservation.

Mark could see the look in her eyes as she scanned the place like a sergeant after a work detail. When she finally looked at him and smiled, he knew their cleanup job must have been pretty good.

"That wasn't half bad," she said

She peeled off her rubber gloves and wiped the itch on her forehead with the back of her arm.

"The place is normally a little neater. I just got behind as midterms were approaching, but I really appreciate your offer to help. Besides, it's nice to be able to spend some time talking with just you."

Sue smiled both inside and out.

While romantic things sailed peacefully through his mind, he moved the conversation to business. He wanted to know more about Forrest Labs and V-World. Maybe without Duncan there, Sue would be less hesitant to reveal what she knew. They all agreed completing the FindIt program was going to take more time. That big idea may not be achievable in time.

"So what are your thoughts on the program, Sue? Can we get it finished in time?" Mark asked.

"If we dropped all classes and worked through the night for a few weeks, maybe. But I'm not sure even that would get us to where we want to be," Sue said.

"I tend to agree, but I don't want to give up on this," Mark said

"We won't give up on you, Mark. And we still have the option of V-World. Maybe what Duncan has will help," Sue said.

"Maybe. If it doesn't, I'll only be seeing everyone here when I'm on leave,"

"Didn't you hear me? I'm not giving up, Mark."

"Thanks. I'm just trying to be realistic."

"I'm not a quitter. We'll make something work,"

"Okay. You're probably right, but I want to know more about how V-World works. I what to know you see as the potential you two have discussed and anything else you can tell me," Mark said.

Mark pulled the tab off another can of beer and handed it to her.

"Sorry, I should have asked if you'd like a glass," Mark said.

"No. This is fine, thanks."

"As I told you when we first met, I've known about Forrest Labs and their work in artificial intelligence. Is what they're doing in that area highly confidential?"

"Oh, yes. I've never even seen any of the internal workings on that side. Just heard the gossip about what they've accomplished, and I know it's a key ingredient on the game side," she said.

"Have you been able to come up with anything that might help solve the riddle of winning the game? When I went in the other day, I couldn't figure much out. Actually, it was pretty boring," Mark said.

"Yes, until you understand a few things, it can be boring. Oh, by the way, I called my uncle and told him about your idea of making the avatars different colors. He liked the idea. He thought they could adjust their artificial intelligence programming to make avatars fear avatars of a different color. Just as you said, that way more fighting might take place. He commented, 'Whoever thought this one up is a marketing genius. Now only if he could program too.'" Sue said, laughing.

"What did you tell him?" Mark asked.

"I told him it was one of my instructors at school and he is a programming genius."

"And?" Mark asked.

"He said to bring him by after he's finished with school, we could use a talent like that."

"Thanks, Sue. Hope you didn't say anything about me being on a lifelong military contract."

"I didn't because I know that we'll be able to get you out of it and my uncle will surely hire you after you finish here," Sue reassured.

"If that happened, I think the government takes annual salary into consideration for the buyout. I guess we better get working on winning in that game; so would you mind just telling me what you know?" Mark said.

"I can tell you how the game works, what others have tried and failed, things like that. None of that is confidential. The policy allows employees to participate and play the game at my level; we just can't win any money. Anyway, employees don't have an advantage because the game is run by the avatars and their artificial intelligence programming. Most of the inputs are coming from those who play the game, not by anyone's actions at the lab," she said.

"Many users have blogs reporting what they've learned and how things work. I can shorten that research perhaps," she explained.

Ignoring the naked nymph lamp, Sue laid down her backpack on the table and pulled out her iBoard.

"This might help. I found some interesting technical documents published in some tech magazines. They suggest the game isn't played within a regular server. It's far more complicated than any other game on the grid," she told him.

"When I logged in, my avatar deleted someone's. That was pretty simple, but it only paid a single Forrester. It would take years to make enough money doing that."

"That's why the winners get followers, the second way to earn points. When those followers make points, the player gets them too," she said.

"Kind of like the relationship between a manufacturer, wholesaler, and retailer. When money goes to the retailer, a portion of it goes back to the manufacturer," Mark suggested.

Sue pressed a few keys that took her to the screen with her work notes. After scanning a few pages and flipping some of her inputs upside down, she finally found the spot she was looking for and began to read:

"Forrest Labs uses an inverse reactive current that operates a unilateral phase detractor automatically synchronizing antimatter relative motion conductors. Those fluxes accelerate data into the transmitter," she read.

"What the hell does that mean?" Mark asked.

"I think it means that the digital programming passes through the global grid and into their system where it is accelerated through what we term a spreader to the place where the game is being played. There is some sort of energy within that space that allows control over relative time," Sue read.

"I wonder what that means?" Mark said.

Sue didn't respond. Instead, she kept reading.

"It's not being played on hardware servers like other grid games. It's being played in a vacuum somewhere at a remote location that only a few know about. I've only heard rumors that it's underground somewhere at the company. I don't know where or how the whole thing works. The user's input comes into Forrest Lab's normal servers and then is transmitted out via a coding system that affects the program through the methodology I just read," she said.

"Go ahead, Sue. Read the rest of it," Mark asked, then added, "Want another beer?"

Mark grabbed two more beers, handed one to Sue, whose eyes were still glued to her iBoard.

She continued reading:

"The original machine had a biteplate of perambulated amulet surmounted by a malleable logarithmic programming archetype that served as its transmitter. Using this process, they've been able to move digital media faster than previously known transmission limitations. Faster than the speed of light," she read with her voice trailing off in thought.

"Faster than the speed of light? Is that in a different portion of the processing?" Mark asked for clarification.

"Yes, I think so. This process moves things to digital unitalitadium, thus going from digital to computational speeds leveraging the unilateral phase detractor," she told him.

"No wonder it hasn't been cracked. It isn't just coding, it's a whole different approach to computation, calculation, and transmission. But why is transmission needed? Transmission to where? How many people even understand how it all works?" he asked.

"There's my uncle, Morrie Crowe the C.E.O. and just a few other engineers who know the entire framework of what it's all about. The rest of the employees work on various sections of the equipment. They only have a small understanding of the entire set up. My job has taken me to all of them, but I still don't understand how it all fits together," Sue told him.

"And as I told you, I specifically asked if it was okay to take a crack at the game, and they told me it is okay for interns like me. I just can't be paid in the same way. I would get a bonus, but not the same payout as a non-employee. There's nothing that says I can't coach you, however.

"You can't do much as a bot in the game, and there are millions of those in there. If you want an intelligent avatar, it costs money. It's a revenue source for the company. But more importantly, it's marketing for the sale of their artificial intelligence programs. Not allowing employees to buy into the game is like telling employees of a soap company not to buy their soap. And as I said, we just can't win the big prize," Sue explained.

Mark nodded his understanding and was thankful she'd resolved that concern. He didn't want Sue to get in trouble helping him. They could move forward with her help if that's the course they determined.

She scanned a note on a scrap of paper then looked up at him.

"I'm not even sure any of that scientific stuff makes any difference to cracking the game. I don't think it's the programming that needs to be cracked; it's the strategy. We'd need to think of it strategically."

"You don't think the code can be cracked?"

"Nobody's found a way yet and there have been many attempts. The artificial intelligence has more of an effect on what happens in game than coding. All the coding does is control the environment of the game, not the avatars and bots. The coding is primarily used to just manipulate things and get messages and materials to V-World. The avatars operate mostly on their own with suggestive inputs from the user," she explained.

"What about the bots?" Mark asked.

"Their A.I. isn't as robust as an avatar. Mostly it just controls basic movement, interactions, and functionality. Users can communicate with them, and they can point them where to go and some other basic things. Still, even if they delete another avatar or bot, they can't earn much in terms of Forresters. As you saw, you got just one Forrester where a subscriber would get a hundred. But if you bought into the game and your avatar is birthed in as an infant, you can win big money," Sue said.

"Birthed in? What do you mean?" Mark asked.

"Just before an avatar or bot is deleted and if you're quick enough to know, you can insert yours into the game. It goes away, and yours is born to one of the female avatars in the game. I was told you can't add matter to the game, only replace it." Sue explained.

Mark could see Sue and Duncan were right that the complexity of this system was so different. Cracking it with programming would be virtually impossible. Sue's suggestion of a strategic approach was the only answer.

"I knew you'd want to know what others had tried, so I asked around and jotted down some notes," Sue continued.

As his spirits were dropping, hers were soaring, and the two, or was it three, beers helped her to become more enthusiastic about this challenge. She looked up and saw Mark looking into her eyes, listening intently. She didn't need to ask if there were any questions, he was waiting for her to continue with her thought. He opened his iBoard and sat it on his lap.

"Come over here," he said, patting the sofa cushion beside him, this time with no dust flying off.

"I'll put another bot into the game and we'll play around with it," he said.

Sue laughed.

"Play around with it? What do you want to do?" Sue smiled as she stood and walked over to sit by him.

As she settled in, she felt the cushion tip toward him, but rather than pull away, she let her body rest against him.

Mark felt the heat of her leg rest gently against his and smelled her fresh scent, even after the work they'd done. Her voice purred some soft explanation of what could happen inside the game, but he paid little attention. His focus was on the softness of her body and the song of her voice.

With the game launched and his bot appearing in the same vacant lot as before, Mark pointed at the clothes pile and his bot dressed. He walked through the fence, but instead of walking in the direction he had before when another bot deleted him, he turned and went in a different direction. After several blocks in what seemed to be an endless city, he spotted some uniformed men unloading suitcases from the back of a taxi and taking them inside a building that looked like a hotel. The sign above the entrance was in the cryptic symbols of the game so he couldn't decipher the name, but he had his bot walk through the revolving door into the lobby.

"Should I take an elevator up to one of the floors?" he asked Sue.

"Sure. Let's see what's up there."

Stepping into the elevator, his bot pressed the top floor and waited as three other passengers -- either bots or avatars, he couldn't tell -- entered and pushed their floors. After making the last stop, he was alone and watched the lights of the floors go by until the elevator stopped and the doors slid open.

His bot stepped out and Mark panned his camera around to see a swimming pool with towel-covered pool lounges around it. Across from the pool were several rooms he assumed were private cabanas. Walking his bot over to the area, he looked inside one of the cabanas.

"What are those things doing?" he asked.

"They're having sex, dummy. Don't you know what that's like?" she teased.

"Ah... No, not for a long, long time," he said, smiling.

"What does that mean? Do you mean you might give me a 'D' if I'm not good at sex?" she asked.

Mark laughed as he reached over and laid his hand on her leg. He turned his head towards her and kissed her soft cheek. Sue responded with a slight sigh as her eyes closed, and her arm slid to his back. His lips brushed her cheek and worked their way towards her mouth. She lifted her head to meet his lips and pulled him up closer. As their hearts beat a wild rhythm and their hands explored each other, Mark reached over and switched off the naked   nymph   lamp.

THE INSIDER

Now it's knocking at your door;
Beware of it, say come no more.
He brings a gift you cannot lose;
Is the offering a deadly ruse?

Through the early morning light Mark propped himself up on his elbows. He turned and watched Sue resting peacefully on his coveted spare pillow. Seeing her lying quietly there made his heart know that was where she belonged. He realized he must do anything to stay with her. Sliding back under the covers, he shimmied closer to feel her warmth. Just as he brushed his lips on the sweetness of her skin, a firm knock broke the blissful silence.

"Damn," Mark groaned.

Sue rolled over and sat upright, pulling the sheet to her breasts.

"What?" she said.

"Someone's at the door," Mark dejectedly replied.

"Damn. It must be Duncan," Sue said then added, "He hasn't been up this early since that new grid game announced they'd come on at eight."

Quickly she stood, pulling up her jeans and throwing on her sweatshirt while kicking her panties and bra under the bed. At the same time, Mark jumped into his pants like a fireman shooting out of bed to an alarm.

Looking down at the bulge in his jeans, he whispered, "I better calm down a little before answering it."

As he stood, it was apparent to Sue he was excited. His breathing was elevated and there were other telltale signals he liked her.

"I'll answer it if you'd like to go freshen up a little," she said, smiling.

"I'll be okay as soon as I see Duncan," he said, walking bent over to the door.

Mark opened the door and saw Duncan standing there with a box overflowing with wires and cables. Stepping aside, Mark ushered him in with a sweep of his hand.

"Come on in, Duncan. You're too late for the clean-up party. Sue was here bright and early to help me."

"This early? She must have been here at daybreak," Duncan replied.

Duncan walked past Mark over to the plywood coffee table, set his box down, and then took a seat on the couch. He began rummaging through the box and began laying pieces of equipment on the table just as Sue came walking into the room.

"Sorry if I'm interrupting anything," he said with sarcasm.

"We were just finished up and were discussing the Forrest Labs game," Mark lied.

He could tell by Duncan's demeanor that he must still have a thing for Sue.

"Remember, Duncan, Sue suggested both of you come to help clean up the place. You were welcome to come, so stop that finger-wagging and let's get to work," Mark said.

"Yeah, sure, okay. Sorry," Duncan replied.

"Sue doesn't think we have time to write all the code we'd need for the FindIt program. What do you think?

"I agree. I've been working on it every day and still have a mountain of coding and testing to do."

"And I appreciate all of the work you two have done, so I've got some good news. Dr. Johnson, who heads that acceleration program, agreed to accept my recommendation of admitting you," Mark told them.

"Yahoo," Sue said, smacking a high five with Duncan.

"So, I sincerely appreciate your efforts toward the FindIt program. When it's completed, you... well, we all, will significantly benefit. We'll be getting a percentage as will the school when the application is finished and sold.

"But for me, time's merely running out. It has boiled down to making a big hit in V-World and maybe even getting a job offer from Forrest Labs to buy my way out of the Military. Other than that, it looks like I'm back in the war at the end of the semester," Mark said.

Duncan didn't notice Sue's head drop down nor the frown on her lips as she fought to hold back a tear.

"Sue's briefed me on some background information for the game, so let me repeat what I think I know to you Duncan, and you two can see if I can get it right. That okay with you, Sue?" Mark asked.

"Sure," Sue said.

Mark went over the technical side of the V-World operation. Sue made some methodical corrections when Mark couldn't remember all the scientific names, but mostly he got it right.

"Winning is a combination of deleting bots and avatars and gaining followers because you get credit for their deletions also. It's a bit like the real world, isn't it?" Sue said.

"I'd say it's exactly like our real world. Our leaders have followers and they use guys like me to delete those orange heads. If our world is that kind of game, President Stevens would be accumulating a heck of a lot of points," Mark offered.

"True. Our world is obviously the model for the V-World," Duncan said.

"So, since cracking the game's code has proven a virtual impossibility and V-World is the only grid game that pays out the kind of money we need, it's the one I'd like to focus on. Do you two agree?" Mark asked.

They both nodded thoughtfully.

"Okay, I have a question," Mark asked, looking at Sue. "Has anyone been successful at planting a virus in the game?"

"I do know that Forrest Labs puts viruses in routinely to control the population. Too many bots and avatars cause lag in the game. And hackers have introduced several, but the A.I. in the avatars eventually eradicates them. The faster the viruses mutate, the quicker that avatar's A.I. comes up with something to stop or slow it down. And even the most effective ones don't delete enough avatars to equal gaining followers and deleting other avatars, and that's where big money lies.

"I don't think we want to go that direction," Sue suggested.

"I agree with Sue for one simple reason," Duncan said.

"What's that?" Mark asked.

"You can't attach credit to a virus introduced by one player. The game is set up so that it has to be an avatar or a bot to gain points. The system isn't designed to recognize where it originated."

"I see. That makes sense," Mark said.

"Duncan's right. So as we've agreed, developing the right strategy is the key. Because of the unbreakable encryption, we don't understand the A.I., the language, or the writing, making it virtually impossible to know what those avatars are doing to gain followers or increase their deletion counts," Sue offered.

"You're right, Sue. We have to figure out how we can understand what's being communicated inside the game," Mark suggested.

Duncan began nervously shuffling his equipment around. After a moment of silence, as the three seemed to be searching for answers, Duncan spoke up.

"I knew most of that technical stuff, Mark. And I've been doing some thinking too. I assembled some things that I think could let us crack V-World. Viruses aren't the answer because they can't be traced back to one avatar. It can't be hacked and not to brag or anything, but I'm pretty good at cracking game codes. I've tried very hard to do it in V-World and can't. Yes, it's a totally different system. Since we don't hear their communications and can't read their writing, there's no way of knowing what works. Why some gamers are successful and some not. We have to understand that world, right?" Duncan offered.

"Yes, that's right, Duncan," Mark said, impressed with his analysis.

"So, since they can't communicate back to us, we have to figure out how to make that happen in a different way. I think I know how we can crack this game," Duncan said.

"Crack it? Do you mean we could win the game?" Mark asked.

"Maybe not crack it and win the entire pot, but we could make millions with my idea," Duncan pointed out.

"Okay. Go on, Duncan. Tell us what your idea is," Mark said.

THE TEST

Space and time somehow connected;
Their time's not our time,
Einstein reflected.

Mark and Sue listened closely as Duncan began. He apparently had stepped up and seemed to become more mature since their first meeting. He was right that communications back to the user from the avatar in the game could be critical. Merely being an observer on how some avatars attain so many game points and others none would be invaluable.

"Your suggestion is right, Duncan. Are you telling us we can put an avatar in the game, and get it to communicate back to us?

"That's kind of right, yes," Duncan said.

"Can you build an avatar that could communicate back to us?" Mark asked.

"Not exactly. Their developed in the game. Some of them have complex artificial intelligence developed by Forrest Labs. I can't copy that. My idea is to put one of us in the game as an avatar and use our own intelligence," Duncan said.

"One of us? Are you crazy, Duncan? Now you're ridiculous," Sue said.

Duncan turned his head to her, then back to Mark.

"No, I'm not. Trust me, it's not impossible," Duncan said.

"How do you know that?" Sue insisted.

"Just go along with me for a minute and look at the advantages. If we could get one of us there, we can give them our knowledge and abilities. Imagine the power to understand opportunities by knowing and reading their languages. With those abilities, we could earn massive points and amass a significant number of followers. Add to that, if we know what avatar has a lot of followers, and we could delete them, we get those points too," Duncan said.

"You make a good point, but still I think we should focus on strategy and what we can do, not something ridiculous," Sue said.

"I know you're doubtful, but remember that one guy who almost won the game early on?" Duncan said.

189

"Oh, yes. That was just after Forrest Labs added avatars and bots that wore different clothes. I think that user got followers to hate and delete those that dressed differently. And I think it was more than that. They may have had a different language and different religion too," Sue said.

"Yes, and he did it using some weird symbol. Look at this," Duncan said.

Duncan went to the games menu and fast scrolled time backward to focus on Hitler with the swastika behind him.

"That operator used his avatar to lead in the deletion of millions, didn't he?" Sue said.

"Yes. And for some reason, everyone seemed to point toward him with their fingers together in some sort of salute. How did he get all of those followers and get them to delete so many avatars?

"Yes, and all of those followers who deleted others gave that guy with the funny pencil thin mustache points. If we were there, we could figure that out and develop something like it. Who knows the possibilities?" Duncan pointed out.

"Go on..." Mark said, encouraging him to expand his thought.

"First, we need an avatar to observe his surroundings, to understand how points can be made. With that understanding, we can plan what we're trying to accomplish. After some time in the game, we bring him back out to brief us. Then we send him back in knowing we're guiding and helping. That way, the avatar would have enormous power."

"Yes, that's all true, but what we have here is the recipe for alligator soup. First, you have to catch an alligator." Mark said.

"I know it can work," Duncan said.

"How do you know that?" Sue said.

"Because I've done it," Duncan said.

"Done what?"

"Put living things into grid games."

"Come on, Duncan. Let's get serious. Something like that isn't possible," Mark said.

"It is and I've done it," Duncan said matter-of-factly.

"What? You've got to be kidding me, Duncan," Sue said.

"I'm not kidding. I did it," Duncan replied.

"Okay. How?" Mark asked.

"The key was something I borrowed from Dad's lab. You know they made things for Forrest Labs, right? Anyway, there were these things that looked like earbuds lying around, so I wondered what they did. I took them home a pair and played with them on my iBoard," Duncan said.

"I started up in my bedroom by cracking the code in the ear buds. I could tell then didn't need to be matched. They could communicate to other software when just one was functioning. I wrote some software to communicate to the earbuds and copied it to another iBoard. By sending code to the ear bud, it could run the program on either iBoard. I taped one earbud to an object and the object to the iBoard and thought I could send them both in and retrieve them. Here, I'll show you the code I wrote, " Duncan said reaching into his back pack.

"Never mind that. You actually sent something into a computer game from your bedroom?" Sue asked.

"That's right. First, I sent a desk chair right into the middle of a football stadium. When one of the players tripped over it, I retrieved it. The player looked back to see what tripped him, but by then, I had it back in my bedroom." Duncan.

"How did you do that?" Sue asked.

"I'm not sure. I did some coding to connect the two computers, and then connected the spare one to those earbud things," Duncan said.

"Go on. What else?" Mark said.

"Well, I began experimenting with various objects around my bedroom, sending them in and then retrieving them. What was interesting, they were still in the room, but in the game too. I could tell because I have an autographed picture of Abigale Flywheel, that famous coder, and it was in there lying on the ground face up. So I quickly teleported it back in case someone stepped on it, and ruined it and I expected the one in my room too. I didn't want to find out."

"Teleported? Where did that come from?" Mark asked.

"It was a term one of the games used when you moved something from one section of the game to the other."

"Okay. What happened next?" Mark said.

"Well, after I became pretty proficient with objects, I wondered what would happen if I could teleport something living. Since so much of Forrest Labs stuff is organic, I thought it could be done. So, after saving up my allowance, I purchased a guinea pig. I told my mom it was for a science experiment at school, and she just nodded her head. She liked it when I did school projects," Duncan told them.

"I used a string to make a little leash for the guinea pig, ran the string through the cage bars and fastened it to the iBoard and earbuds and sent my new friend off. The guinea pig was in his cage, but rather than moving around sniffing, it seemed to just stand zombie-like, in a coma-like state. In the game, it was scurrying around, chomping on the grass. The guinea pig was in the game and in his cage at the same time."

"What happened to it when you brought it back into your room?" Sue asked.

"Actually, I couldn't bring him back like with the objects."

"Do you mean he was lost in the game?" Mark asked.

"No, he came back with that iBoard, but not from anything I did. I turned around and poof! He was there with that spare iBoard and earbuds. I discovered after reviewing the recording that the critter was walking across the keyboard. I realized I'd set up the iBoard to initiate the program when any key was pressed, so it disappeared from the game and came out of its zombie state in his cage."

"I see. You have both iBoards programmed with the code you'd written," Mark said.

"That's right. It was just a matter of copying one to the other."

"Did you tell anyone what you'd done?" Sue asked.

"No. I didn't want to get in trouble for doing experiments. Besides, I wondered what would happen with something bigger, so I coaxed the neighbor's barking dog over to the house using some cut up wieners and snuck it in the back door. Once in my bedroom, I hooked it up like the guinea pig and transmitted it in. The dog sniffed around and lifted its leg in a few places, then came over to the keyboard and started sniffing. I'd rubbed some wiener smell on the keyboard, so it came back into my room when it began licking the keyboard. I quickly got him back into his neighbor's yard before he lifted his leg on my bed," Duncan told them.

Sue and Mark were gawking at Duncan in wonderment. Obviously, he was a fantastic programmer with an intriguing, curious mind.

Duncan went on.

"I wondered if it worked with a guinea pig, and with a dog, could it work with a human."

"Don't tell me..." Sue said.

"Well, I thought about it for several days and reasoned if it worked with animals it seems logical it would with a person. I wasn't sure how to go about it. My first thought was to kidnap the neighbor's kid and try him," Duncan laughed.

"I wouldn't have done that, but what about my weird friend Rick? But I didn't want Rick to even be in my room. That last time he was there, he broke three things messing around with them.

"Finally, after considering as many options as I could, I decided I'd have to try it on myself the same way all scientists do. And, because these were earbud things, I just placed on in my ear and left the other taped to the silver iBoard."

"I made some adjustments to the program to ignore inorganic materials, so it would only recognize organic. The key was the earbuds. I even found the program in it and made that change. Placing the black iBoard on my lap, I typed the command in the silver one on my desk, and the next thing I knew I was in an outdoor setting in a strange place with the black iBoard lying at my feet. It shocked me so frantically, I touched a key on that black iBoard and just as quickly came back into my room," Duncan explained.

Mouths opened slightly, Mark and Sue looked at each other dumbfounded.

"You've got to be shitting me," Mark said astonished.

"No, it's the truth. I was surprised how effortlessly it went and didn't even know I'd been teleported until I reviewed the recording and saw myself in the game.

Duncan went on to tell them that after a few more experiments, he was ready to crack some games. He was doing great until his mother came into his room and saw him sitting there looking half dead. She'd called emergency and the paramedics were examining him when he transmitted back out of the game.

When he realized he was back in his bedroom, he asked the emergency workers why they were there and what this was all about. They told him he'd been in some sort of coma and asked if he'd been taking any illegal drugs. His mother, who was angry and hugged him at the same time, held him close when she noticed the metallic objects protruding from his ears and demanded to know what they were for. He told her they were some new jewelry the kids are wearing.

"Fortunately, they didn't take them off or confiscate them or we'd be dead in the water on this idea," Duncan told them.

"So, what happened next?" Mark asked.

"Mom called the grid authorities about the dangers of the grid, and their investigations showed some of the hacking I'd done in games. They wrote to my parents with a warning for potential fines and/or imprisonment if I continued the practice."

"So, that's when you enrolled in school; right?" Mark asked

"Yes. I know I did something risky, but I also know it works."

"If you could really do that in one game, I wonder if we could use it in V-World?" Sue asked.

"Could be. As we've concluded it's strategy we need more than cracking the code. We have to understand how the avatars communicate, what all the writing is, and why some avatars gain followers and others don't. With that information, we could develop a very good strategy," Duncan said.

"When I tried out the game, I could type in directions, but the bot didn't seem to react. Do avatars reply to your questions? Is there any way of getting information out while someone's in the game?" Mark asked.

"That's the difficulty of the game. You can send in instructions and watch to see if they're followed. Many times, nothing happens, as if they're ignoring or don't understand what you wrote. Sometimes they may send a message back, and it appears on your screen. But that doesn't happen all the time. I guess sometimes the A.I. in the avatar gets confused. I think it could be their programmed instructions don't match with what is sent in via an iBoard."

"Interesting. If you knew what they were saying, that would definitely be an advantage. In the game, they have to be able to read the writing. If they could just communicate it back to us, we'd be in business."

"I still have some questions beyond the safety of doing this. Let's assume we could get me into the game. Am I going to have to wear one of those earbud looking things all the time?" Mark asked.

"The silver iBoard is programmed to control things through that black iBoard and those opal earbuds. The earbuds don't have to be worn for it to work, they just have to be near the iBoard. That's why I taped it on," he proclaimed proudly.

Carefully, Duncan placed the black iBoard on the table, taped the earbuds to it, and then switched on his silver unit. Pressing a key, he brought up V-World and navigated toward a wooded area his in-world map identified as empty.

"Watch this," he said.

With a few keystrokes, the black iBoard and single earbud disappeared.

"Where'd it go?" Mark asked, pointing at the place the black iBoard had been.

"That's it... there in the game," Duncan told him, nodding at his screen.

Next, he typed in a few commands, and the black iBoard again appeared sitting on the coffee table.

"Amazing," was all Mark could say.

When he finally got over the disbelief of what he'd just witnessed, Mark asked, "And you can send biological things that way too?"

"Yes, organic things, but not exactly like that. It worked with the earbuds, but, as I said, you don't have to wear them. If you're just near the programmed iBoard and earbuds, it works.

Something I read in my dad's lab suggested the earbuds can convert chemicals into some type of matter. Ninety-nine percent of our body is comprised of six elements: oxygen, carbon, hydrogen, nitrogen, calcium, and phosphorus. There's also a smattering of potassium, sulfur, sodium, chlorine, and magnesium. I think what happens at Forrest Labs, those elements are broken down and somehow transmitted. Then they're reassembled by their program at the destination. Just holding the black iBoard and earbuds would work with organic materials. Then we just move them to someplace secure until the person in the game goes to them and teleports back out."

"What would happen if the iBoard malfunctioned, was stolen, or wouldn't work?" Mark asked.

"I could just copy the program into another iBoard and send it in," Duncan said.

"What about the earbuds?"

"That could be a problem. As I said, I only have this one set. If something happened I'm sure I could find another set around dad's lab, but I'm not sure," Duncan said.

There was a period of silence as the three began thinking. Finally, Sue came up with something.

"I don't think we could assume that V-World would work as other simple games. Just putting someone in there wouldn't be that easy. Remember Forrest Labs has two types of avatars: bots, and their premium avatar version. They insert artificial intelligence in all, but the premium one operates at a higher intellectual level. So, I don't know how that would interfere with our inborn intelligence. Would it cancel it or would it be additive to what we already know?" Sue asked.

"Good question. We just don't know, do we?" Mark said.

"You said you could program any key to activate a macro, and they'd come back, right?" Sue asked.

"Yes, if they're with the earbuds and iBoard," Duncan said.

"Good question, Sue," Mark said then went on.

"Do you think we could transmit me into that V-World game as a test?" Mark asked.

Sue didn't answer right away. She ran her fingers through her hair in deep thought.

"Possibly. But just as Duncan said, we don't know if someone couldn't transmit in there with the same intelligence we have here. The Lab's system inserts an artificial intelligence program when the avatar is birthed."

"Birthed? What do you mean?"

"That's how you get a super intelligent avatar. It's just like we're birthed. In the game avatars copulate and impregnate just like we do. The avatars created by that process have superior A.I.

"Duncan used earbuds to move back and forth in the other games. V-World is different and just going in with our mine we still couldn't understand their language. We'd have to be birthed into the game," Sue said.

"No 'they', Sue. If we're going to do this it will be me," Mark said.

"Let's think this through. I wouldn't have the earbuds that could help me transmit back out. If I'm birthed in, I'd have to become old enough to find where we hid them. How long would that take?" Mark asked.

"You can move time in the game so in our time, not long. But there are a couple of things you have to consider. Other users in the game may catch on to a fast riser. They may move time ahead and see someone earning points then go back in time and delete them. We can help guide the one in the game, but we can't sit around here until he or she is eighteen. Remember too, the matter in the game is always recycled. To add matter, you have to remove an equivalent or greater amount. Forrest Labs continues to cull the population in the game to make room for new players," Sue said.

"How does that affect what we're considering? And stop saying, 'he or she' it will be me. What do we need to do?" Mark asked.

"We cause an accident where one avatar is deleted as another is born. Bots don't have that much matter so we could run someone in as a bot, force them to be deleted by accident, and have ours... okay you, Mark, berthed," Sue said.

"I understand. We'd have to bypass the system and remove the matter ourselves. Let me get this right. You're saying we put in a bot and have it deleted, then birth our avatar into the game, right? Mark asked.

"Possibly... What do you think, Duncan?" Sue asked.

"Yes. Then if that birthed avatar would accept instructions from us, we could fast forward the game and get Mark experience. We just have to check with him as we move along to warn of dangers. I can program an alert in my iBoard as we move him along in age. Once he has a feel for the system and can read their language, we bring him out, review his notes, then send him back in. We could get you into leadership positions, generate followers, and maybe even start a war and get millions deleted," he suggested.

"That's true only if the avatar understood the situation, and the A.I. programming wouldn't block it," Sue told him.

"Question: If that avatar in the game was given an iBoard, could they communicate back here?" Mark asked.

"That I don't know; it's possible. The program is linked to the one here, so maybe. But the one in the game would have to understand how it worked. Remember, their memory will be erased and replaced with an A.I.," Duncan said.

Again, they paused and stared into space thinking.

"Going in and out is risky. Doing that, your memory might be erased and you'd have to start over. There's another danger. We don't know how many of those, what did you call them? Teleports? We don't know how many our bodies could take. It's too risky," Sue said.

"Maybe we should do a test in V-World. You've done it in other games, but not V-World so let's send something into V-World. Let's plant the black iBoard and the earbuds somewhere in the game for later recovery and see if it works. If it does, we go into the game," Mark suggested.

"I've gotten myself into too much trouble doing that and promised my mom I wouldn't mess with it again," Duncan said.

"I understand, Duncan. You don't need to risk anything for my benefit. And Sue, you can't be the one either because if something should happen, you might be able to fix things at Forrest Labs. That's why I keep saying me. I have nothing to lose. What are the potential shortfalls or dangers if we can get me into the game via the birthing process?" Mark asked.

"Assuming we can get you in, the biggest danger is getting you back out via the process we discussed. Hiding our transmission devices and directing you to them," Duncan said.

"If I'm in there, you just keep sending me messages repeating that I need to get to where they're hidden and what I need to do," Mark said.

"Let's not get ahead of ourselves. Let's do the test," Mark suggested. "We'll try it with a guinea pig and if that works, I'll go in as an avatar. Our only value is to see if we can put me in there and return me in one piece as an avatar," Mark clarified.

"Okay, we'll do that, but we still don't know what would happen to your presence here if you're an avatar, or even your bot if we transmit you in and are deleted. Would you die in this world too?" Sue wondered.

"Let's not let that happen. All I know is that if I have to go back to the war, I'm a dead man anyway, so doing this is worth the risk. Go get a guinea pig, Duncan." Mark said.

THE ENTRY

Get him in and see what goes;
Run the test like science joes.
It's risky, yes but he must do it;
Or off to war he'd get right to it.

Mark looked at the equipment, wondering if it was worth the risk. Could he trust this kid's word that it would work? He obviously was bright with an excellent pedigree since his father was a scientist involved in some top-secret artificial intelligence experiments. But based on his experiences with students and young soldiers, lineage was only part of the performance equation. He needed reassurance to have his body broken down by a computer program and transmitted by a device none of them knew anything about. The thought of him being transmitted through space, or some unknown medium, to get into a game seemed impossible. They'd sent in the guinea pig Mark asked for, and just to be safe, a stray cat that meowed its way in as if crying, "I don't wanna go!" Those things worked as Duncan claimed. Maybe this would too. Sue and Duncan came back the next day and laid out Duncan's equipment. The two iBoards, one silver and the other black, cables, the earbuds, and an oval crystal bowl.

Looking at the bowl, Mark asked, "Is that where the flowers go at my funeral?" Mark asked.

"That's not funny, Mark," Sue said.

"That's the transmitting amplifier. You know that crystals resonate at a specific frequency and that we generate an electromagnetic field; right?" Duncan asked.

"Yes, I understand that," Mark replied.

Well, the program I developed combines those two things and the sensors on the iBoard pick them up, convert them to a signal that is broadcast to Forrest Lab's system. Their magic then goes to work and teleports the organic objects closest to the crystal vase to the destination I select on my iBoard. So, we just put the black iBoard and earbuds along with the organic material, which would be you, close by and they go into the game," Duncan said.

"Why didn't you have it for the animals?" Mark asked.

"Because their mass was small. You're bigger so a boost will help," Duncan said confidently.

"Tell me again how I get back out of the game," Mark asked.

"The earbuds in your ears do the amplification needed, so you just wear them and hit any key on the iBoard," Duncan responded.

"I hope that stuff works right with as much mass as I have. Cats and guinea pigs don't weigh as much as me. Are you sure your calculations are right?" Mark asked.

"Yes. I've taken everything into consideration. You'll be fine," Duncan assured.

Mark did have some concern, but going back into the war with survival rates at fifty percent was ludicrous if there were other options he could take. First step in an attack was to knock out the eyes of the enemy. They always targeted radar and communications, the brains of an attack. And that was exactly where the electronics were housed, the job he'd have when reentering.

"Okay, if we go forward with this, how's it going to work? What do we need to do?" Mark asked.

"Let's do it the safest way we can, Duncan," Sue said.

Mark looked over at her to see the same fear on her face that he'd seen with soldiers going into battle. She wasn't crying, but he could see the pale appearance of her skin and watery eyes, expressionless face gazing at nothing.

Her eyes quickly shifted to Duncan.

"Don't mess this up, Duncan. You're sure it can work?" she said.

"I'm pretty sure. I've done it myself, just in a different game. So, even though we only did animals into V-World, the process of teleporting is the same," he said.

"How is this first test going to work?" Mark asked.

"We can send you in as... you said avatar, but I think we should just do this test with a bot. We're only making sure we can get you in and back out. If it works then we can do it with an avatar. We'll put you in an isolated area where there'd be no chance of someone trying to delete you and see how it goes," Duncan suggested.

"Okay. Let's give it a shot," Mark said.

They began preparations with Duncan bringing up V-World on his silver iBoard. Using the camera in the game, he began scanning around looking for a place where no other avatars or bots would come near. After pulling his system camera back and moving over the round bluish globe, he zoomed into the middle of a landmass where there were only wheat fields. There were no grazing animals, one indication it wasn't a farm, and there were no avatars or bots in sight.

He handed Mark the earbuds.

"I think you should securely fasten them to the iBoard. I don't want to be responsible for that, Mark. You'll need to wear them when I bring you out," Duncan said.

Mark double wrapped that tape over the earbuds and to the black iBoard saying, "That'll do it."

"Now, just place the iBoard on the vase and touch it or the vase, it doesn't really matter," Duncan instructed.

Mark slid his fingers under the iBoard and grasped the vase.

"Will this work?" he asked.

"That's good, but you just need to be touching the vase, not hang onto it, you can't take it with you," Duncan replied.

Duncan pressed a key combination on his iBoard. There was a slight pause, then Mark and the iBoard/Earbud combination momentarily disappeared.

Sue's attention was drawn to Duncan's iBoard screen, where she saw Mark appearing there in the game. Her eyes shot over to see where Mark had been sitting. Something she'd never seen before began happening. Piece by piece, pixel by pixel, his form reappeared sitting comfortably in his apartment chair.

"Is that him in the game?" Sue asked, with eyes glued to the screen.

"Yes. He's a bot,"

"But it doesn't look like him," Sue said.

"Look closer. It does look like him if you look close," Duncan said.

"Move the camera closer to him, Duncan."

As the camera moved in closer to the bot's face, Sue shouted, "Oh my God! You're right. It's him, but he's sitting here," she said, pointing at Mark sitting in the chair. "How can that be?"

"I don't know the answer to that one, but he's there."

"How does he know to pick up the iBoard?" Sue asked.

"I'll type in some instructions and tell him to."

Duncan typed in his instructions and watched the screen.

The bot in V-World representing Mark scratched its head, looked around behind him then stood with hands on hips.

Again, Duncan typed in the same instructions.

This time the bot jumped. It walked over to the iBoard and pressed a key. Instantaneously the bot disappeared from the screen.

In the apartment, Mark's frozen appearance changed, and his eyes blinked and began to shift around in his chair.

"Okay. I'm ready. Let's do it," Mark said looking between Sue and Duncan.

"It's over."

"Huh? What do you mean it's over?" Mark asked.

"We sent you in the game."

"I was in there? Oh, yeah. I kind of remember a field or something and thought it was a dream."

"Did you get my instructions," Duncan asked.

"What instructions?"

"I told you to press a key on the iBoard," Duncan said.

"I was a bot?"

"Yes, you were in the game for a couple of minutes," Duncan said.

Mark thought for a minute. "Damn. I do remember something telling me to press a key on an iBoard. I thought I was here and you needed help or something. Was that in the game?"

"Yep."

"Then it worked. It just seemed so quick," Mark said.

"Remember time is different there," Duncan said.

"Let's try leaving me in there longer and giving me some other instructions to see what happens. Tell me to do something specific, but don't have me wander too far from the iBoard," Mark said.

Again they went through the process. Mark's bot was back in the field, and his real self was in the apartment sitting there unmoving other than the slow rise and fall of his chest.

"Bring him back," Sue pleaded.

"He wants us to give him some instructions, Sue."

"Make it simple instructions and do it quickly, please."

"It'll be fine," Duncan responded.

Duncan wasn't hesitant to have Mark take the risk, but Sue had feelings of doubt.

Working with Mark on their joint project helped her understand him as a man and as a lover. The process made her feel like she'd never felt before with any other male. She'd fallen in love and didn't want to lose him to the war or to this quest.

"Let's have him do something that will be left there in the game. When he comes back, we can look at it together," Duncan suggested.

Sue looked at Mark in the game, then back at him in the chair, breathing slowly, as if he was peacefully asleep. The calmness of him helped settle her nerves and her mind went into a puzzle-solving mode.

"I've got an idea," Sue said. "Let's have him walk around in that field and make a pattern. When he bends it over, it will show up from above, and we can show it to him when he's back. Just don't make it too big so he can't find the iBoard," she proposed.

"Good idea. I can pull up a concentric circle formula and transmit it to him and see if he'll walk it," Duncan replied.

"Don't let him get too far from the iBoard, though," she reminded Duncan.

"I won't. I can put him on a course to come right back to it."

Duncan sent commands into the iBoard, and the two watched as Mark began walking away from the iBoard, then turn and start walking in a circle far, but not too far, from the iBoard. After each pass, Mark move out further making the circle appear wider and wider. When the circle was wide enough, Duncan sent a command to return to the iBoard. In the game, Mark stopped and waited then walked along the path from the circles back to the iBoard. Duncan sent in the command to press a button on the board, and Mark immediately responded and disappeared from the game.

In the apartment, Mark shook his head.

"How'd it go?" he asked.

"Take a look," Duncan said, sliding the iBoard over to him.

"I made that pattern? I didn't know I was that artistic," Mark said.

"Well, I'm not quite sure how that worked, I just sent a pattern to you, and you were able to copy it walking. Pretty cool, huh?" Duncan said proudly.

Duncan ran the recording of Mark's bot walking the pattern, neatly laying the straw on its side, looking like the letter O with a line through the middle at an angle.

"I kind of remember being there. It was a wheat field," Mark said.

"And I sort of remember having the urge to walk in specific directions. Those were commands you gave me through that iBoard?"

"Yes. Well, I didn't give instructions in writing, I just sent them to you as a picture," Duncan said.

"So when we birth you in, we'll let you mature then direct you to the earbuds and iBoard, and you'll be back here," Duncan said.

"Okay, let's do it. Do we need to put money into the game to send me in as an Avatar?" Mark asked.

"Just use my account," Sue said. "I don't have to pay to put things in the game."

Duncan navigated over to Sue's account, inserted her username and password, and got the system set up.

"We're all ready to go. Here's the birthing option right here," Duncan said, pointing at his screen.

"Okay, we're going to birth you in. This time you won't go with the iBoard and earbuds for obvious reasons. We don't want a woman giving birth to you and to an iBoard with earbuds taped to it. Once you're safely in, we'll find a safe place and hide the bundle there for safekeeping."

Duncan looked at Mark for confirmation then over at Sue. Neither said anything.

"Ready?" Duncan asked Mark.

"Let's do it," Mark replied.

"Be safe," Sue said, really wanting to hug and kiss him.

With a few commands from Duncan's keyboard, the magic happened. Mark was in his sleep-like pose as Sue and Duncan watched their iBoard screen. The iBoard was on the floor of a room with a pregnant woman and a female doctor attending here. Everyone was so busy helping the woman deliver Mark, they didn't notice the object on the floor. With a couple commands on Duncan's iBoard, the black iBoard and earbuds in the game appeared next to his machine.

Satisfied, Mark was safely inserted into the birthing process, they began scanning around V-World and spotted what looked like a vast city. Zooming in, they saw some interesting and identifiable landmarks and made a note of their coordinates. Duncan navigated his camera to the basement of one of the two tallest buildings in the city. There he found a platform above a ventilation pipe that appeared full of dust.

"Nobody's been here for a very long time. Check the coordinates, Sue, and we'll transmit this iBoard and the earbuds there," Duncan said.

Duncan shot the coordinates over to Sue's iBoard for backup and safekeeping, then immediately passed them through his program. Without a sound, the black iBoard, earbuds taped to the top, now appeared on the hidden dusty spot they'd discovered.

They were now safely in the game where they could remain safe, undetectable, and secure until Mark, in his avatar guise, would be able to grab it and return. The process would take a couple of weeks, and then they'd   all   be   set   for   life.

THE TOWERS

From where the voice chants from afar?
Lyrics of disaster come beckoning me.
Warning and whispering, a noxious mar;
Murmured with a macabre glee.

"Hello, Mary?" I said into the payphone.

"Hello, Rasheed. How are you doing?" Mary said.

We chatted a little about how things were going. She asked if I'd been given any warnings or instructions recently.

"I did get a strange instruction, yes," I told her.

"What was it?" she asked.

"I was told to pick up a package behind some store's dumpster off Market Street," I said.

"That doesn't sound strange. Why do you say it was strange. What was in the package?"

"Money."

"Wow. How much?"

"I haven't counted it yet, but that's not the strange part."

"Oh? What is?"

"I was told to catch a flight somewhere, but the voice didn't know exactly where," I told her.

"How could you catch a plane to 'somewhere'? Is that all it said?" she asked.

"It gave me a description of a city, and that's all," I told her.

"What is the description?"

"It said take a plane to a city that is a long way away from where I am and closer to where the sun rises. It has two very tall identical buildings close to water. Across the water is a statue of a woman holding a torch over her head. That sounds like New York doesn't it?" I asked.

"That's the only place I can think of too, Rasheed. When are you supposed to go?"

"Right away is all I know. It only said, 'go now' and repeated that. It said if I don't go now, it will be too late, so I guess it's urgent," I told her.

"Did it tell you what you had to do there? Is it a target to delete?" Mary asked with a worried voice.

"No. It said I had to retrieve an object in one of those tall buildings."

"What kind of object?" Mary asked.

"It didn't say, it just kept saying I needed to go now," I said.

"Well, then, you better go. Let me know how it turns out, Rasheed. Do you need my help with anything?

"Yeah. Where do I get an airline ticket to New York?"

"There's a Delta Ticket office over on 5th Street. You can get one there."

I thanked Mary and told her I'd keep her posted, then walked over to get a ticket on the soonest flight to New York. I told the woman behind the counter I had to leave as soon as possible, but she said the soonest she could get me out was first thing in the morning.

The "red-eye" she said was sold out.

"But I have to get there as soon as possible. Can you help me?" I pleaded.

"Let me check a couple of the other carriers for you," the nice lady said.

I waited as she made some phone calls that only took a few minutes.

"United and American are full tonight too, I'm sorry. You could go out to the airport and wait for no shows, but if you want to be assured of a seat you should be booked on a flight," she explained.

"Okay, book me on your first flight in the morning, " I told her.

"Sure. Round trip or one way?"

"Just get a one-way ticket," the voice came in.

"One way, please," I told her

I guess when the message came in my facial expressions changed. The ticket lady gave me a funny look and said, "Okay. When you want to come back just give us a call and you can pick up your ticket at the airport. It would be less expensive to by a round trip now, "she told me.

"It's okay. I'm not sure right now when I will return."

She was right about both things. It made sense to have a seat on some flight so I reached in the bag, pulled out cash enough for the ticket. But I couldn't be a round trip because I didn't know what I was going to do in New York after I retrieved what I was being sent for.

She printed it out and gave it to me, and stuffed it into the bag with the money. It seemed to be enough for dinner, so I headed over to McD's and grabbed something before heading to my doorway to sleep.

*****

"Come on. Wake up," the voice said, pulling me out of my dream.

"We have to get you there now. Don't be late and miss the flight."

I had no idea why I had to go to New York. Things were working out pretty well in San Francisco, so why leave? Without question, I grabbed my belongings, hid my shopping cart, changed clothes, and grabbed a cab for the short trip to the San Francisco Airport. When I arrived, it was two hours before my 7:00 AM flight.

But something was wrong. The voice to change clothes and clean up, but it didn't ask me to bring any extra clothes or even a toothbrush that I used at least once a week. Was I going to be in New York for just the day? When was I supposed to return? I knew the voice would have something in mind, and everything would be okay, so I'd just have to wait and see what it wants.

The cab dropped me off at Terminal 1 in front of the sign marked Delta. Inside I looked up at a board that showed the flight to New York was leaving from gate 45. As I made my way down the long concourse, I began thinking I might be walking to New York. Even though the number was a big one, thankfully, the gate was the first one I came to.

The terminal seemed pretty busy for so early in the morning, but no flights had left gate 45, so I sat and found a newspaper lying next to me and began reading. There was clear weather in the East where I was heading. San Francisco weather was never severe except to tourists who expected warm balmy weather like they have in Miami. I remembered how cold it was in July of '95 when I got here.

The paper had a piece about how one of the San Francisco churches was opening a hospitality meal for free to anyone wanting one. I wondered if they all did that, but it made my mind go back to those discussions with Luther after Mary's lab for religious studies class. There are literally thousands of religions on earth, each with its own unique way to help. I wonder if there are real answers to all these questions within just one of those religious beliefs. If so, are the others wrong?

I guess if you are a devoted, sincere believer in your own faith, the others have to be wrong. I know Jafar thought they were all wrong and were out to get him and Islam. He ruined my faith in religion and I've become an open-minded thinker since that short time with Luther. He made me wonder about our existence on earth. Was I so different than those well-dressed people walking into theaters or going to restaurants? Did their life begin like mine? I seemed as smart as any of them, yet I was different. Why?

"I guess this flight's going to be full. Look at how many are here already," the woman behind me said to her seatmate.

"Looks like it," he sighed.

"Why is everyone looking up at the television monitors? What's going on?" I heard her ask.

I turned and looked up at the monitor hearing the murmur of the crowd beginning to get louder.

Passengers were beginning to rise from their seats. Some were heading for the baggage claim area for some reason.

Glancing up at the clock I saw it showing just past six and calculated it was a little after nine in New York. I still had an hour and a half before my flight, so let my mind drift off into a peaceful place if I could find one. Mary came to mind, but then there was someone else. Another girl with a beautiful face and curvy figure, but I couldn't come up with her name. My feeling toward her was different than I felt about Mary. It was a strange feeling, one I didn't understand. I had a longing to be close to that someone, something I'd never experienced living alone on the streets. I could almost smell the sweet scent of hair and its softness against my face, even though that had never happened in my life. Then as my heart began to race and soft music began to stir deep inside, the name Sue popped into my head. The feeling of light euphoria was broken with a sudden thought of terror. War. It felt so real I began cowering down, expecting ordnance to start falling from the heavens.

The woman now sitting where the Chronicle had lain asked, "Are you all right?"

That pulled me out of my trance.

"Yeah, I was just scratching the back of my leg," I told her.

What were all these images in my head?

Sue… that's her name, I thought.

There was something else. That term iBoard was familiar, but I couldn't place why. I seemed to recall it had something to do with the things a company down the peninsula was doing. I reached for the name then remembered the bite out of an apple. Yes, Apple, I remember. The voice said something about iBoard, but this Apple company had a machine that made calculations that anyone could do.

This trip has something to do with that iBoard thing.

I'll just have to go and hope it gives me some instructions when I get there. This wasn't like most messages I got from the voice. This time the voice seemed more insistent than what I'd ever felt before.

"Oh my god," she said, pointing at the television monitor.

I glanced up and looked at the flight and gate number monitors and saw all of them canceled.

"What's going on? They're all canceled," I said to her.

"No. Look at the television monitor. What's happening?"

I turned and looked at the television monitor and saw smoke coming from one of the World Trade Center buildings. Just as I was about to ask her what it was, I saw an airplane fly into the other building. I glanced at the clock beside the television and saw it was 6:04, 9:04 in New York. Black smoke was billowing out of an impression in the side of the building that looked like the outline of an airplane. As we watched, pieces of the smoldering building began falling to the ground. Near the monitor, a woman shrieked, and virtually everyone in the area stood and stared at the monitor in complete silence.

"What's happening?" someone shouted.

"It's the World Trade Center. I was watching the news when they cut to this. I saw one of the Trade Center buildings with the silhouette of an airplane buried in it. As I was looking, a plane flew into the other one," a woman said.

Most of the crowded concourse began standing in front of the monitors watching and waiting. For what, I wasn't sure. Others started walking toward the lobby of the airport. I knew I had to get to New York, so I checked the monitor for flight schedules. I pulled out my ticket to ensure I had the right date and flight number. It showed the date, 9/11/2001, and my flight, DL237. Looking at the board, I saw my flight switch from a boarding time of 7:30 to "Canceled."

Dejected, I wasn't sure what to do. I waited for some message from the voice. Nothing. I made my way with the rest of the crowd up toward the lobby. As the concourse emptied into the entry foyer, over in one corner was a group of youth singing a song with a soft, comforting melody. It went:

I open my mouth to the Lord, and I won't turn back.
I open my mouth to the Lord, and I won't turn back.
I open my mouth to the Lord, and I won't turn back.
I will go; I shall go to see what the end will be.

THE UNCLE

There is an answer,
She knows just where.
It's in the darkness,
She'll find him there.

The faint early morning predawn light cast an image of a grainy black and white film on the tall corporate office building. Palm trees lined the cobblestone driveway that stretched from the entry gates to abstract chrome monolith at the companies entrance. Susan Harvey was familiar with this beautifully landscaped entrance, having made the trips several times going to work. But that was usually in the afternoon after classes at school. Today, it was early morning, and she was on her way to meet with the company C.E.O., her uncle Morris Crowe. Before the turnaround, Sue made a hard-right at the cutoff leading to the employee's parking lot. Her windshield sticker and her identification would allow access through the security gate.

As she drove in, she spotted her uncle's vehicle parked in the covered executive area just as she expected. He was always early and seemed to always be the last one leaving. Even when they had holidays, Uncle Morrie would be late because he had an "important" work assignment to complete.

Her uncle, the brother of her mother, was fun at family gatherings, unlike the stern C.E.O. at work. At home, he'd play with the kids and clown around making practical jokes. At one family dinner, someone teased him about putting gravy on everything. When grandmother's apple pie dessert was served, he asked, "Pass the gravy, please," and poured it over the pie. He had the knack of being enjoyable when the situation called for it while being stern, objective, and driven at work. He'd helped Sue land a part-time job at the lab not because she was a relative but because she was an exceptional talent. But he didn't want anyone to think she'd come aboard because of the relationship with the boss. His Chief of Staff, Connie Parchman, suggested he say she'd won a competition at the local high schools. Their surnames were different, so nobody would know they were related. Sue had called ahead on Morrie's private line to see if he would see her before work but hadn't told him what it was about. She said she'd be discussing something far more severe than her working environment. She wouldn't bite on his probes for more information telling him it could wait until they were together. She wasn't sure how she'd approach the subject, but unless she came forward and explained honestly everything that had happened, he wouldn't be able to help. And without it, she was sure the man she loved would die.

Duncan would simply allow Mark to wither away sitting there in his apartment in that frozen state he'd helped induce. Mark's lookalike avatar wandered around aimlessly trapped in some distant place. They knew Mark didn't understand where he was, who he was, or how to escape the prison that held him. They desperately needed to communicate with him to provide instructions on how he could return. But Duncan didn't care. In fact, when the disaster happened, the first thing Duncan did was ask her to attend that stupid war movie. He seemed happy his competition for her was no longer around. To Sue, Duncan was no competition at all. While she worked with him and found him brilliant, he possessed that typical immature, socially clumsy teenage boy.

As she approached the employee entrance, she swiped her card in the security door. She paused for Leroy, the building's security system, to recognize her and unlock the door.

"Good morning, Sue. You're here unusually early today. I don't have permission to grant you entrance during these nonworking hours. What is the reason you are requesting entry?" the computer asked.

"I'm here to see Mr. Crowe before I start work," she answered.

"May I inquire as to the reason for your visit?" Leroy asked.

"No, you may not. Just tell him I'm here, please."

"As you wish," Leroy replied unemotionally.

A few minutes later, the door unlocked and Sue made her way into the building. She crossed the shiny black stone floor to the bank of elevators toward the rear of the building and pressed the up button.

At this hour, she didn't wait long for an elevator to appear. Stepping in, she pressed 47, the top floor where the executive offices were located. There was a sudden upward acceleration and, within a few seconds, the doors swooshed open. Sue looked in at the large reception area with a vacant desk that, during regular hours, would be staffed by Carrie Jo, the bubbly receptionist. Sue walked over to the counter and touched the screen that replaced the absent Carrie Jo. A list of names appeared, and she selected the top one, "Mr. Morris Crowe, C.E.O." and waited.

Within a moment, her uncle's face appeared. "Hello, Sue. Come on in. I'll unlock the door."

She heard a click on the large oak door to her left. She made her way through the stately entrance and down the long hall decorated with historical photos and soft lighting coming from seemingly nowhere. Of to the sides were Vice President offices along with his Chief of Staff. All of them vacant at this early morning hour.

Morrie stood at his opened door at the end of the hall.

"Come on in, Sue. It's good to see you," he said.

Morrie's office was at the end of the building with a view of the company's wooded landscaping and the massive lake occupied by a few white swans and other smaller water birds. Just across the way was the meandering Woodward River occupied by a single small sailboat.

Can I get you a cup of something?" he asked.

"No, I'm fine, Uncle Morrie. Thank you." She said.

"Everything going okay down in the security department?" Morrie asked.

"Yes. Everything is going well at work. I like the people and the work I do.

"Nobody has a clue that we're related, so thanks for arranging the opportunity for me clandestinely, Uncle Morrie. I was so afraid I'd be labeled as a freeloader," Sue said.

"You're welcome. Everything good with the family? I've been meaning to call my sister, but I've been so busy here at work. Is she doing okay?" he asked, realizing how bad he was taking care of personal business.

"Yes. Mom's fine, and we're all looking forward to the next family get together," Sue said.

"Well then, everything is good, yet you call and tell me it's urgent. What is it, Sue?" asked Morrie. Sue didn't know where to start. She was afraid if she began with her concerns for Mark, she'd start crying. The only logical thing she could do is start at the beginning and explain how she got into this mess.

"At school I went to our local off campus break place and saw a friend setting at a table so went over to say hello. The place was crowded and he was at a table with another person I assumed was a student. As it turned out, he was one of the instructors in my major, computations. He was there as part of a military assignment and introduced himself as Mark Gorman. He seemed like a very knowledgeable, intelligent man and we both were interested in what he had to say. My friend, Duncan, and I were discussing our futures and Mark offered us an opportunity for preparing ourselves for the schools accelerated graduation program, so we all were working together on this project," Sue said.

"What kind of project?" her uncle wanted to know.

"Well, Mark had an idea in banking and investments that would generate the potential for a new business, but needed coding done quickly to make it work," she told him.

"Okay, so you were going to help him code this idea and he'd help you what?"

"Help us get into that accelerated graduation program," Sue answered.

"Go on," Uncle Morrie said.

"We worked on it for quite a while together, but there was a problem and Mark needed some money quickly."

"Quickly? Why?"

"He was at the school because the military gave him a couple of years off after he was badly injured in one of the battles in the war. He was under a lifetime obligation to the military that, because of a recent congressional decision, could buy his way out of the military. Time was running out for this program and he wanted to move on with his life," Sue told him.

"Yes, I read something about that."

"Well, because of the deadline and the challenges with his idea, Duncan suggested we work on winning money in V-World," Sue confessed.

"That's a long shot, Sue. We've put up a lot of money in that game, but not very many win anything," Morrie told her.

"I know that, Morrie, but Duncan had an idea and a unique approach. He was at school for trouble he got into cracking into grid games and knew a lot about them. He proposed something that was dangerous, but would almost ensure Mark could make the revenue he needed to buy out his enlistment," Sue explained.

"Okay, go on. This interesting Sue."

"We began working very closely together and I became very fond of Mark. He was different than any other boy I'd ever known. He wasn't a boy, he was a man. Smart, brave, strong, secure with himself, all the things I admire. Much like you, Uncle Morrie," Sue admitted.

"I thought you were seeing some football player," her uncle commented.

"That's been over a long time," she said.

"And he's a very bright programmer. You'd like him, Uncle Morrie. He had that idea about making some of the game bots different colors," Sue said.

"Yes. A great idea. We're working on that one, but we think the colors we have there now are fine. He probably just hasn't run into any black, yellow, or red bots. We get those groups fighting all the time."

"He hasn't been in the game much so he probably missed the fighting or I'm sure he would have joined.

"Anyway, the reason we started working with him was that business program that matched litigations with stocks institutions may have owned during the period," Sue clarified.

"That sounds like a great idea, and it must have been an honor for this Mark guy to think you could write such a program."

"Yes, I was honored. And we were making some progress, but as I said there were complications in getting the data we needed, so progress was slow, and the deadline for his military buyout was approaching. We had to look at other options," Sue said.

"Sue, why were you willing to help this man, Mark."

Sue gave the question some thought. In the beginning, it wasn't because she loved Mark, so she went back to when it all started and explained it to Morrie.

"He offered to help tutor us and we offered to help him and get our diplomas sooner. And if his program sold, we'd share in the revenues," Sue said.

"Ah. I understand. That sounds like a solid plan. So, you don't think you can finish that project, right?" Morrie asked.

"Not in time, no,"

"Okay. What's your plan now? You think V-World is an option?"

"Well, yes, but in a different way. Let me explain what we decided to do. I hope I'm not in trouble for this, but Duncan suggested he knew a way to crack V-World," Sue said.

"But you'd have no better chance of winning in that game than anyone else, Sue. It's so randomized nobody can really control what happens in there," he said.

"I know that, but Duncan thought we could beat the game if we utilized something he'd discovered playing with some things he found in his father's lab."

"What things? What lab?" asked Morrie.

"They were earbuds. I forget the name of the lab but they're some sort of transmitting device. Duncan figured out a way to utilize them for cracking into the game. Originally, he didn't even know what they were for," Sue said.

"Earbuds… hummm. Could it be Shannon Labs? We have them under contract. They have some earbud looking-mechanisms that allow transmitting biologicals through…" he stopped.

"Yes. Shannon Labs that rings a bell. Through? Through what?" Sue asked.

"That's top-secret, honey," Morrie paused, then went on. "I didn't mean to call you 'honey,' I shouldn't treat you like my little niece in the office, I'm sorry. Anyway, even as my niece, it's something I can't discuss. Not because it's proprietary to our company, some of the things are top secret with the government."

"I'm not offended by you talking to me as your niece. In fact, it's exactly what I want you to do because this is more personal than business. I need to talk with you as my uncle, not as an employee, okay?" Sue asked.

"Sure. You know I'd do anything I can to help you," Morrie said. He looked across the desk and could see a tear tumbling down Sue's cheek.

"Uncle, he's in desperate trouble. If I don't find a solution, he will die, and I can't just let him sit there and die. Please. Please, Morrie, I'm counting on you to help us out of this mess."

Morrie could see something on Sue's face that he'd never seen before. She was always the cheerful one at home and ever the one to break the solemnness of a situation. Even when she talked about boyfriends, it was matter-of-fact. Now her face seemed to show a combination of fear and concern. What she couldn't hide was that look of love.

"Okay, Sue. What do you need to know? And what can I do to help?

"Maybe we should get something warm to drink, and I'll explain it in detail. Can you take the time?" Sue asked.

"For you, sure."

Uncle Morrie picked up his phone and left a message for Connie to hold all calls and cancel any morning appointments until he gives the go-ahead.

Sue walked over to the pot on the office bar and poured two cups of coffee. She handed one to her uncle and took the chair on the other side of his desk. She talked about Mark's military experiences and his nightmares. Even though he missed his buddies and wanted to support them, he also wanted to stay out of the war. He feels his time is up because he's almost been killed more than once. He told me that the war is meaningless because it's a civil war and we've picked one of the sides. He told me he had significant concerns for his survivability in the war zone. After losing friends to death and capture the future was up for grabs. We have to save him," Sue said.

"What do you mean, save him? Is he sick?"

"No, it's nothing like that. He's stuck...," Sue stopped not knowing how to express her thought.

"Stuck? Where is he?" Morrie asked.

Before answering, Sue took a sip of coffee. She had rehearsed how she would tell Morrie about the situation so that it didn't come across like a bunch of fools playing games. Maybe they were, she wasn't sure. Finally, she just blurted it out.

"He's in V-World," Sue said.

Morrie sat nodding his head silently, not saying a word. He leaned back in his chair and waited for Sue to say something. There was a period of strained silence. Sue thought perhaps he didn't hear her.

"Did you hear me?" she asked.

"Yes, go on. How did he get there?" Morrie unemotionally asked as if people get teleported into grid games every day.

"Duncan's program and the iBoard and earbuds," Sue told him.

"Duncan's a very creative guy. We can use him too when he's out of school," Morrie said.

"This is serious, Uncle Morrie,"

"I know it must seem that way. And I'm taking this very seriously. Let me just feedback what I think I heard you tell me," he said.

Morrie repeated verbatim everything Sue told him.

"Yes, that's it," Sue confirmed.

Morrie expected he knew the answer, but he asked, "Sue, why such an interest in this instructor?"

Sue was still hesitant to take this to a personal level. If Mark was just another instructor, would she have the same passion? Probably not, but she would still try to help.

"If he was just a business partner, I'd still be here."

"I know. That's the way you are, Sue."

"With Mark, it's that and more. I care for him deeply. He's the only guy in my life that I've ever felt this way about, Uncle Morrie. Maybe its love, I don't know, but I have to do anything I can to save him," Sue said.

Her uncle tipped his chair back and looked into Sue's face. Now, more than before, he could tell she was deeply in love with this soldier. He understood how love could be an overriding motivation to accomplish something. She'd never give up the fight for him, and she was blood. He couldn't let her down. But still, there was the secrecy of what the scientists at Forrest Labs developed. He had to consider how much he could divulge and even if what they had could help. He didn't doubt they found a way to get someone in the game. The company did that all the time, but their technology was far superior to anything anyone else could develop. There might be a way to help.

"Maybe I can help. I think I understand what's going on. When I brought you aboard, I started the process of getting you a top security clearance like some of our other employees. Those clearances require background checks, including research into the family, questioning acquaintances, neighbors, teachers, etcetera. I'd be sticking my neck out to allow you to know these secrets without that security clearance. Let me give this some thought," he told her.

"I understand. Anything you can do for me within your powers is appreciated. Please…" her voice dropped off.

Morrie broke into her sentence.

"Why don't you take a little break and let me make a phone call," Morrie said.

Sue rose, turned, and left the office. She slowly closed the door as Morrie picked up the phone and punched in a code. She walked down the hall to the ladies' room to powder her nose. She'd never really ever powdered her nose, but that's what they said in the movies.

The morning sun was close to lifting its head above the horizon. A faint orange glow revealed the company lake and the drifting Woodward River. Birds circled below dipping for minnows, and the sailboat leaned its way downstream. In an hour, the rising twin suns would brighten the day and hopefully shine on a solution for Sue.

Morrie laid his phone back down on his desk, pressed a button next to it, then swiveled and watched the windows transform from the misty clear to a dark shade of gray.

Sue knocked on the door and stuck her head in.

"Come on in, Sue. Let's talk about this situation a little more. How long has he been in the game?"

"Almost two weeks," she replied, walking over to her chair in front of Morrie's desk.

"What's been going on in the game during that time?" Morrie asked.

"We rolled the game back in time and looked for our interactions with Mark. In the game, his name is either Billy or Rasheed, but we don't know exactly because it changed over time. Anyway, we followed him along from his birthing deeper into the game. We even looked at the woman who took him in and found she had no history of interest, so we assumed she is a bot. There is a man who is a different story. He was someone named Jafar and was being controlled by a group of gamers planning to delete thousands by flying airplanes into a couple of tall buildings."

"What tall buildings?"

"They were two identical tall buildings in some huge city on a peninsula. I'll get to that in a moment because it's part of why I'm here. Jafar's game operator would have made a lot of points if Mark hadn't deleted him. Instead, it was Mark who earned those points because of Jafar's association with that group," Sue explained.

"How did you know his name in the game?" Morrie asked.

"Good question. Most of the language in the game is encrypted, yes. Duncan figured out that breaking the encryption for names using the earbuds. He said it was pretty easy," explained Sue.

"Yes, we knew that. It's those earbuds that help to crack the encryption. We have upgraded models here and are trying to understand some of it ourselves. Those writings were developed by the A.I. we plant in all avatars, not by us.

"So, you have him in there and you're deleting this Jafar guy to earn some points. Is that right? Morrie asked.

"Yes, we guided him through that deletion to gain maximum points, not even knowing about the bonus. We weren't around for the next one he deleted, so he must have acted on his own," Sue told Morrie.

"What was going on with that one?"

"He got a ride with a trucker, and even though Mark was smaller, he did something to outsmart or outfight him and got away. The guy was sexually perverted, so Mark earned bonus points again. I don't think I told you he was the "All Military" heavyweight mixed martial arts champion. That skill must have carried over to his avatar," Sue supposed.

"Yes, some of those things could carry over. Go on, Sue. What else?" Morrie asked.

"Well, he got to some beautiful city with bridges over a bay and found a job. At some seminar, he met this woman named Mary and she began helping him. At first, Mark didn't realize she had mothered him as an infant, but when he found out, they became close friends. During that time, Mark became a target and Mary helped him through that issue. We assume it was because of how many points he'd accumulated and it set him up as a target for bonus points."

"Yes. Having accumulated a lot of points either by what Mark did or gaining followers does put a price on your head. Others are going to come after your avatar to get those bonus points.

"If you roll back the game to the beginning, you'll see several avatars that had a tremendous following and became targets for deletion. Some were deleted in horrendous ways. One they called Jesus of Nazareth was nailed up on some posts if you can imagine that," Morrie explained.

"How awful! Was he then slain?"

"No, they let him suffer there with spikes through his hands and feet until they thought he was deleted. They took him down and put in him a cave. His user pulled one over them when he brought in an identical bot and put it in that cave. Boy, did that create a scene."

"Did that happen to others who had large followings?" Sue asked.

"Yes. Many were either deleted or took their own lives before someone could earn points for deleting them. An example was an avatar named Hitler. He amassed enough points to almost break the bank by gaining followers and ordering the deletion of millions of bots and avatars he put in camps," Morrie pointed out.

The two went on discussing other famous avatars that became targets and deleted. Then Sue changed the subject.

"Uncle Morrie, what about this Mary; she must be an avatar too because she knew Mark was a target. She must have stopped following her game operator's orders because she stopped following the delete commands."

"Could be that her operator doesn't play the game so she's just not being guided. She may just be sensitive to things being broadcast others don't hear," observed Morrie.

"Could be because she was warning Mark and helping him hide."

"Well, we built free will into them. It's part of their artificial intelligence, but let's not get ahead of ourselves. Take me back to the beginning and tell me how this all worked. How did Mark get into the game with super intelligence?" Morrie asked.

"We birthed him into the world by deleting an avatar and inserting him into the womb of a woman. He knew who he was for a while but quickly began losing memory as the artificial intelligence began taking over. Now he seems to have lost all of his past, so even when we type in commands, he doesn't understand who we are or who he is," Sue said.

"And now you want to get him out of the game? Why?" Morrie asked.

"Our plan was for him to earn enough Forresters, and as I said, if he gets a good job offer, he gains his release. The chances of survival in the war are slim, so he was willing to take the chance. We did some calculations on our side and thought we could bring him out safely," Sue explained.

"How were you going to do that?" Morrie wanted to know.

"We got him in the game with those earbuds and an iBoard with Duncan's program. We'd done some tests and knew we could get him back if he had those two items in his possession. We couldn't give it to him when he was birthed, so we pulled it out of the game then reinserted them in those tall buildings in that big city. As he got older, we gave him instructions to go get it, but by then, the buildings were destroyed, and the iBoard and earbuds lost."

"So your Mark fellow has no idea his real existence is here, not there..." Morrie's voice drifted off.

After thinking a minute, he added, "Gads, Susan. If anyone else was telling me this story, I wouldn't believe it. The three of you have accomplished something only Forrest Labs has done.

"If you're not a gamer and haven't played V-World, it would seem strange to realize there's an identical self in our game. If he knew it was his avatar in the game, and knew the game objectives, he could dominate it," Morrie said out loud.

"Of course, that's why we sent him there," Sue said.

"Why didn't you just delete him in the game?" Morrie asked.

"I couldn't do that, Uncle. I don't even play those violent games on the grid. Besides, several others in the game tried and couldn't delete him. I'm not sure how to do it. I can't kill the man I love, Uncle Morrie," Sue moaned.

"What's in there is an avatar, not your Mark. He's here."

"Huh? I don't understand what you mean," Sue said.

"You have an avatar in there. So do I. If someone deletes them in the game, we'd still be right here just as before. Heck, it may have already happened, but we're still here. The thing in the game is an artificial representation of the real us.

"What you did is force a birth into the game to get the highest level of A.I. It may act like natural births in the game, it may not. We just don't know. When someone is born here, they're also born into V-World. Just because they are deleted in V-World doesn't mean they die here. Your Mark is a new and different case, but I don't believe it would be any different than a natural birth," Morrie expressed to Sue.

"Okay, but we can't wait around for someone to delete him. We're nearing his deadline for the buyout application. If he doesn't submit his application and is still in V-World when he's called back to service, he'll be AWOL and in trouble with the military," Sue pointed out.

"Okay. I understand the situation, Susan. I called my contact with the government, and they said as CEO I could give you a temporary security clearance, but you can't reveal anything you see. Not to your other programmer friend nor to Mark. Agree?" Uncle Morrie said, looking sternly across the desk at her.

"Yes, of course."

"Come with me," Morrie said.

THE ANSWER

The observable universe,
Is way out there,
Much further than we can see.

But what about the one inside,
Where quarks and liptons will be?
It's the unobservable universe,
So close that we cannot see.

The first of the twin suns tipped its hat to their world as it slowly lifted above the horizon. Morrie and Susan stood gazing out the window in deep thought. Morrie wondered how he could explain the operations to Sue without overcomplicating things. Sue was thinking about Mark and how to save him. She didn't know if her uncle could, or even would, help. They'd done something outrageous and she knew it. But she also knew that Mark couldn't leave her life and go back to something that that would cost his life. She couldn't lose him. Morrie broke the silence.

"This is going to be strange and complicated. I don't want you to get the wrong impression of the business venture we have here. Artificial intelligence is our primary business and what I'm about to show you will seem strange based on your experience with the firm so far. Trust me, what I'm going to show you is vital to our success and goes beyond the outward appearance of the company. Let's go," he said.

His administrator, Connie, was at work by then, and as the two walked past, Morrie stuck his head in saying, "We'll be right back, Connie. We're heading over to Building C. If there's anything urgent, let the guard know. Otherwise hold my calls for later."

Morrie and Sue got into the elevator and Morrie inserted a key and turned it.

"What's that thing, Morrie?" Sue asked.

"It's called a key. Some new technology our tech people came up with watching a thing some bots in the game were using. They'd go up to a lock and instead of a beam like we have that stuck in a device called a key. Our AI must have helped them come up with it," responded Morrie.

After Morrie turned the key, another light lit up. Pressing it, the elevator started down. Sue watched the lights flash as they passed each floor in the building. As they got to "G," the ground level, the elevator didn't stop. That light went out, and she could feel the elevator continue down.

"Where is it going?" she asked Morrie.

"This is the top-secret area I told you about. We're down a few hundred feet below the surface for security reasons."

When the elevator stopped, the doors slid open, and they were facing a small room with a platform. Uncle Morrie slide his badge over a counter on the wall and a small levitating coach pulled up and stopped. As the two stepped inside, the coach rocked slightly, the door closed and it began moving.

"Better sit down. This thing travels fast," he told Sue.

The digital counter overhead began reading off their speed and when it reached 750 it went back to 1.

"What is that telling you?" Sue asked pointing at the counter.

"How fast we're going. The 1 gives us a Mach number, or the speed of sound. The tub we're in becomes a vacuum a little further down and we'll reach over Mach 5, so the trip won't be too long.

The counter began falling off and the tunnel began getting lighter. As it fell below 100, the coach slowed even further and came to a stop. The door whooshed open and the two exited the machine.

"That was quite a ride, Uncle Morrie. I hope we don't have to walk home," Sue laughed.

In the foyer of the platform an armed guard sat at a desk. Behind him was a series of monitors that seemed to be looking down hallways except for the bottom four. One of those was in the coach they'd just rode, one was a room with a large black ball-looking object, and the third a room with rows of people sitting in chairs, motionless.

"Hello, Mr. Crowe. It's nice to see you again, sir," the guard said.

"Harold, good to see you again too. How's the wife and kids?"

"Everything's good, thank you. Are you going to be working inside or just giving the young lady a tour?" the guard asked.

"She has a new top-secret clearance, so no badge yet. She's one of our new techs I'm showing around," Morrie said.

The guard glanced at Morrie, then at Sue, and simply nodded, saying nothing. An outcropping on the desk had two keypads mounted on a stainless-steel frame. Morrie slid his key into one slot; the guard did the same with another. Both turned their keys simultaneously, and a bank-vault-sized door next to the guard station began slowly swinging open.

"Follow me, Ms. Harvey," Morrie said, motioning Sue to follow.

The two strolled down a long hallway past several rooms. Sue could look through the glass windows at rows of computers and people tapping keyboards as they watched the bright screens. At the end of the hall, Morrie stopped.

"What's in here is something our founder developed years and years ago. As you know, Mr. Forrest wasn't a physicist as we know them today. He didn't get a degree from a prestigious university or work for a deep-thought science program. He had a theory and after being fired from a chemical firm, he began work on that theory. It had something to do with what we now know as quantum physics. In other words, he theorized that there were particles smaller than the atom and things more extensive than the universe.

He needed funds to build the equipment required to investigate his idea so he developed and sold several mechanical ideas that made him millions. With that money, he could procure the equipment needed to build his model. No records of what he developed exist, so nobody is sure how he did it. But right here, deep underground, he was able to accomplish something never done before.

"What was it?" Sue asked.

"I'm going to show you. As I warned you in my office it will be hard for you to comprehend. Give it time to sink in."

Morrie stuck his finger into an opening beside the door and the keypad beside it lit up. He pressed a series of numbers, and the door slid open to a large darkened room with one small light in the ceiling that seemed hundreds of feet above. Sue noticed a catwalk that appeared to extend to the left and the right with slight bends indicating that it was circling something.

"Where does this go?" she asked, pointing along the catwalk.

"It goes in a circle around that," Morrie said, pointing straight ahead.

Sue looked more closely and could see a huge dark object that appeared to be a wall. On closer examination, she noticed it was a sphere that seemed to be gradually rotating.

"What's that?" she asked.

"That's V-World," Morrie said.

"What? You mean it's an actual world?" Sue said, puzzled.

"It's a combination of many things, Sue. It's partially physical and partly chemical and partly electronic. It's matter and it's dark matter and it's energy and space. It's all of those things compressed into the size of this cavern. Whatever device he had, he was able to bring the entire world compressed down into this space."

"Entire world?" Sue asked.

"More than our entire world. It's actually the entire universe that includes our entire world," Morrie answered.

"What? How?"

"We don't know how, we only know it's there and it is where our artificial intelligence is being tested. It's on a scale that is so small it is virtually undetectable by anyone outside the walls of Forrest Labs."

"V-World is inside this sphere. Does that mean Mark is in that sphere too?" Sue asked.

"Not exactly. Remember, what's in there is an identical representation of our universe. So he's in there, but it's a representation of him there in his apartment. That's where he is now, right?"

"Yes. He's just sitting there." Sue said.

"Come with me. Let me show you something else," Morrie said.

The two left the room and walked back in the direction they'd entered. A few feet up the hallway was a door on their right. Morrie opened it, and they walked in. Inside there were rows of people sitting, just like the monitor she'd seen at the guard station.

"Look familiar?" Morrie asked.

"Yes. That's what Mark looks like. He's just sitting there. What are these people doing?" Sue asked.

"These are our monitors. They manage and control the game," he said.

"Just sitting there? How do they do that?" Sue asked.

"It is confusing, I know. While in the game, the managers assess many things. Each has a special assignment in different parts of the world. They make deletions of avatars or bots as appropriate, particularly of avatars that have gained followers and are gaining too many points," Morrie explained.

"Do you mean the game is fixed?" Sue asked.

"No, no, no. It's managed. Players still make good points just like your friend did. Our managers just control things that have grown out of order," Morrie explained.

"What do you mean out of order?" Sue wondered.

"The population is one thing. When the world in there becomes too large and is consuming too much energy, we introduce viruses to help cull the population," Morrie calmly explained.

"Dr. Forrest discovered the secret to dark matter, something that consumes 85% of all matter, and with his equipment compressed a copy of our universe. That machine, a Quantum Universal Anatomical Compensational Kinetic-omatic or QUACK for short, stored it in that sphere. He let it run for a period of time then began probing electronically inside and found a place that looked almost identical to our world. As he looked closer, he found actual living beings on a planet identical to ours. It wasn't long after that we began testing our artificial intelligence on the

223

beings there. Doing that, we discovered similarities to people we knew here. In fact, almost identical copies," Morrie told her.

"That's utterly amazing," Sue said.

"Well, there's more you need to know. As things began growing, we realized it could all collapse because of the consumption of organic matter. The whole system was overwhelming energy. We're now trying to make that system smaller so it won't devour so much energy. We don't know what would happen to our universe and our world if that one becomes overloaded," Morrie explicated.

"How many are in V-World?" Sue asked.

"We have about a hundred at this location, but we have around eight hundred locations worldwide with fewer employees, but they have the same system set up. They all get in and out of the game several times a day. I think my last data showed two-thousand of our bots are deleted, then reemerge, each day. We're talking around four hundred thousand a year," Morrie said.

"I didn't mean from Forrest Labs, I meant how many total avatars and bots are in V-World?" Sue clarified.

"Oh. As many as there are here on our planet, about seven billion, but only about nine or ten million avatars have duel representations. When Dr. Forrest discovered his machine, it copied all matter. That means all our world was copied into the system and made into avatars identical to us. Yes, there are bots too. The difference being simply the level of artificial intelligence. Avatars have higher levels than bots. That doesn't mean a bot cannot become an avatar. They can if the game player puts them in and purchase the higher A.I. For simplicity, we simply call all of them avatars," Morrie explained.

"They all have representation here in our world?"

"Not all. You can create one in the game, but many of them have one here. It's just that not everyone knows they have an identical being somewhere else in the universe. The game continues developing more and more avatars because when people here had children, their avatars had children in the game too.

Not everyone in our world plays the game and gives commands to their avatar in that world. We believe that there is a small group in the game that believe they have an identical being somewhere else, but they have a relatively small following. They're close, but not quite accurate. I was told they believe their avatar was created in the image and likeness of a God and since God is spiritual, so are they. That's pretty close, but we're sure not Gods, " Morrie told her.

"In a sense they are right, just not accurate," Sue said.

"I guess that's true," Morrie offered. "They were created in the image and likeness of someone here. Some of our citizens think they are God," Morrie chuckled.

Sue had another thought.

"You said even I was in there, so what if my avatar's deleted?"

"Just to be clear, yes there is an avatar that is you, but she may not look exactly like you look here. In rare situations, it could even be male instead of female and because you weren't helping it along it may have been deleted with one of our culling procedures to keep the population down. So, to answer your question, your inworld self just switched over to another avatar. That said, you could be in there as you are here."

Sue thought about that for a minute and realized he was right. If her avatar was deleted, she'd just regenerate it like they did Mark's bot in his test. For it to be him, he had to be born into the game.

"Can we talk about the people working here?" Sue asked.

"Sure. What questions do you have?"

"What do they do in the game? And how to they go in and come back?" Sue wanted to know, thinking she could use the same strategy with Mark.

"They aren't born into the game like Mark. They have those earbuds developed by your friend Duncan's father's firm. They know exactly what their objective is in the game. They seek out and delete avatars that are accumulating too many points. If we didn't do that, we'd go broke. Second, they carry out our culling process by depositing and dispensing viruses we've developed here. They take them into the game and infect as many avatars as possible who then infect others. With exponential growth, the number of new cases each day constantly increases. It's an ongoing effort because we didn't realize how our own in house developed A.I. is smart enough to come up with an antivirus," Morrie explained.

"I guess that's why we need so many programmers, Morrie.

"So, they go in, but how do they get out of the game?" Sue asked

"There's a couple of ways we can bring them back. Because they're what we'd term bots, not true avatars, it's a little easier. Duncan had the prototype earbuds we rejected because they were too large to actually wear. The new ones are smaller. They're worn by the employees as they go in and are set to automatically return them at a specific time. He or she gets a warning and deletes themselves and are back here," Morrie told her.

"Deletes themself? Do you mean they commit suicide?" Sue asked with a slight shrill.

"It's the only way to pull them out, so yes," Morrie answered.

"In your situation with Mark, you kids did great hiding Duncan's father's prototypes in a building and directing him there. Someone ingeniously deleted about two thousand by flying an airplane into those buildings. Sadly,

Mark's earbuds and the iBoard were in those buildings, but don't worry Sue, he'll be back in just a little while," Morrie said.

"What do you mean?" Sue asked.

"Remember I was talking about our A.I. in the avatars figuring out how to develop an antivirus?" Morrie asked.

"Yes. Go on," Sue said.

"We had to come up with a different type that's being carried into the game now. The matter is out of control. Things are heating up which could cause the whole system to overheat. The problem is overpopulation. So, we're carrying in a virus programmed to continually delete avatars. Yes, they'll develop an antivirus, but this one will change form when it's detected. We think it will be far more successful than past attempts," Morrie explained.

"Are you thinking in the past Mark had one of those viruses, but his A.I. defeated it?" Sue asked.

"Either his own or something other avatars developed and injected into him," Morrie said.

Susan considered the virus question but if he'd evaded others in the past, wondered if it would work now.

"There have been numerous attempts on his life, but nobody has been able to delete him. He seems to always escape. If we can't kill him -- I mean delete his avatar -- how will we get him out?" Sue said with a tear trickling down the side of her cheek.

"He'll be deleted soon, Sue. This new one will get him. Don't worry, he should be back within the week," Morrie said, handing her his handkerchief.

"How can you be so sure? Nothing has worked so far," Sue said, now crying

"This new one is designed to take out half the population in the game. It's passed on by contact with other avatars, so all you need to do is put him in contact with one infected. He'll get it, and he'll be deleted. You'll have him back in no time."

"We can't wait for him to get sick, Morrie. What if he doesn't. I'm concerned his real self that's sitting there in his apartment will die," cried Sue.

"I understand," Morrie said as his voice drifted off.

"I have an idea. Why don't we put you in the game and you take him to a place where he gets positively exposed to the virus. The leaders in the game now require the bots to wear masks to stop the spread, but if you took him to a place where people are yelling and screaming without masks, his odds of getting exposed are greater," Morrie told her.

Sue considered the suggestion. Now that she understood more about the inner workings of the game, Morrie's idea made sense.

"Okay, how do I get in? I have no idea where my avatar is now," Sue explained.

"Let's check something. Mark has a friend there that he trusts. I wonder if anyone is claiming that avatar. What was her name in the game? Mary, I think," Morrie thought as he sat at a monitor and began typing. After a minute of searching, he turned to Sue.

"That friend Mary is an avatar and has nobody here controlling her. You can join the game with your company account and begin sending Mary messages. Maybe she'll convince him to do something that will enhance his chances of getting the virus."

"They're friends, Morrie. I'm not sure I can send in any messages that would make her do that," said Sue.

"I can't let you use those earbuds to get into the game in our system. It's too dangerous and takes about six months of training. You need something sooner than that," Morrie confirmed.

"Yes, that's true."

"Then maybe you should find your avatar and take control of it. You could befriend Mark and delete him once and for all," reasoned Morrie.

"I don't think I could delete him, Morrie. To me that is just too violent."

"I guess I understand that. Then set him up to get exposed to the new population culling virus. I'm not sure how, but if you get to your avatar, she or he will know where the dangerous places are to contract that deadly virus."

"That sounds more humane than the way I've seen things get deleted in the game. How do I even find my avatar?" Sue asked.

"We have a system you can use to track her down. Let's go into the room across the hall, and one of our people will show you how it works."

Sue took Morrie's hand and left the room with the workers with earbuds. In her anticipation, she almost pulled Morrie across the hall. Morrie approached one of the monitor stations and tapped the worker on the shoulder. She turned around and saw the two standing behind here.

"Yes, sir? How can I help you?" the worker asked.

"Hello, Margaret. I hope your day is going well," greeted Morrie.

"Yes, it is. Thank you, Mr. Crowe."

"I'd like you to help get this woman set up to find her avatar in the game. Can you do that for me?"

"Yes, of course," Margaret said, standing up.

"This is Sue, Margaret. She works over in our security department and will be coming aboard full time once her schooling is finished. We want her to understand everything about our system over here, so please help her out," explained Morrie.

"Yes, sir. I'm happy to."

"Sue, come on up to my office and let me know how it goes when you're through here. Margaret knows everything there is to know about getting you into the game. She'll be a real help to you," Morrie said, causing Margaret to blush.

"I don't know everything, Mr. Crowe," Margaret said.

"Well, you're the best we have, Margaret," Morrie said as he turned and left.

"Pull up that chair and come sit by me, Sue. Let's get you started," Margaret said.

Sue grabbed the closest office chair and rolled it up beside Margaret who was sitting in front of two computer screens. Looking over at Sue's company ID badge, she logged into the system and found her profile.

"To do this, we need your DNA to find your avatar in the system. It has some identical DNA markers as you do here. It's how we find our employees working in the game too. The system puts a small round dot on a map, and we just scroll into where they are and feed messages into them," Margaret explained.

She handed Sue a small probe, covered it with a paper-looking cover, then held it out to Sue.

"Hold this in your mouth for fifteen seconds, the system will beep, and your DNA will be loaded into our company profile."

Sue complied, and in fifteen seconds a beep came from Margaret's machine and a long series of numbers came up behind a heading in her profile marked, "DNA."

Margaret explained some of the software options that Sue recognized as similar to the public side of the V-World game.

"I've been here before, Margaret, so I understand how this works," she told her.

"Okay. The link I'm going to give you will let you in the game in a different way, so why don't we just walk through it," Margaret suggested.

On Sue's iBoard, she placed a link to the software on the company website's secure side.

"You'll be able to do things in the game that you can't do entering through the public side. To find your avatar, notice there's another option on the menu that you don't see on the public version of the game called ADMIN.

See it?" Margaret asked.

"Yes."

"Open it,"

Sue did as she was asked and saw the options drop down in a long vertical column. Things Sue knew nothing about like, Force and Error, Render Tests, Render Metadata, Network, Recorder, and World. Beside each item was a triangle. Pressing the triangle opened more drop-down options.

"Press the World option," Margaret instructed as she watched Sue's movement on her own system that was now linked to Sue's iBoard.

Sue did as instructed and saw another long list of options. Right below one called, "Dereneder all animesh" she saw what she was looking for: "Find Avatar."

"That's where you can find yourself in the game," Margaret told her. "Why don't you go on in and find yourself. It will be a fun experience. You can roll on over to that spare table and play around with it. Any questions, let me know."

Sue thanked Margaret for her help and rolled over to the desk and began her search.

Satisfied she could now develop a plan, Sue walked back past the security guard to the underground railroad and back to the main office building. Going back up in the elevator didn't require the key Uncle Morrie used coming down. As she entered, she pressed the top floor. The elevator started slowly, then gained speed as it ascended. In less than ten seconds it glided to a stop and the doors slid open. Sue walked over to the reception desk seeing a smiling Carrie Jo tapping away on an iBoard.

"Hello. May I help you?" Carrie asked.

"Yes. I'm here to see Mr. Crowe. Is he available?" Sue asked.

"Is he expecting you?" Carrie inquired. She wasn't a screener like the robot at the entrance. Her job was to be polite and friendly.

"I think so, yes."

"Your name please?"

"Susan Harvey."

"Let me check for you, Ms. Harvey," Carrie Jo said.

Carrie picked up the phone and Sue heard her call Morrie's Chief of Staff to see if he was available. After a few words she sat down the phone and looked up at Sue.

"You can go right in," Carrie told her, pointing toward the door that led to Morrie's office.

Sue walked down the carpeted hall to Morrie's door and slowly opened it.

"Got a minute?" Sue asked.

"Yes. Come on in," greeted Morrie. "How'd it go? Did you find your avatar?"

"Yes. I found it and I'm sorry I didn't find it earlier. With administrative access to the game I can read the signs. That should make it easier to navigate," Sue told her uncle.

"Yes, that's what the software does. Where did you find her?"

"The name of that city where we hid the iBoard and earbuds is New York and that's where she is. She's been a homeless person there for a while," Sue explained.

"How do you know that?"

"I saw her avatar. It does look like me," Sue paused in mid-sentence, then added, "Well, that would be me wouldn't it?" she laughed. "She was on a street with a bunch of lights and signs with her hand out, poor thing. I haven't been there to help her," Sue explained.

"Did you get her name?"

"Yes. It's Judy."

Uncle Morrie came over and gave Sue a hug. "Honey, you'll have your Mark home in no time. It will be easier to guide Judy and get her to San Francisco now that you understand how things work. Get her to know your friend Mark and the two of you get yourselves exposed and you'll both be deleted."

"There's another interesting observation I made," Sue told her uncle.

"What was that, dear?"

"Judy is Mary's daughter."

"Mary?" Morrie asked.

"Mary White, that friend of Mark's. When I get Judy to San Francisco we can have a family reunion and invite Mark there for Mary to introduce me to him," Sue said with a smile.

"You're on your way to success, kid!" Morrie smiled.

Sue thanked Morrie for all his help. And thanked his Chief of Staff too. As she walked by the bubbly receptionist, Carrie Jo, she smiled.

"You have a striking resemblance to my hairdresser. She's confident, smart, and beautiful, just like you," Sue said.

"Thank you," Carrie said as she watched Sue step into the elevator.

As the doors slid closed, Carrie could hear a very loud "yippee."

Inside, before the elevator reached the bottom, Sue heard the elevator music playing the familiar national anthem:

I open my mouth to the Lord, and I won't turn back.
I open my mouth to the Lord, and I won't turn back.
I open my mouth to the Lord, and I won't turn back.
I will go; I shall go to see what the end will be.

Made in the USA
Monee, IL
01 December 2020